From Spark To Fire

An Anthology of Creative Prompts and Responses

From Spark To Fire

An Anthology of Creative Prompts and Responses

Sacred Circle Writers

Moonlit Press
ANTHOLOGY

Williams   *Flagstaff*   *Doney Park*

First Published October 02015

From Spark To Fire:
An Anthology of Creative Prompts and Responses

by
Sacred Circle Writers

Printed in the United States of America

Original front cover art with permission by
Laurie Wilson Fatland: http://www.lauriefatlandart.com/

Original back cover art with permission by
Al Brown, Technical Artist: http://webdustworld.com

Interior photographs with permission by
John Fatland: http://jfatty.wix.com/jfatland-photography

Cover Design by Al Brown

al.brown@moonlitpress.com

in cooperation with:
Web Dust World: Designing, Developing and Delivering Usable and
Sustainable Tools, Techniques and Technologies

Edited and Curated by Terryl Warnock

Published by:
Moonlit Press LLC
P. O. Box 126
Williams, Arizona 86046

http://MoonlitPress.com/

ISBN-13: 978-0-9894698-4-5

ISBN-10: 0-9894698-4-0

Library of Congress Control Number: 2015916137

Dedicated to Dave Becker

Your words, your humor, and your spirit will live on.
You are missed.

Photo Credit: John Fatland

I AM

I write,
Therefore I am.

My soul leaves tracks across the paper.
Wisps of thought wend
Amongst the wilderness of words,
In hopes someone will follow.
And see the essence of me.

Brush strokes of simple syllables
Masterpiece or child's scribble
May touch another's inner life
And turn who knows what tide.
In word there is eternity.

I am,
Therefore I write.

        Laurie Wilson Fatland

Table of Contents

Poetry of the Sacred Circle...223

Editor's Picks...................249

First Words..........................275

Gratitude List....................329

INTRODUCTION

You hold in your hands the truest of collaborative efforts. The lone author's name at the beginning of each piece of writing is wonderfully misleading. Without intent to deceive, of course. We each claim our own work, but ultimately this collection is the work of a group of people who are deeply connected with one another, not only as writers, but as human beings. It was our love of writing and good food that brought us together in the first place, but beyond that surface connection we have since discovered and developed deeper kinship. We have found our clan. We have each entered the Sacred Circle and been transformed by it into a greater whole.

We have helped write and rewrite, edit and organize these pieces for each other. We have prompted and prodded and argued our points. We shouted right out loud what we liked best. We care for each other deeply, so we have been gentle with our remarks about what we liked least. The core of this book is made from the best responses to our weekly creative writing prompts. We have corrected each other's spelling, grammar and plot. We have checked facts for each other and given encouragement when the going got tough. We became so encouraged we set off on larger projects and in different directions. We grew bold and started writing poetry and books.

We place our hearts in your hands.

WE ARE THE SACRED CIRCLE

Photo credit: John Fatland

Terryl Warnock

Terryl Warnock lives and works with a happy heart in a small town in Northern Arizona. She's had an interesting go of it so far in this lifetime, acquiring two and seven-eighths degrees and half-dozen disparate careers along the way.

Terryl is settling in to contentedly write out the twilight and is proud to be affiliated with Moonlit Press. She wasn't even aware she was homeless until the Sacred Circle Writers asked her in and she felt as though she'd come home at last. She is looking forward to the publication of her first book in 2016. *The Miracle du jour* is a collection of fables, parables, short stories and yarns seeking hope, peace and acceptance in this world and in this lifetime. Why wait till the afterlife for salvation?

mailto:terryl@moonlitpress.com

Photo Credit: John Fatland

Katarina Karjala

Katarina Karjala was born in Slovakia, where she spent the first forty years of her life. She holds Masters Degrees in History, Social Studies and the German Language from Comenius University in Bratislava. She is a former high school teacher who likes to share her knowledge and experiences, so profoundly shaped by the social changes in, and the eventual breakup of, Czechoslovakia. Moving to the United States is also reflected in her writing. She writes short stories, children's books, and historical fiction. Katarina lives in Flagstaff, Arizona.

mailto:katarina_karjala@hotmail.com

Photo Credit: John Fatland

Laurie Wilson Fatland

Laurie Wilson Fatland grew up with a love of books. Escape from the long, hot days of summer; the reward after a boring day at school; a nighttime ritual of reading, all became essential parts of her life. "The good ones leave a mark on your soul and come back to touch your life in ways you can't foresee," she has said. To her, opening up a new book was like opening a gift, each one a promise of something unique to treasure and unwrap, little by little.

It was the bad books, though, that inspired her to write. She started out writing poetry; it was a love of hers in elementary and high school. But an active imagination caused her to constantly think up stories and share them with her daughter and other children. The bad books made her want to try her hand at writing for adults and she helped create the Sacred Circle Writers.

Laurie Wilson Fatland was born and raised in California's Central Valley. She spent part of her youth in both Northern and Southern California, attending California State Fullerton where she studied art. After several years on the Navajo Reservation, she now lives in Flagstaff, Arizona with her husband, daughter, four dogs, four horses and a head swirling with stories to tell.

http://dontreinmein.wix.com/lauriewilsonfatlandauthor

Dave & Marley

Photo Credit: Keli Becker

Dave Becker

Dave Becker was born in San Francisco, California and grew up to study physical education at California State University, San Francisco. He worked for the California Department of Transportation in Half Moon Bay as an equipment operator. It was there he met, Keli, the love of his life and made her his wife. The Beckers moved to Flagstaff, Arizona after Dave retired, and he enjoyed working around their small farm. Dave and Keli lived in Northern Arizona for ten years until cardiac arrest took Dave much too soon. Dave and Keli would have been married 35 years.

Dave enjoyed golfing, reading, going for walks, good food and exploring. He discovered his love of writing while recording his Technicolor dreams. He was always willing to try something new. Dave was wise and kind and had a soft spot for abandoned animals.

He is sorely missed by all who knew him.

Photo Credit: John Fatland

Keli Becker

Keli Becker was born in Oakland, California, and grew up in many cities around the San Francisco Bay area. She met and married Dave Becker, the love of her life, while working for the California Department of Transportation Maintenance Division in Half Moon Bay.

Keli loves Dave, reading, cooking, gardening, and is deeply involved in the rescue of abused and abandoned animals. She has been writing most of her life and has a deep passion for it.

Cardiac arrest took her beloved husband too soon.

mailto:kelijbecker@hotmail.com

Photo Credit: John Fatland

PROMPTS AND RESPONSES

THINGS

Things. A universal part of the human endeavor involves surrounding ourselves with things, the artifacts of our culture. We acquire and display not just things we use, but things that make us comfortable and things that articulate our unique style. Ultimately they're just things, they have no voice or personality. They are not important to us in the fundamental way, say, relationships or beauty or place are, and they don't mean much to people who have a healthy relationship with them. There are, of course, those who are sick with things; those who are avaricious and hoard and would surrender their souls to and for their things. For the rest of us, they remain merely things. Or are they? Turns out they aren't always mute, they speak volumes if we care to listen. It is these unique things—the inanimate with their whispered stories—that have captured the imagination and attention of the Sacred Circle Writers this week.

Laurie Wilson Fatland explores the connection through time certain objects can have in *The Ring*; Terryl Warnock shares the history of a thing that speaks to different people in different ways in *The Moose Hat*; and Keli Becker spins a delightful yarn about a statue that is more than meets the eye in *The Gargoyle*.

The Ring

Laurie Wilson Fatland

Allison loved old things. She spent all of her spare time combing through antique and second hand shops, searching for treasures amidst all of the junk there. In a way, she was an archaeologist, sifting through people's detritus to find the meaningful piece that opened the doors to the past.

For Allison was never content to just own a piece, she wanted to know everything about it. She searched a plate for identifying marks, or a chair for initials that might reveal the maker and the place it was created. Allison was a collector of history.

Entering her apartment in a remodeled building from the 1800s was almost like entering a museum. The walls were covered in old art, and delicate furniture crowded the floor. Sometimes Allison envisioned them as old ladies in a tearoom, each decked out in their finery and trying to outdo each other for attention.

Her job as a librarian gave her plenty of time to research her discoveries. She would painstakingly follow the clues she discovered until she understood everything about the era and the place her newly-found acquisition had come from. When she sat alone in her quiet apartment at night, she looked at each item and knew it intimately. This was the only way she could surround herself with friends.

Middle aged, short and round, Allison was not the sort that attracted people. Her conversations consisted of long lectures about the details of history which most people found excruciatingly boring. She had pretty features though, and lovely blonde hair that she kept bound in a severe bun. Allison could have been pretty, if she had cared enough to cultivate what God had given her.

On her way home to her little haven in Brooklyn, Allison made her usual stops at second hand stores along the way. There was nothing new to see. On a whim she decided to take a different route home and see if she could find something to add to her collection. There! Down a shadowed alley, she saw the sign for a little shop, Hidden History. Now this one looked promising.

The bell on the door tinkled as she stepped into the dusty shop. The owner, a little man with horn-rimmed glasses peered at her from behind the glass counter. "Welcome," he said, in a small rusty voice.

Allison smiled at him and began to browse through the bric-a-brac, checking under plates and statues for interesting marks. She worked her way up to the counter, which displayed several trays of antique jewelry. Nestled in velvet and surrounded by old necklaces, an emerald ring caught her eye, sparkling beautifully even in the dingy light of the shop. "May I see that emerald ring?" she asked.

The owner, pulled out the tray to show her, "You've a good eye, Miss. This one is rather special." He carefully handed her the ring.

Allison saw that it was a stunning square cut emerald; the setting was gold, swirling around the emerald to hold it and show it off. The workmanship was impeccable. She looked closely for marks and inscriptions. There was the 18 karat mark for the gold, and on the inside she found some faint writing. "It says, Allison, love Mark. Funny, that's my name, Allison."

"Well, it must be meant to be then," the man chuckled in his squeaky voice. "Slip it on."

Allison slid the ring on her finger, a perfect fit. "Do you know anything about its history?" she asked.

"I bought it from an old lady in Brooklyn. She said it was given to her mother by a famous mob boss in the late 1880s. I never followed it up though. Just thought it was a pretty piece. She did say the ring was cursed and brought her mother bad luck. That's all I know," he said.

This intrigued Allison even more. Here was a little treasure from the past, with its own past, something whose history she alone could uncover.

She bought it on the spot, even though his price seemed high. She admired its sparkle on her hand as she stepped from the shop.

Suddenly her vision went dark and she held onto the wall to keep herself from falling. When it cleared she couldn't believe her eyes! Horses and carriages were rumbling down the street. Men in top hats and women in long period dresses were strolling along the sidewalk. She ran to the end of the alley to see if this were some sort of parade. But no, it seemed she had stepped back in time. Everywhere the city had changed.

Allison looked down at her feet, she was wearing kidskin boots, and a full skirt of blue satin sprung from her waist. She stopped by a store window and was astonished to see herself; thin and fashionably dressed, her golden hair piled on top of her head. 'Why, I'm beautiful!' she thought. Just then she saw the ring sparkle on her finger and pulled it off to look at it again. The darkness returned, as if she had closed her eyes.

When she looked up, everything had changed again. She was once again the drab, boring Allison, and the city had reverted to its usual self. I must be getting sick, she thought, and slid the ring into her pocket and trudged home.

That night, Allison sat alone, holding the ring and pondering the strange afternoon. Could the ring be cursed? Well, that's silly. I must have let my imagination run away with me. Just to be sure, she closed her eyes and slipped the ring on again.

When she opened her eyes, she found herself in a pink and white bedroom, large and luxuriously furnished. She looked down at her figure; she was the thin and beautiful Allison again. While she was trying to make sense of this, the door opened and a tall, handsome man walked in. He had dark hair and a little mustache which twitched when he smiled at her.

"Hello Allison, my sweet," he said as he walked by her, pausing to run his fingers over her cheek in a tender gesture. Allison had never been touched like that in her whole life. It made her tingle all over.

He tossed his coat onto a nearby chair and a monogrammed handkerchief slid out, M was embroidered on it. He must be Mark, she thought as he went into the next room.

Testing the waters, she called out "Where have you been all day, Mark?" She heard him slam something down and his heavy footsteps as he stomped to the door.

"How dare you question me, you bitch," he snarled as he rushed across the room toward her, slapping her so hard she fell from her chair. She saw him raise his boot to kick her and she covered her face in fear. His boot made contact with her hand and she heard the crunch of bone as her finger broke.

Mark screamed at her, "Never, ever, question me! I told you to never ask me where I have been. Do it again and I'll kill you." He stormed out of the room, locking the door behind him.

Allison lay on the floor in pain and confusion. After awhile she struggled to her feet and lay on the bed. She examined her hand as she tried to take off the ring, gingerly to avoid more damage to her finger. It would not come off. Her hand was swollen and bruised. She knew then she was trapped.

She heard a whisper, "Tell them. Tell them. Tell them." Where was it coming from? She listened carefully and realized the whisper was coming from the ring!

Just then the door opened again and Mark slipped in, locking the door. "Allison, I've come to a decision." She just looked up at him questioningly, afraid to speak.

"It's time we part ways, my dear. I can no longer trust you." He smiled at her sweetly as he approached.

"Fine", Allison said softly, as she got up and moved to the door. "Just unlock the door and I'll go, I won't bother you again."

Mark smiled as he pulled his brass topped cane from behind his back. "No, you won't bother me again", he said as he swung it toward Allison's head.

Allison went down like a rock when the cane hit her in the temple. She blacked out completely.

She had no idea how much time had passed when she started to come to. It was cold and raining and she was sopping wet. Allison realized she was being carried, the scratchy wool of a man's coat biting into her cheek. She kept her eyes closed and breathed softly, afraid of what would come next. She felt the blood seeping from her aching head but dared not move. "Goodbye, my love," she heard Mark's voice whisper softly as he laid her down and pushed her into the river.

Allison held her breath as she slipped into the water; playing dead until she floated down the river far enough to be out of sight. She struggled against the long skirts in the icy water, but was able to make her way to the end of a pier and haul herself up the ladder to collapse on the old wood.

As she gained strength, Allison checked her hand and found the swelling had gone down from soaking in the cold river. She gently tested the ring on her injured finger and was relieved to feel it slip off into her hand.

Looking up, Allison knew she was safe. The modern city lit the night sky all around her, it had never seemed so beautiful.

She made her way to the closest hospital, got her broken finger set and bandaged and returned home to hot tea, dry clothes and a soft bed. She slept a dreamless sleep until morning.

Allison headed off to work, the ring in her pocket. She was determined to find out what happened to the other Allison. She hoped the newspaper archives would reveal everything.

After hours of searching, Allison discovered a famous mobster named Mark Snyder. He ran all the gambling in Brooklyn during the last half of the 1880s. As she searched through the years, she discovered an article on Allison Slater, long time mistress of Mark Snyder. She had been found floating in the river, dead from a blow to the head. It was decided by the city coroner that she had committed suicide and had hit her head as she fell into the water. Case closed. Mark Snyder had walked free.

Allison put the ring in a box and hid it in the back of a drawer. But it did not rest. Every night, as Allison lay down to sleep, she heard it whisper, "Tell them. Tell them. Tell them." Over and over again.

"How?" she thought. "Who would listen?" Finally she knew. She was a librarian. She knew books. She would write this story, she would research the truth. Someone would listen and Allison would finally find peace.

The Moose Hat

Terryl Warnock

Winter Solstice

My Dearest Friend;

I can take a hint. I know you love my hat and I know you want it. I'd gift you with it but I can't do that. Perhaps when I share its story with you, you'll understand why.

I first met this hat early one morning at the top of Lift #3 at Wolf Creek Ski Area. I'd just been up on the top tower adjusting the counterweight tension.

#3 is a wild ride. It's a detachable poma; an antiquated sort of oddity in itself. That it ran up a 100% slope (45 degree angle) at an extremely high rate of speed made it dangerous and seductive into the bargain. There was a sign at the bottom of the lift, cautioning the foolhardy that #3 serviced advanced and expert terrain only, but the sign was really pretty superfluous. It took a dang good skier just to ride #3—if they had the skills to make the trip up, they were most likely going to be just fine on the way down. It was a heckuva launch, too—zero to full speed, instantly. People who weighed less than a hundred pounds often caught air at takeoff, and those who couldn't make the trip up rarely made it much further than the end of the loading ramp.

Lift #3 was old and tired by the time I came to know her; she was cranky and irritable, slow to start and quick to take a break. It took a delicate and understanding touch, like that of a lover, to keep her going. I had that touch and so I worked #3 almost every day that season.

Adjusting counterweight tension is tricky on any lift. The counterweight is an enormous weight, a cement block the size of a storage shed in this case, suspended to counterweight the bullwheel assembly. It functions to keep tension on the cable so it won't fall to the ground if the lift should derail. The bullwheel at the top of Lift #3 was free-floating, suspended from guy wires rigged between the two topmost towers of the lift. The terminus of the lift was an angled tower situated on the brink of the Continental Divide with the counterweight dangling from the back side of it. To adjust the counterweight tension you had to climb that skewed top tower with a heavy pack full of tools, entwine your body in and around all of the various rigging, hook a come-along to the counterweight, drop a measuring tape, and raise or lower the counterweight to the appropriate height, working with frozen, sluggish fingers.

Tramway board regulations required this be done before anyone could ride (except lift ops who are, of course, beneath mention), so counterweight adjustment was an opening gig in the morning when the tower rungs were invariably heavily rimed and very slippery. Like most spooky work, it becomes as comfortable as it can with familiarity and besides, there is absolutely nothing on the planet more breathtakingly beautiful than that first tender caress of the sun's warmth and light on the vast splendor of the sleeping, frozen Rocky Mountains.

Well you may ask what any of this has to do with the hat. Well, the morning I met this hat was spookier than usual because a snowcat was grooming Alberta Face. You gotta know Alberta to love her. She be steep, wide open, and right beside Lift #3 so everybody riding up can watch her eat you alive. The mountain manager only groomed Alberta a couple of times each season, if at all, even though she cleaned up real nice and we all loved skiing her when she was groomed. It was only done once and again because grooming Alberta was a dangerous and delicate business, and it took a masterful cat driver to do it. Since Alberta was so steep and the snowcat so heavy, grooming Alberta was a matter of a controlled slide on the part of the machine. To make things more interesting yet, the pitch down her left shoulder was such that Alberta tended to shrug the cat off sideways into one of the lift towers—tower 13 as luck would have it.

So there I was, clinging to the topmost tower watching a huge, roaring machine slide sideways towards the 13th tower of the very same lift upon which I was so precariously perched. If the cat were even to just barely nick tower 13, my life was in serious jeopardy—it would create a slingshot effect, you see, with high-tension 2" steel cable as the slingshot and me as the projectile. It was early in the season and I hadn't met this new driver yet, much less come to know him well enough to trust him with my life.

Legend had it that Lift #3 had lost her 13th tower on a couple of different occasions to newbie cat drivers. Those legends didn't happen to mention whether any lift ops, being beneath mention, had lost their lives on those occasions or not. My world stopped turning as I watched the drama play out downslope. It was an infinity from one heartbeat to the next. Ice crystals lazed past in agonizing slowness as I sucked in a frosty, aching breath I was unaware of holding, treasuring it as though it were my last. It occurred to me how strange it was to be sweating so profusely in the 20 below chill with my heart hammering in my chest, and how odd it would be were that my last thought, my last sensation, in this lifetime. Was this that infamous pre-death "flash before your eyes" I'd heard of?

As you can probably surmise from the fact that I'm writing to you today, whole and healthy, the moment passed without incident. The driver missed the tower with millimeters to spare and as soon as my gelatinous knees would hold me up again, I finished my counterweight, climbed down and started shoveling my ramp, amazed, somehow, that the world had started turning again as though nothing of note had happened.

When the snowcat came back around for its next pass a few minutes later, I waved the driver in with a thermos of steaming coffee.

~

This moosehat crawled out of that snowcat atop the head of one John Braun, a.k.a. John "Dawg" Braun.

"Hiya! I'd like to buy you a cuppa for missing that tower." I chirped, "You scared the shit out of me."

"What are you, some kinda **fucking wimp**!?" He bellowed in return, his roar drowning out even the considerable baritone purr of the idling diesel and the rubber squeaky of the now-running lift. He fairly shattered the sacred, dawning stillness of my magical mountain wonderland with his boisterous, loud self. "Nobody ever told you life in the mountains was going to be **easy**, did they?" He crawled down off that machine chewing me out like he was my drill sergeant. "If you can't handle it, maybe you ought to be at the bottom, or in the kitchen, or home with your soap operas with the rest of the **girls**," he spat. "I take mine black," he tossed over his shoulder as he barged into the lift shack and impolitely plopped down on the best seat in the house atop the propane heater.

There's something about cat drivers. Nobody can say why, but they're almost always a bit odd, especially during season. A perfectly normal person off-season can take a job as a groomer and become strange in a way that only working all night can do. If you've never worked all night you can't possibly know, and if you have worked all night, well, no explanation is necessary. It's even worse on cat drivers though because they work all night in the cold and dark—alone. Their jobs involve more time for ingraining idiosyncrasies than any human was ever meant to have. It renders some of them introverted and shy; when they come out into the bright light of dayside human companionship they're dazzled and blink owlishly in confusion. Some are philosophers and some savants, some brilliant musicians and some deeply spiritual. They're almost all deep thinkers on some level or another. There are those few, however, that the job renders caustic, grouchy, smug, intolerant assholes. From the first moment I met him there was no question whatsoever in my mind which professional persona had mastered the Dawg.

"What do you think this is, some kinda fucking coffee shop!?" I roared back, just as indignantly as I could. "It comes with cream and sugar or not at all." You can't let these guys think for a minute that they can intimidate you. "Hey," I said, trying to turn the conversation in a more congenial direction, "that's a really cool hat. I've never seen one with mooses on it before, where'd you get it?"

"They're elk, you dipshit, are you blind as well as gutless?!"

For the most part, cat drivers generally seem to consider lift ops and ski instructors some sort of lower life form. Bottom feeders beneath mention.

"They're moose, jerk off. Look at those noses! Did you ever see an elk with a profile like that? Look, I happen to spend a lot of time contemplating mooseface you know. I may never have seen a live moose, but I drink a lot of Moosehead beer. Besides, I was just trying to compliment you on your hat, you asshole. Sheesh, get over your cheap self."

"OK, OK." he groused, with just the hint of a smile tugging at the corners of his eyes, "If you like this hat so much, I'll trade you for it. Gimme your hat and we've got a deal."

~

There was a stunned moment of silence while I groped for a response. He might just as well have slapped me.

~

"Jesus Christ!" I finally sputtered, "I can't swap you for this hat, it's my uniform hat!"

"So what?! A ski area uniform hat and fifty cents will get you a **decent** cup of coffee anywhere in town. Besides I just know you don't think I'm gonna work the rest of my shift, this early in the season, bareheaded, just so some snippy little lift op can pilfer my favorite hat. You're not **that** ignorant, really, are you?" His voiced dripped poisonous sarcasm.

"We aren't in town, and if you don't like the coffee I'll drink yours. I didn't lug it all the way up here just so you could talk trash about it. Since you're a newbie here you obviously don't know what lift ops had to go through just to get uniform hats this year! You trying to get me in trouble with my boss?"

He crossed his arms over his chest, his eyes narrowed, reassessing. "You scared of your boss?"

"Duh, yeah I'm scared of my boss. What the hell do you think? I got rent to pay! Um, you're not scared of your boss?"

"Nah, my boss can't live without me and we both know it. Oh, all right all right," he said as he tossed me a real smile for the first time. "Candy ass. Stop your whining. My shift is nearly done anyway. What else you got to trade?"

I squared my shoulders, crossed my arms over my chest, and planted my feet. "I've got a summer hat with me, but it's really special to me and if you want to trade for it, you've got to give me the moose hat and some Moosehead beers to go with it."

I fished my treasured, battered felt hat out of my pack and offered it up to him.

"Ha!" he scoffed, "What's so special about that? It's beat to shit. Got any more coffee? It's lousy, you damn sure wrecked it with the cream and sugar, you know, but at least it's hot, and I'm near froze up."

"Oh you poor thing." I sneered as I poured him another cuppa, "Nobody ever told you life in the mountains was going to be **easy** did they? See, lift ops were never previously issued hats by the area, this is the first year. Early last season, we were trying to get the area to provide us hats as part of our uniforms like any other mountain staff, but they refused—guess they didn't think we were worth it or something. Lift ops matter less than other mountain staff, you know, who cares if we freeze to death? So we pooled our meager resources and had our own hats made, custom. They were godawful—by design. They were puke orange with big garish purple stripes running through and had WOLF CREEK LIFT CREW in an absolutely disgusting off-yellowish brownish color—puce, I think they call it—across the forehead. We only had enough made for ourselves and we wore them every minute of every day, even when it was hot, just to irritate the bosses. They were SO ugly! The bosses hated them. They were great! When the bosses would gripe about them, we'd just shrug and remind them that if they didn't like our taste in hats, they should provide us whatever kind of headwear they thought appropriate."

"Yeah, yeah," he said slurping his cuppa and discourteously lighting a cigarette in my confined space without even asking, his scorn as noxious as the second-hand smoke. "Asshole bosses at a ski area, now that's breaking news. What's that got to do with this tired old hat you're trying to trade me for my elk hat anyway? **Will** you get to the point?"

"Well, see, as the season wore on last year, those butt-ugly liftie hats became quite the thing. They caught on. They became symbolic of bucking the system—wearing one was like flipping off your boss, right to his face. They became coveted by every employee here who has a bad attitude, who, as I'm sure you know by now, are legion.

"Anyway, after a great deal of negotiation, I swapped mine with Russell for this summer hat of his. You don't know Russell, he's not teaching here this year. Russ was an instructor here last year and he did not get along with the ski school director. You know what a jerk Barry can be, especially when he gets on that "ski better by being born-again" binniz. Russ just couldn't gag it down.

"Boy, Russ really got Barry's goat with that tacky hat, it was such great fun to watch! That awful hat clashed so horribly with Russ's bright green ski instructor's jacket it'd choke you. Mind you, Russ was in trouble with Barry long before the hat anyway, mostly for his love of doing inverted aerials off the roof of the ski patrol shack, but also for his unorthodox teaching methods. Russ never did buy off on that PSIA (Professional Ski Instructors of America) line of horsecrap. He said if you let them, PSIA would ruin your skiing for life. Wearing that ugly hat was only the last of many, many straws between Barry and Russ.

"Russell was a friend of mine, still is. He's a damn fine ski instructor and a damn fine person, and I won't ever have the pleasure of working with him at this area any more. He made it through last season by the skin of his teeth, but Barry made it clear he needn't come back for clinic this year. That's why this summer hat is special to me, and that's why the deal stands."

~

The Dawg shrugged, snagged Russ's hat, tossed the moose hat on the counter, got in his cat and drove off with nary so much as a by your leave for drinking up all my coffee. Cat drivers can be rude that way.

We became fast friends over those Moosehead beers, though, oddly enough, The Dawg and I did. He never would admit that they're moose on the hat rather than elk and it became a standing point of contention between us. Nevertheless, in the ensuing seasons he always gave my lift a little extra special attention with his cat, taught me the exhilarating joy of long skis, ultimately helped me through my first ski school clinic, and became one of my very, very favorite skiing buddies. We became partners in crime; skiing out of bounds, going on road trips, drinking too much, and wreaking as much havoc on the ski area's political pecking order as we possibly could. He took care of me after I wrecked my knee, and it was only under the lash of his sharp tongue I found the guts to tough out the therapy and get back on skis. He felt like the only friend I had in the world when my forever relationship *du jour* was falling apart, and he was there, usually with a Moosehead beer or two in tow, to help ease my fears and frustrations as I made the transition from ne'er do well ski bum to responsible restaurant manager.

~

So you see, if you'd like this hat, it's yours, but you've got to swap me a hat for it in return.

Love,

T

The Gargoyle

Keli Becker

I was just another tourist in beautiful San Francisco, doing the stupid things most tourists do: buying stuff we didn't need, sightseeing, and holding up traffic, both vehicular and pedestrian. Understandable to us, annoying as hell to the city residents.

San Francisco was a really wonderful city with its eclectic mix of building styles: modern, Italianate, Stick, Queen Anne, and the widely known Victorian style buildings, the amazing "Painted Ladies." It was a feast for the eyes. I think I would have made a phenomenal architect except I hate math. Self-defeating, but I can still appreciate a beautiful building when I see it.

I was ogling the incredible structures with their gargoyles and grotesques. I was fascinated with the gargoyles. I pulled my gaze away from the roofs and stumbled on the best place in the world: "Gargoyles-R-Us." It was a funky little store with every imaginable kind of gargoyle. I expected plastic statues made in China, but the statues were made of resin with the dust of fallen gargoyles mixed in. They were portable and shippable for jazzing up your lawn, house, or mansion. This was the place for me!

There were lions, eagles, snakes, monkeys and even monks doing things monks shouldn't be doing. Weird looking little fat men picking their noses and other bodily parts. The Green Man. Darth Vader!

I had to get one. It could sit next to our front door. One of the duties of gargoyles was to provide protection. Who couldn't use some of that? I looked around the store for one I liked. I wasn't crazy for the monkeys or little fat monks. I could take or leave the goats and eagles.

But coming around a turn at the end of an aisle, I heard a gravelly voice bark at me. I thought it might be a service dog.

As I started up the aisle, I heard that bark again. It sounded like a dog barking into a revolving metal trash can with gravel in it. What the...?

I looked around. The gargoyles were as motionless as monuments. Except for one. A small bat-winged dog crouched on the floor under two sturdy shelves. It was wagging its tail in the gravel dust. It sounded like a cement mixer. It smiled at me. I swear.

"Pick me! Please, please pick me! I miss the outdoors and watching people and I've been here sooo long. Please pick me?" the little thing said plaintively.

I was shocked. I looked around. There was no one near me to hear what was going on. I didn't know what to do.

I walked closer to the little stone dog. It was grinning! And the bat wings were spreading out from its shoulders as if it was ready to fly. Although it had a bat-like face and ears, it had the demeanor of a dog and stood about three feet tall.

"Hey, there." I reached out to pet its head, but thought better of it. I was questioning my sanity at that point, and maybe my judgment wasn't the best it could be. "Hi, little guy. Good boy?"

"I happen to be a girl but that's okay. I guess it's hard to tell, right?"

"Yeah, just a bit. Say, how come you can talk to me and none of the others can?"

"I have a secret they don't. When the cornerstone was laid for the cathedral where I was made to be, a worker was sacrificed. He was bled and his body buried under the cornerstone. The man's blood was sprinkled over many of the stones that were to be used in the building of the cathedral. I was the last stone, smaller than the rest. One of the stone masons decided to make something of me. He made me like this to remind him of a dog he once had." *Must have been a pretty ugly dog,* I thought to myself. The statue went on. "That was so, he told me as he made me, every time he passed by the cathedral and looked up, he would see me and think of his best friend.

"When the cathedral came down during an earthquake I broke apart. My stone mason came and picked up my parts. He kept me in a wooden box. I was passed from person to person in the family over many generations. Then I was sold to the owner of this store. He made a mold of my doggie self and had me ground up to be added to the resin. Because of the life that was part of me and the love the stone mason put into my creation, I'm able to talk to you. I can protect you. I will take care of your property. I will protect all of your soft bodies. Please pick me."

I was fascinated. A talking gargoyle. How many people had one of these? And I could have her shipped back home to be waiting for my arrival, just like my real dogs are waiting for me!

I wondered how my real dogs would react. Well, I decided, I'll cross that bridge when I come to it. I paid for the gargoyle and arranged for shipping with a surly young female clerk. I went back to see the little bat-winged dog one more time before I left. She was so cute! Her tail beat staccato on the dirty floor.

"I have a building and people to protect again! I'm so excited!" she said, "And I'll eat all of your garbage"

I located the shopkeeper and made sure she knew which gargoyle I wanted. She seemed relieved. "I was wondering when that little sucker was going to go."

"Have you had her long?"

"Her? How can you tell?" She eyed me with suspicion. "People have been saying they hear it talk to them. Nuts, right? Did she talk to you?"

I'd had enough of the woman and her sarcasm. "If you would just get the statue mailed to my house. Thank you."

"Look, lady, I'm sorry. I've been working here since Corny opened the place up, about three years ago. Corny—his real name is Cornelius—is my second cousin, and helped me out when I couldn't find a job, but I didn't think I'd be here this long."

Who was I, True Confessions? I started to edge away but she followed me, an old broom in her hands.

"I sweep up after these things every day and next morning it's like someone has come in and dumped dust and gravel all over the place. Like these damn things have a freakin' party every night." Did the little dog gargoyle lie to me about her being the only one who could talk? Or party?

The woman was talking faster now, as if she had to get something out before I walked away. Before it was too late.

"I've been saving money to go to a community college or trade school so I can get out of here. I'm getting the creeps working here. I hear someone, or something, talking when I'm here alone. Not soft, like me and you are talking now, but rough, like rocks in a tumbler."

The clerk sounded frantic. I continued to try to slip sideways along the aisle toward the door. She reached out to grab my jacket. I was shocked to immobility.

"Corny, he says its the rocks in my head tumbling around. He doesn't believe me." Bright tears glistened in her eyes. One escaped and painted a silvery trail down her cheek. "I know I'm not crazy, lady, not yet but I will be soon if I don't get out of here!"

Just then, a short, balding, overweight man came through the doorway. The young woman quickly let go of my jacket.

"What are ya doin', Susan? Buggin' the customers again? I told ya to stop with that nonsense, didn't I?"

"Yeah, Corny. We were just talking, honest. Right, lady?" Her eyes pleaded with me to agree.

"I hope it wasn't any more of that 'The gargoyles are talking to me' stuff. It better not have been." Corny was glaring at Susan with bug-eyed irritation.

I felt compelled to come to her aid. "No problems. We were just talking. Susan was giving me directions to a restaurant I wanted to try while I was in the city." I glanced at Susan who nodded her head rapidly.

"Yeah, Corny, that's what it was."

"Well, you're not the tourist info center. You should be sweeping and cleaning up this place. I don't know what you do around here all day. It's always a mess," he groused at poor Susan. Seemed she couldn't do anything right. She should want to get away from 'Cousin Corny' even if the gargoyles didn't party every night.

Then Cousin Corny gave me one more reason to like him even less. "If you need directions to a restaurant, I could take you there myself. Show you around a little, you know?" he said with a nasty leer.

Eww. He was disgusting.

"No, thanks, I'm good. I'll just be on my way." And I quickly whispered to Susan, "Good luck."

Susan smiled back at me through the tears coursing down her cheeks.

The next morning, while reading the local newspaper, drinking some of the best coffee ever while scarfing down a basketful of pastries and bagels from Room Service with my husband, Russell, I came across a story in the local news that turned the coffee to acid in my stomach and the pastry to dust in my mouth.

A young woman, Susan Martin, shop help at Gargoyles-R-Us on Van Ness, was savagely attacked last night. Her mauled body was barely recognizable but Cornelius Martin, her cousin and proprietor of the shop, identified the remains. He said he had gone down to the store to see if Ms. Martin had any trouble the night before, as she had previously discussed hearing strange noises after hours in the store with him. He called police immediately after discovering the remains, he said. Mr. Martin is being looked at as a 'person of interest.

I felt nauseous. I told Russell what happened the previous day, leaving out the part about the talking, partying gargoyles. I felt pastry forcing its way back up my throat. I just made it to the toilet in time.

I didn't really feel like sightseeing after the dreadful news, but we were headed home the following day. We wanted to see the waterfront area, try the world famous sourdough bread and fresh seafood, and visit the now empty prison island just a short boat ride away.

The incident at 'Gargoyles-R-Us weighed heavily on my mind. I talked with Russell about going to the police and telling them what had happened the day before but Russell pointed out that Susan hadn't been making a whole lot of sense and Cousin Corny would shoot down anything I said. Russell also pointed out that if the police ignored Corny and believed me, I could be at the police department all day.

After a short deliberation, we decided to forego the cops and leave for our final day of tourism. I tried to tuck Susan into a distant corner of my mind. She popped back into my conscience every so often. I did consumerism proud. We got to see and do everything we set out to do and went back to the hotel a little poorer, but sated.

We spent the next morning stuffing clothes and souvenirs into our bags. I would be squashing a trinket wrapped in a new T-shirt into my suitcase and think about my gift to myself waiting on the porch at home. It always brought me back to Susan. Surely some creeps from the streets had broken in and done the deed. The cops would find them and justice would be served.

Not that it would do Susan and her dreams much good. I felt a guilty twinge. Was there anything I could have done to save her? I didn't think so, but my conscience nagged me.

The flight home was tiresome; hurry and wait, hurry and wait. Our 18 year-old daughter, Sarah, picked us up from the airport in our king cab truck. She had been corralled to animal and house sit while we were gone and was thrilled we were home. I wondered how many plants had died, and if any of our dogs had run away. Sarah talked non-stop. You would have thought she had managed a spread of thousands of acres instead of just ten, and taken care of herds of cattle and horses instead of five dogs, four horses, a mule, and a bearded dragon. When we reached the house our dogs, all accounted for, greeted us like we had been gone forever. We dragged our over-stuffed luggage into the house and sat down for a breather. Sarah offered iced tea which we gratefully accepted.

"Was there anything delivered recently?" I asked Sarah.

"Yes, ma'am. It's out on the porch. It's kinda big. Is it for me?"

"Unfortunately for you, it's not, but I'll leave it to you in my will."

"Thanks bunches, Mom. And I could have sworn it barked. I mean, I know you wouldn't send a live dog in a box like that." Pause. "Would you?"

"Of course not, but I am anxious to open it." Would the gargoyle talk to anyone else? Or had it singled me out? Was I still sane?

"Let's open it," I said eagerly.

"Yeah!" enthused my daughter. She ran to find a pair of scissors.

Sarah returned with the scissors and we went to work on the box. Whoever packed the gargoyle (probably poor Susan) had gone just a little mad with the fill material. There was more than the object called for, but I was grateful. I didn't want anything to happen to my new little buddy. We finally got down to the gargoyle and I was afraid the wrong one had been sent. The one I had picked out was crouching down on her front legs with her booty up in the air, a 'come play with me' posture.

This one was sitting up as if begging. But when Sarah looked away, the bat-dog rolled stone eyes at me and winked! I let out a bark of laughter in surprise. Sarah turned back quickly. "You alright, Mom?"

"Yeah, just something in my throat. I'm fine."

Sarah looked at me dubiously. I tried to look like everything really was just fine.

"It's cute, if you like ugly," was my daughter's opinion. "Where are you going to put it?"

"Her," I said automatically.

"What?"

"Her. It's a she."

"Are you okay, Mom? Seriously."

"Yes I'm fine. Seriously. I just thought she looked like a she."

"If you say so. Look, you and dad are probably exhausted after the plane ride. Why don't I fix dinner for you guys, then I'll get out of your hair and let you get some rest. How's that sound?"

"Like an angel came up with it. Thanks, honey"

"No problem. I'll get started on that right away. Would you be up for some bacon and eggs?"

"That would be heavenly especially since I don't have to do it. Go, be off with you; work your magic in the kitchen, oh child of mine." I flapped my hands at her.

Sarah scooted off. I turned back to the gargoyle, who was now sitting on her haunches.

"I didn't know you could move like that."

"You didn't ask."

"Yeah, well. I'm going to put you here, next to the front door so you can protect me and mine."

"Protected you shall be. And speaking of eating, I could also use some food. Dog gargoyles were linked to the deadly sin of gluttony. I am a dog. I'm hungry. I can eat throw-away, too."

"Well, you'll have to wait. I'll check the garbage can and see what we have. More than likely Sarah didn't take the trash out so you may be in luck. Did you get fed at the gargoyle store?"

"No," the statue replied.

I started to pet my new porch ornament, but pulled my hand back quickly. A gut instinct had stopped me. "Is it alright to pet you?" I didn't want to find my hand caught in stone jaws.

"I have had my head petted by sticky-handed little humans and big humans. I can't say I particularly enjoy it, but since I'm with you now, you can pet my head. I may grow to like it." I was sure I wouldn't be petting her any time soon. "I also need water," my new acquisition stated.

"Why do you need water?"

"I was created as a spout for directing water away from buildings and to remind illiterate peasants of the Seven Deadly Sins. You already know what I represent." The gargoyle's voice had gotten increasingly snarky. "Now that you have me, I can help you remember not to want too much of anything, especially food."

Great. A gargoyle diet. The latest, greatest diet fad. Everyone should try it. I was getting annoyed at this thing's tone of voice. "I'll water you later."

"Come and get it! Din-din!" Sarah saved the day. The savory smell of bacon wafted out to the porch and made my mouth water.

I hadn't had anything to eat since San Francisco, at least 8 hours ago.

"See you later," I tossed off as I hurried inside. I thought I heard a gravely growl behind me.

The bacon, eggs, and fresh hash browns were as delicious as only simple fare can be when you are really hungry.

Sarah said, "I heard you out on the porch. Your voice sounds funny. And when did you start talking to yourself?"

"When I had you, dear."

There were still a couple of bags left in the car, so we let the dogs out in the front yard while we went to get them. We were deeply engrossed with our task and catching up on neighborhood gossip; only one more trip out to the truck and we could get our pj's on and relax.

I heard a yelp and counted tails. Ralphie, one of our Chihuahuas was missing. He had been with us just moments before. He wasn't one to wander off.

The three of us looked everywhere outside we could think of. No Ralphie. I decided to check the house. As I ran up the porch stairs, I glanced at the gargoyle. Hanging out of the 'goyle's mouth was a tail. "Ralphie?" The tail wagged. The gargoyle wagged her tail, too. I would have sworn she smiled.

"Okaaay, open your mouth and let the dog out." The 'goyle's tail wagged harder; it grated on the porch boards and scratched them terribly. The mouth did not open. "Ralphie, are you okay?" I asked in a stage whisper. Ralphie's tail wagged harder.

"Open up or I'll get a sledge hammer."

Reluctantly, the gargoyle's jaws ground open and Ralphie tumbled out, covered not with spit, but with dust. He shook himself vigorously and a small cloud lifted off of his little body.

"Why did you try to eat my dog?" I asked crossly.

"I am here to protect you and your home from harm. This creature seemed to pose a threat, so I seized him. Besides I'm hungry. And he peed on me."

"Alright, alright, I'll feed you. Just don't eat the dogs." I paused. "What do gargoyles eat?" I was a little afraid of the answer.

"I am a dog gargoyle." She sounded like she was tired of explaining the obvious. "Whatever your dogs eat is good. Garbage, too." She sat there, smiling. "I won't be too picky."

"How much do you eat?"

"Just keep it coming. I'll let you know when I've had enough." Her tail ground back and forth in joyful anticipation.

"Mom, are you hitting the house with a rock, and, if so, why?" I could hear Sarah walking toward the front door.

Just moving the gargoyle around to a better spot." I glared at it. "I hope you're not going to be more trouble than you're worth," I whispered.

"What, Mom? Are you talking to yourself again?"

"I do seem to be doing a lot of that lately. Nobody listens to me when I'm talking to them, now everybody hears me when I'm talking to myself."

"Go to bed, Mom. I'll take care of feeding the horses and dogs, so you can relax before the real world intrudes tomorrow."

I sighed. What a kid. I wondered what she would say when I told her the damned gargoyle could talk? And would anyone believe me? And not have me committed?

Sarah headed down to the barn. I crept into the kitchen and opened the garbage. I got a paper plate and picked out egg shells, some old Chinese food, wilted lettuce and half a baloney sandwich that was turning colors. I walked softly to the laundry room where the dog food was kept in a plastic tub.

Sarah walked into the laundry room and I jumped guiltily, thrusting the loaded plate behind my back. "Mother, what are you doing?" She sounded exasperated. "I said I would feed the mutts so could go take a load off. How often do I do this for you anyway? You sure are acting funny. Is the jet lag that bad?"

I jumped on the excuse. "Yeah, that's it. I just don't feel like myself," I lied. "I've got a few things to do then I'll go lay down."

"That sounds like a good idea. Go get comfortable. I'm leaving and don't wait up for me. I'm going to Marcy's birthday party and don't know when I'll be home. And before you say anything else, yes, I've got my cell phone. Love ya, Mom."

"Thanks for everything, Sarah. Bye and have a good time." I was secretly relieved to have Sarah gone. I didn't know where Russell was, but he usually whistled when he went around the place, so I'd probably hear him coming. I would have to tell him pretty soon about the gargoyle, but would the gargoyle cooperate and talk to him?

I took the plate of scraps and dog food out to the front porch. The gargoyle was lying down like a lion in front of a library, surveying her realm. She surveyed the property as if it was hers. I put the plate down between her paws. "Is this all?" she asked with a snotty attitude.

"Yes, this is all." I said, "For now."

"I'll need more than this tomorrow. Protecting a property is hungry work. I need lots of food, especially if you don't want your dogs to disappear." She looked at me slyly. "We wouldn't want another accident like today's, would we?"

This thing was a despot! Now what was I going to do? I wanted to send the little demon back to the shop in San Francisco, damn the shipping cost, but there had been that sign by the cash register, 'NO RETURNS – ALL SALES FINAL'.

And mine wasn't even the worst one! Look at what the ones left behind had done to poor Susan!

My gargoyle calmly began munching on the plate's contents. It seemed that she ate slowly but the food was gone in nothing flat. The sound of her stone jaws was horrifying. The grinding got on my nerves in new and awful ways. When I thought about what might have happened to little Ralphie, I broke out in a cold sweat.

"Everything alright?" the monster asked sweetly.

"I have some things I must do before I go to bed tonight. I'll just pick up this plate..." The plate disappeared as I reached for it.

"I eat garbage, too. Remember?"

"I won't forget," I muttered. Her muzzle had actually left a kind of road rash on my knuckle. Tiny beads of blood rose up on my abraded skin. I'd had enough of this creature for the day. I stumbled to my bedroom, put pajamas on and went to bed.

I heard Russell come in the front door just as I was falling asleep. Sarah must have told him I wasn't feeling well before she left for her party because he considerately turned off the light and didn't bother me.

During the night, I woke to the sound of rocks, one at a time, being dropped on the bedroom floor. The thuds kept coming, closer and closer. Russell was snoring. How could he sleep through that noise? It was loud and getting louder.

The pounding stopped at the foot of the bed as if deciding which side to pick. When it started again, it was headed for my side. I kept my eyes tightly closed. I was so afraid. I felt the bed jar as something bumped against it. The noise stopped right next to me. I heard a pebbly sounding murmur in my ear. Dust fell on my face. I had to open my eyes, a stone mouth was moving in on my throat!

I screamed and thrashed wildly. I struck out with clenched fists to get the monster away from me before the muzzle could clamp down. My fists made contact with a boulder. As it grabbed my wrists, I shrieked louder and fought harder.

"Easy, babe, easy," the monstrosity said, pressing my hands down gently. "You've had a nasty nightmare. Just take it easy," the soothing voice continued. That wasn't the voice of a monster.

I ventured a look with one eye. My husband was holding my wrists and murmuring soft words to me from his side of the bed. "Where's the monster?!" I yelled. "Where is she? She was going to rip my throat out!"

"Nobody is going to rip your throat out. You just had a bad dream." He released my hands. "Are you okay now?"

"Yes, I'm okay." My throat hurt from screaming and I could feel pain in my knuckles. It was all a dream. That stupid gargoyle was giving me nightmares.

I swung my bare feet to the cold floor and stood up on something sharp. ROCKS! Right next to my bed! It was no nightmare! That misbegotten pile of stones was trying to kill me! The gloves were coming off. The sledgehammer was coming out in the morning. That bitch was soon to be rubble.

I went back to bed and was soon dozing. I finally fell into a deep sleep that lasted into the morning. When I awoke, I felt much better than I had the day before in spite of the disturbances in the night. I was refreshed and ready to take on the demon spawn on my front porch.

I went into the kitchen for breakfast. Sarah was eating cereal at the island. She had also made bacon and scrambled eggs for me and Russell. "Feeling better, Mom?"

"Yes, much better, thank you." All I needed was a good meal and a good night's sleep."

"Dad told me you had a whopper of a nightmare. Are you okay now?"

"Yeah, when I finally fell asleep, it was deep." I decided to take the plunge. "I have a favor to ask of you."

"Tell me first, then I'll let you know."

Typical. "I'm going to get rid of that gargoyle. It's evil."

"I know it's ugly but I thought you really liked it. 'Her,' sorry."

"She almost ate Ralphie, she wants to be fed constantly, and she almost ripped my throat out last night! I realized I sounded like a raving lunatic. Sarah stared at me with wide-eyed amazement, an unchewed spoonful of cereal in her open mouth.

"Easy, Mom," Sarah managed to choke out. "It'll be okay. I'll just go get Dad..."

"NO! He won't, he won't..."

"Understand? Mom, I don't understand! What's going on?" A knowing look came over her face. "Are you going through...the Change?"

"No, I am not going through the Change. I've got something to tell you and you can't tell your father. He would think..."

"That you're acting crazy?! What is going on?"

"Okay." I took a deep breath. I ran down the whole story for Sarah. Her expression ran a gamut of emotions from incredulous and disbelieving to awestruck and deeply worried.

"And this thing really is alive? And talks? And eats?"

"Yup. If the damned thing will cooperate, I can show you. Come on." My poor daughter followed me, no doubt convinced I was off my rocker. I was wondering about that myself. "Let me go first and you hide around the corner. I'll get her to talk. Then you'll know. Then you can help me figure out what to do with her."

We approached the front door. I was certain the gargoyle wouldn't say or do anything, and I would be committed. She was standing guard to anyone else's eye, but I knew better. She was lying in wait. Probably for me. For me to feed her. I could play on that.

I walked out and stood in front of her. "Well? Are you hungry? What do you want to eat?"

No response. The damned thing just sat there like she should have all along. I stood there, determined to wait her out. I hoped Sarah had enough patience to wait her out, too. After a couple of minutes, I heard a small grinding sound and looked down. The thing's eyes were swiveling to meet mine.

"Yes, I am hungry. I need to be fed soon, or I'll find another source of food." The memory of Ralphie's tail sticking out of her mouth came back to me.

"All right, all right. What do you want?"

"I can eat just about anything. I smell eggs and bacon in the house. That should be fine. I want lots."

I scooted back into the house, eager to see Sarah's face.

Sarah was backed against the island with a stunned look on her face. "Mom. That thing really talks. It talks! What are you going to do?" There was panic in her voice. "We have to tell Dad!"

"No. He'll think we're both crazy. I need to do something about this gargoyle but I need help. Please help me?"

"Okay. We'll figure all of this out. Just take it easy. We can do it." Calming me down calmed her down. "You got it from a shop in San Francisco, right? Can you send it back?" Hope was edging into her voice.

"We can try. I don't know how we'll be able to get her back into the box. She'll probably fight us."

I looked through my purse for the receipt. I had rubber-banded all of the trip receipts together. "Gargoyles-R-Us. Here we go." I hadn't paid much attention to the receipt before. It was on a cheap paper strip that would probably disintegrate before I got my bank statement. The ink from the machine was already bleeding out, making the figures on it look like it had been put through the washing machine. Cousin Corny had spared no expense in his store. The phone number of the shop was barely legible already.

I dialed the number. The other end rang once, twice, and then the discordant notes with the mechanized voice came on the line to tell me that the number was disconnected and no longer in service. Great. "Well, returning the beast is no longer an option. What now?"

We were thinking hard when a loud obscenity accompanied by a big crash sounded on the porch. We hurried to the door and opened it to a great cloud of dust. Russell was swearing a streak that could have set the house on fire.

"That damned gargoyle! I swear it tried to trip me every time I passed it." Sarah and I traded knowing looks. "I'm really sorry. I was moving it to a different spot and it felt like it was fighting me to get back to its original place on the porch. I was attempting to position it closer to the bannister and somehow it ended up falling from the porch. I can try to fix it with some cement..." He spread his hands apologetically.

"No!" Sarah and I yelled at the same time.

"No, it's okay." I said, "I'll just see how much damage there is and let you know." My husband looked at me strangely.

"I know how much you wanted that thing, ugly as it is. I'm really sorry."

"Don't worry about it." I tried to keep my voice sorrowful but inside I was rejoicing. Sarah was trying not to smile. "You go finish your chores and I'll take care of this." Boy, oh boy, would I take care of this!

A look over the side of the porch revealed a pile of gravel. Some parts of the gargoyle were still visible as a leg here and what might have been a tail there. One part that had survived intact was the head. It lay a little way from the remaining parts of its body.

"Let him put me back together." That gravelly voice still had the nerve to order me around! "I was just playing a little joke on your husband. He should have to repair me."

"What kind of joke?" I was curious about what this creature considered a joke.

"I just put my foot out whenever he went by. He always tripped but didn't fall. It was funny! He never caught on, either."

"Why should you be put back together? You are not a nice gargoyle."

"I can still protect your property." The voice had become a bit plaintive now. Maybe this rotten thing was sorry for what it had done.

"You won't order me around anymore or try to hurt anything on this ranch?"

"I will do as you ask. I will do my duty and nothing more. I promise. Please put me back together?"

So I talked Russell into fixing the thing. What he did with it was amazing. It was rough in some spots but he rebuilt it, and the gargoyle behaved during the whole process.

It was placed on a stump just inside our property gate, out of the way and unable to harm anything. Once in a while, I go to the gate with a bit of a sandwich or an apple core. The 'goyle is polite and happy for the treat and the company.

Sarah found out there's more to the world than she had ever known, and I learned that getting what you want can be worse than not having it.

Photo Credit: John Fatland

HORROR

Something about the cooling and darkening of the fall, and the spectacular way vegetation crisps to ghosts as it dies off for winter, has spurred imaginations to the macabre for the length and breadth of human history. Halloween looms and after the plenty of summer, people hunker down around the fire where it's safe, light, and warm; they dig out their favorite old ghost stories to thrill the nights that blacken so early. Some people, like the Sacred Circle Writers, come up with new ones.

Dave Becker's creepy Shirley Temple Doll, far from being a comforting toy, shares its nightmares willingly in *The Doll*. What could possibly be scarier than spiders and snakes? The way they move fascinates us at the same time it inspires phobic fear for many. If Laurie Wilson Fatland's *She* doesn't keep you awake tonight for fear of dreaming, nothing will, and *The Innocents* will have you keeping a close eye indeed on your children. Keli Becker teaches us the high cost of callous disregard in *Restless Spirits Cemetery*.

The Doll

Dave Becker

At last Grandma passed away. She never went anywhere. She didn't eat right. She never took care of herself and had no interest in anything but watching TV. She had no true friends, and the friends she did have, she criticized all of the time.

The only person I truly ever saw her attach to was my daughter, 7 year-old Josie. Grandma gave her anything she wanted and fed her as much junk food as she could. Many times I had to intervene and cut the junk food off, hiding it from Josie once she got home.

The one thing she gave Josie that wasn't junk food was her beloved Shirley Temple doll. The doll was grandma's favorite thing; she said it reminded her of herself when she was a little girl. The frilly clothes, curly blond hair and blue eyes. When she was young Grandma said she danced just like Shirley Temple had in her old movies.

Josie loved the doll because it came from Grandma, and reminded her of her Grandma. Josie immediately set up her old crib next to her bed so the doll could sleep next to her.

After a couple of days I noticed that the doll was on the couch where Grandma had always sat every morning.

I asked Josie why the doll was on the couch every morning and not in her room. Josie said that the doll would end up in bed with her, fidgeting and growling and keep her awake. So Josie would get up and put the doll on the couch so she could get some sleep. After that Josie didn't even take the doll to her bedroom anymore, but opted to just leave the doll on the couch every night to begin with.

This went on for about a week until one morning I noticed a knife next to the doll on the couch. I immediately said something to Josie but she said she had nothing to do with the knife. In fact, she said, that's why she put the doll on the couch in the first place. It gave her the creeps.

Several more mornings went by and the knife was next to the doll every morning. I kept putting the knife back into its butcher block holder on the top shelf of the kitchen cabinet. But the knife was always sitting next to the doll in the morning, and I would put it away again...every morning.

Now the doll had started to give me the serious creeps too, so I decided to put it in the back room and lock the door. But the next morning the doll was back on the couch with the knife next to it.

I confronted Josie about the movements of the doll, but she didn't know anything about it so I dropped the subject.

I thought that maybe it was time to get rid of that ragged, frayed old doll once and for all so I put it in the garbage can for the next day's garbage pick-up.

To my surprise, when I got home, the doll was back on the couch again with the knife next to it. I immediately took the doll out to the car, threw it in the trunk and closed it.

The next morning it was again on the couch with the knife next to it. I picked it up by the hair, took it to the car, threw it in the trunk again, went back into the house to get Josie, and off to school we went. When I got to work, I parked next to the dumpster, tossed the doll in and went into the building.

I could see the dumpster and my car from my office window and didn't see anything suspicious going on. The refuse company came to empty the dumpster. I went out to look...no doll. Maybe this little nightmare was finally over.

I got off work, picked Josie up from school and went home. To my surprise, there was that damn doll sitting on the couch, with the knife next to it. What next?

I went in to take a shower before fixing dinner and helping Josie with her homework. Maybe I could come up with a good idea to get rid of this thing once and for all.

When I came out of the shower, the doll was at my feet, slashing at my ankles with the knife. I dropped the towel to cover my ankles and kicked the doll across the room. It hit the wall and was barely stunned. It came at me again, and I kicked it again, harder. It hit the wall harder. The arm with the knife in its hand came off and continued gyrating on the floor. I picked up the doll by the curly cues on top of its head, took it outside, and threw it into the BBQ, and locked the lid.

I breathed a sigh of relief until I realized I was standing in my backyard for the neighbors on either side of my house to see. I was still naked, bleeding at my ankles, and getting the most curious look from my daughter standing at the back door.

I went back into the house, got some clothes on, and went back into the bathroom to retrieve the gyrating arm still with the knife in its hand. I stepped on the knife and yanked the hand away from it. I took the hand and arm back out to the BBQ. I quickly tossed it in to join the rest of the now definitely pissed off doll.

I turned on the gas on the BBQ, lit the burners, and turned each knob to "high." Within minutes the temperature gauge read 500 degrees. The BBQ began to shake, smoke, growl, pound, and spin around. To keep it from tipping over, I pushed it into a corner of the stone seating area, and wedged some large rocks around it.

I went into the house where it was safe and watched the BBQ for about two and a half hours until the propane ran out.

I didn't have the nerve to open it up. I loaded it into my neighbor's pick-up and took it to the metal recyclers.

I don't know what was worse for Josie: losing her doll; seeing me naked in the backyard; or watching the BBQ almost melt away. Either way, all was forgotten in a couple of weeks. A trip to TOYS R US and a gallon of ice cream cured us both.

She

Laurie Wilson Fatland

She did not think, not in the conventional sense. Hers was the finely honed instinct of a predator; the end result of millions of years of evolution. Her kind had lived quietly among mankind, hunting and killing and being killed from long before the writing of history.

Now, however, man's tampering with the earth had given her the advantage and accelerated evolution's slow progress. In the dark spaces of the nuclear waste dumping grounds, the tiny predator had changed. She had grown.

Her cave arched over an underground lake. A lake that humans did not know existed when they began leaving their hot waste behind. The lake was fed by rainfall and seasonal streams that percolated the unnatural soup. When she first hatched she fed on insects and small blind water creatures, who themselves had been changed by their frightening environment. The people who came and went above ground were fully shielded by nuclear protective suits, scared of what they had created; the creatures who lived here had no such defense. They absorbed the radiation and became something new.

As she grew, she slurped the blood and flesh from the altered fish in the lake. The changes were subtle, not visible to the human eye. A strand of DNA here, an extra protein there, it was enough that she was recreated into a being far beyond her predecessors.

She continued to grow, far past the parameters of her kind. She grew hungry, far past the capacity of the cave to satiate her. It was time to move to better feeding grounds.

As she approached the opening of the cave she instinctively held back until darkness blanketed the surrounding forest. Her four pairs of eyes did not like the light; they were adapted to discerning movement and the faint shadows of black and white in the night. She ventured out cautiously, moving quickly through trees and bushes, the soft scrabbling of her claws was like the rustling of dry leaves. The scent of meat was strong and compelling. She found a rock outcropping and perched to wait. Her kind excelled in patience.

Eight eyes searched the forest for movement. Eight legs were poised to sense tiny vibrations in the forest floor. She hovered next to a game trail, heavy with the meat smell, her hunger heightening all her senses.

A lone deer ambled along the trail, alert to any movement or change in the scent of its surroundings. It smelled the darkness and the earth around it, but she was just another of the forest smells. Perhaps the deer picked up the smell of the cave, but it was not alarmed, it stopped to graze the tender grass along the trail.

Her leap was perfectly timed. Faster than the human eye could register she engulfed the deer in her legs and sank her fangs into its tender abdomen. Size was not the only change her putrefying environment had wrought on her. Necrotic venom dripped from her fangs that could liquefy flesh in minutes. She held the deer tightly while it struggled as the venom turned it into an ooze of flesh and blood and fluid she suckled eagerly.

Satisfied, she returned to her perch to await the next meal. When daylight came, she crawled under the rocks and rested, gaining strength and growing until the next hunting.

And so she dwelled, deep in the forest, gorging on any animal that came near. When the prey grew scarce, she moved to the next trail, following the smell of the meat she craved.

Time passed, and the prey no longer came near, so she kept moving, hunting and killing and drinking. She perfected her technique. Nothing was safe from her, her cunning and intelligence grew with her speed, and no animal escaped her fangs.

As she traveled, she moved from cave to cave and rock pile to rock pile. In one of them she encountered a large male spider. Not as large as her, but big enough that the desire to mate overwhelmed her. The mating was quick and mechanical, a necessity of survival, after which she ate him to help nourish her children. Soon, she laid her eggs and spun a swaddling for them, a silken egg sack that she held close and carried with her as she moved.

Now she had new purpose, she must continue to feed and care for her eggs to ensure their survival. Her hunting became even more aggressive and frequent. The meat disappeared. Her hunger grew, and her wanderings took her farther and farther from her origins.

When the egg sack grew too difficult to maneuver, she settled into another cave to await the arrival of her young. She grew ravenous as she waited. But her reward was to see her children as they crawled from the nest and climbed onto her back, their black legs clinging to her hairy body. When they had all emerged it was time to move, time to satisfy her hunger and feed her children until they could hunt for themselves.

The young ones clung to their mother, watching and learning as she found new prey. They eagerly climbed down to suck the liquefied flesh along with her, and they too grew. But the prey became scarcer and scarcer, and they all grew hungrier. And so she moved, searching for new smells of meat, coming at last to the edge of the forest, where mankind dwelled.

The lights of the village bothered her at first. She hung back in the darkness, watching and listening. Soon, though, the meat smell drew her closer and closer, the children moving excitedly over her back as they caught the scent too. In the dark of night she found the prey had hidden itself in shelters of wood, she smelled them inside and she contemplated how to remove them, climbing over the houses and exploring with her legs and claws.

Soon she found that there were openings in the shelters covered with soft material that her claws could tear and thin, hard surfaces that broke when she tapped them. She reached in and snared one of the prey. It screamed but she silenced it quickly with a bite. The soft gel it became from the venom was barely enough to quell the pangs of hunger. But there were many of them and she moved from shelter to shelter eating them all. Some even came running out as they heard the screams and the children leapt on them and devoured them, honing their hunting skills to take them down.

The village was emptied and she moved on, following the scent to the next one. She had learned. She had found an easy source to satisfy her hunger. And her children had learned. They spun small webs and used the winds to scatter themselves along the edges of the forest. Their primal survival drive made them know instinctively that there was not enough meat to satisfy them all, that they must move on.

The forests near Chernobyl grew empty. The villages grew empty. Mankind began to wonder what was happening, but it always happened under cover of darkness. All that could be found were dried sacks of skin left behind. No flesh, no blood, no bones.

Meanwhile the children grew. And they multiplied. They traveled under cover of darkness and emptied village after village. They closed in on cities and began to move through the darkness. It was too late for mankind. The survivors hid themselves and tried to find ways to destroy this threat. But the children studied them, and they learned, and they were many. The meat smell always drew them near.

The Innocents

Laurie Wilson Fatland

It was too easy, really. And the bastard deserved it. Granted, we both had a taste for the soft, smooth flesh of children, but he left them scarred and crippled for life, I simply left them dead.

I come from a long line of spell casters; my talents have been passed down for centuries and honed to a particular intensity in my generation. I am the final one. My gift to the world will be the end of my line, but that doesn't mean I won't enjoy the time left.

Oh, I've tried to assimilate into the general population. Live, love, laugh and eat as they do, but the hunger is much too strong. For years I denied myself, but no longer. The hunger threatens to swallow me if it is not satisfied and after all, what is the cost of a few more lives in mankind's long history of gore? My contribution is a tiny one, and for the greater good, after all.

If you met me, you would not recognize me. I am the sweet old lady in your neighborhood whom everyone loves; a harmless, gentle lady who bakes cookies and offers them to the children. I am everyone's idea of the perfect grandmother. Interestingly, I am often asked to babysit for families nearby, something I gladly do to further my research and to bask in the scent of innocent children.

I have long studied how to indulge my desperate hunger for roasted child without inciting the rage of the populace. So many times I failed, moving every few years and changing my persona to hide amongst you and try again. It was a wearying life. Finally, though, I stumbled upon Wayne Frithers and my problems were solved.

The day I found him was overcast, yet warm; a perfect day to walk in the woods and gather noxious mushrooms and plants for my spells. I was carefully pulling up the roots of water hemlock when I saw them. Mr. Frithers had the child pressed into the ground, half unclothed, forcing himself onto the crying little one. Disgusting. I was sickened. What a waste of a beautiful child. I should have stepped in and stopped him, but it was too late for that child, who was now so pitifully damaged.

No, a greater plan came to me and I stepped back, unseen, into the shadows of the woods. Mr. Frithers whispered his threats to the child, who was sobbing and trying to cover itself. He seemed well practiced, and confident that his intimidation would keep the child from revealing his terrible secrets. The child stumbled away, broken and afraid. Mr. Frithers sat back in the leaves, more disgusting than any slime-covered toad, no doubt reliving his abominable crime and doubling his twisted pleasure.

When he finally walked away, I followed. His home wasn't far from mine, it was a rundown old clapboard in need of paint, with a littered and weed-filled yard. It took me very little research to discover his identity and his job as a home appliance repairman. I began to understand that he used his job as a way to discover and stalk his prey. Well, now the hunter would become the hunted.

I kept a close eye on Mr. Frithers after that. My reputation for taking long walks around the town made it simple for me to watch him. Every day I began my walks passing by his house, and I noted where his work truck was parked when he did his repairs. At each house where there were children, I saw how Mr. Frithers found excuses to elongate his repairs until the children came home from school. What other people saw as friendliness, I saw as a predator, trying to lull his prey before he struck.

These became the homes where I harvested my children. I did my gathering at night, when the children were dazed with sleep and their parents lay oblivious in their beds. A simple spell outside an open window, a drop of potion in a bedside glass of water was all that was needed; they were now in my complete control. Spellcaster or witch, whatever you wish to call me, I am talented at my craft. It is the subtle things that matter, the devil is in the details and I made sure every detail was covered. No one ever suspected, no one ever saw me.

My pattern was established. Mr. Frithers did the hunting for me, he was the one whose presence was established at every scene. Missing children became the focus of the town; it was the topic of every conversation and the nightly fear of every family. It was only a matter of time until Mr. Frithers was implicated.

Meanwhile, the sleepy, delicious children followed me home willingly and were barely aware when I snapped their little necks, cut them up and popped them into the oven. Afterward, when the hunger was stilled, I always baked cookies for dessert; spicy, strongly flavored cookies that helped mask the distinctive smell of roasted child.

It wasn't long before parents began to suspect the repairman. There was a much longer period of time before he was arrested, as the police searched for evidence to tie him to the crimes. Of course, I knew there was no evidence; I'd made sure of that. Meanwhile, I continued my harvesting and butchered some of the children and froze them to keep me satisfied during my upcoming sabbatical. It wouldn't do for children to go missing while Mr. Frithers rotted in jail.

It was, truly, a brilliant plan. I indulged my hunger while sparing these children, each of whom would have been cruelly victimized by Mr. Frithers, a lifetime of suffering and pain. They were mercy killings in truth. And, ultimately, I removed a child predator from society. My plan really benefited everyone. Humanity would never acknowledge it, but I was their avenging angel, their savior.

My supplies are beginning to run low, however. I will have to move on soon. There can be no more harvesting here while Mr. Frithers languishes in prison. It shouldn't be too difficult to find my next location. After all, child predators exist in almost every town. These monsters have given me the perfect opportunity to dispense my special kind of justice and satisfy my needs.

Child predators have their own unique scent, I have discovered, and I am honing my skills to hunt them down in the time remaining for me. And children, my soft, plump children, I am coming. Have no fear little ones, I am coming to help you, to grant you a merciful death, to save you from your worst nightmares.

Restless Spirits Cemetery

Keli Becker

The cemetery sat in the center of town like a great diseased toadstool at the junction of two streets. It was two acres in size and avoided by residents of the settlement. Their excuses were not the usual ones people vaguely uncomfortable with the dead used. People went out of their way to go around this cemetery because they got accosted when near the place.

Pinched, jostled and poked, the citizens of the town hated the spot even though numerous loved ones were buried there. Many came away from what should have been a calming, reassuring visit with their deceased family and friends with bruises and blood blisters that took an uncommon amount of time to fade away.

The cemetery, named Rosco Barnard Street Cemetery, was situated on an ancient site sacred to the Mishmash Indians. They had performed healing rites, banishment ceremonies, and foretelling of events at the place where Roscoe Barnard Street and Clara Barnard Streets joined. The native Mishmash were forced out by the loggers who came to inhabit the town, and the Mishmash holy man placed a curse on the land.

The Barnards made fast money by putting their money on the railroads that were coming into town. They built a house on the Mishmash's sacred spot in 1859 when the lumber business was in full swing. It was a grand house, overseeing the town like a castle on a hill. Troubles plagued the building of the house and more accidents occurred during construction than could be accounted for logically.

The lingering artifacts of the Mishmash were generally destroyed, or kept as souvenirs. The pots were particularly preferred as they were masterfully designed.

Rosco Barnard was sinfully rich according to the town's citizens, and flaunted his wealth, associating only with the equally rich, of which there were just enough for a ruling class to form.

Only the wealthy held official positions in city government and of course, the laws passed favored only the well-to-do. The poorer folks worked to keep the affluent in their lofty situations, and suffered while the rich got richer.

The townfolk were therefore very interested when news of the Barnard's troubles with their house filtered down through the household servants. Orbs were seen floating in hallways. Cold spots were felt in most of the rooms. Objects were moved from one place to another. Human forms floated throughout the building, giving more than one fright to the staff. Even the staid butler was affected. He refused to deliver meals to the master's bedroom because the tray was tipped out of his hands every time by unseen spirits. Other servants were tripped going up and down stairs and prevented from doing their duties. Household accounts inevitably went wrong; silverware went missing, plates were flung around the dining room by unseen hands to crash and mar the rich woodwork of the furnishings.

The house became infested with rats. One of the younger children ingested poison set out to kill them and almost died. Business suffered, too. Mr. Barnard could not work at home. Transactions went wrong, payloads were lost without explanation, and papers disappeared for which no cause could be found.

One of the Barnard's children tripped going down the grand staircase and broke his neck. The servants and visitors to the house would see the specter of the little boy around the house. Guests soon stopped visiting.

It became impossible to maintain a household staff, and the Barnards moved to another town. The house fell into disrepair and started deteriorating at an unusual speed. Granted the winters were rough, and the winds damaging, but you could almost see it disintegrate before your eyes.

The Barnards, in their generosity, gave the house and the land it sat on to the growing town to do with as the town government wanted. The civic seats had been gradually taken over by regular citizens who decided to build a church and a cemetery on the plot of land. They felt the spirit of the Lord was needed on the blighted area.

The land was cleared and the church went up at record speed. The men building it wanted to be done and away from it as soon as possible. Unusual accidents happened during construction that no amount of careful handling could avoid. Men were pushed from ladders and trusses when no one was near them. Hammers were yanked from hands and pounded on those same hands.

It got so bad that the township had to offer high wages for the era just to keep men on the job and lure workers to the area. There almost weren't enough uninjured citizens to finish the job. Finally the church was finished. A minister performed a public blessing ceremony to ease the uncertainty of the citizens.

As time went by, the incidents grew fewer and an uneasy peace settled on the site. The first turnout wasn't great. Church attendance increased gradually as the weeks went by and the community's unease was gradually put aside.

Eventually the building was purchased by the Catholic Church and renamed Our Mother of Perpetual Sorrows which, for reasons known only to the Church, which seemed apt. Eight gargoyles were placed on the roof for protection. They were also supposed to be reminders of the Seven Deadly Sins. No one seemed to know why there were eight gargoyles instead of just seven and in light of the "accidents" no one wanted to take them down. Most of the parishioners didn't know about the deadly sins anyway, and those who did only knew the gargoyles were supposed to be protection, which it was well known the plot of land sorely needed.

The rest of the land behind the church was designated as the Church cemetery. Nobody objected; things at the site had been quiet since the first minister had performed the blessing ceremony.

All went well for 100 years. Then came the day the powers that be decided to move the cemetery to the other side of town in order to build a school on the old Mishmash site behind the church. They declared a Christian school was necessary so the kids whose families could afford it would get a proper education.

The bodies in the cemetery were carefully dug up and transported to the new plot. The deeper the workers dug in the Mishmash cemetery, the more artifacts came to light. The men started to feel uneasy and minor accidents began to occur more regularly. There wasn't one man on the crew who didn't have a wound of some kind.

Tales of the accident-prone building of the church a hundred years ago had been forgotten. At first, the supervisors laughed it off as clumsiness, but grew concerned when even the most careful workers got hurt. Again the work was rushed. The new school was built and classes started.

Things were quiet for a year and students and teachers got comfortable and in a routine. Then strange things started happening.

The priest would go into the church in the morning and find candles lit when no one had been around to do it. The building was kept locked at night. Parishioners felt themselves being jostled in the pews and while going up to the altar to receive the Sacrament. Footsteps were heard in the aisles and movement was seen behind the altar when the priest and altar boys were not near it. Human-like shadows moved around the confessionals and penitents felt cold while confessing. People heard voices other than the priest's while telling their sins. Items on the altar would be moved from place to place during mass.

The adjoining school was not without restless spirits either. The body of a small boy was found while the school was being built, somehow overlooked in the rush to move the cemetery. It is said to this day that his ghost runs up and down the halls during classes, pinches girls on their way to the restroom and tugs painfully on their hair. All of the sports balls are scattered around the auditorium after hours. Bouncing balls can be heard by the janitors late at night. "I'll be back," is written on chalkboards throughout the school.

The misplaced souls do not enjoy their eternal rest. The mischievous boy and the curse remain waiting for the unwary. One of the gargoyles is missing from the roof; no one knows what happened to it and no sign of it was ever found anywhere on the grounds.

Once ousted from their land, the Mishmash moved to unknown canyons and have never been seen or heard from again. The Barnards lost most of their money and prestige on bad deals. They invested in an outsized trading post and a large cattle drive. The other investors were con men and absconded with the money, trading goods and cattle, leaving the Barnards with just enough funds to open a boarding house. The Mishmash site remains haunted.

Photo Credit: John Fatland

MOTHER'S CRAZY

The Sacred Circle Writers are a gentle critique group, lovingly offering feedback to each other towards both improving writing technique and polishing individual pieces. The business part of the meeting is frequently brief, incidental to the sense of friendship and community we know with each other. We sit down, perfunctorily swap writing for comment and critique, and then get on to the important stuff: enjoying good food and conversation. Sometimes we don't even get around to deciding on a prompt to write to for the week. The Sacred Circle Writers is a circle of incorrigible and unrepentant storytellers.

One day the conversation wandered to the topic of the complicated relationships between mothers and their children. One of the Sacred Circle writers told tales of his mother that were so bizarre and scary we could hardly believe they were true. We had our prompt for the week. The stories that follow were inspired by the same strange, crazy, perhaps even evil, woman.

Whence came the archetype of the evil stepmother? Or mother/mother-in-law in this case? What motivates evil? Is it a selfish desire for some perceived gain? Or is there more? Is it an effort to control, or a malicious, uncontrollable desire to hurt?

You can't make this stuff up. Or can you?

Laurie Wilson Fatland's *The Box* explores the communicable nature of the disease and the full-circle craziness such hurtful people can infect others with, and Keli Becker's *The Darkness Beyond* plumbs the depths of fear and cruelty inherent in such relationships.

The Box

Laurie Wilson Fatland

Last night I dreamed I was a child again. I was locked in an old chest, my childhood toy box, screaming for help while my mother cackled maniacally and refused to release me. I wished it was just a dream but I was reliving a memory.

I woke up with a simmering resentment toward my mother. The memory had rekindled the hatred for her I nurtured all those years. I had convinced myself those feelings were put aside, but my subconscious must have been keeping them around. My shrink would have a field day with this, but I wasn't about to tell him about it.

Meanwhile, my weekly visit with Mother now loomed uncomfortably in front of me. It was difficult enough when I was feeling charitable. The old bat was 80 now and she had no choice but to rely on me for help. She refused to leave her house. Both of us knew she wasn't physically able to take care of things, and I suspected, she was not mentally capable either. So, I made my visits every week to make sure she had food, and that all the maintenance was done on the house. After all, it would be mine someday.

I can't say I am really a dutiful son. I'm 50 now, single, never married. I live in a drab apartment and work as an accountant at a local factory. Mother has nothing to brag about. But I am responsible. I'll make sure she has what she needs and no one can blame me when she finally goes.

The wind was blowing and clouds were gathering for the first storm of fall when I left my apartment. My old, dented Ford sedan rumbled to life on the first try, maybe a good omen. The drive over to her house was uneventful and I pulled up in front of the old clapboard house a little before noon. But I was in no hurry to get out of the car. I sat, looking at the house with its overgrown, patchy lawn and neglected flower beds. I can't see any point fixing up the yard if she's not going to take care of it. I did give the house a new coat of white paint last summer, so it didn't look too bad. I started envisioning it as it would be when I finally moved back in: bushes, flowers and a nice green lawn. Maybe I would even find some kind woman my age who would want to share my simple life. There is always hope.

My life with women has never been very successful. No doubt Mother has something to do with that. I've had a series of awkward dates; most of them never went beyond the first. I just don't know what to say to women. I keep waiting for the verbal abuse to start.

"Ralph, you damn fool, get out of the car and get in here!" My mother was shrieking from the front door. I'm sure the whole neighborhood heard.

I opened the car door and walked into the house as calmly as I could, knowing what lay ahead. "You stupid idiot, sitting out there like some retarded boy who don't know where the door is." Mother had a way of spewing venom.

"Mother, people don't say retarded anymore," I said blandly, hoping to get under her skin.

"I don't give a shit. If the shoe fits, it fits. . .." She was her usual charming self. "I've got my grocery list here, ya gotta go get me my groceries and some other stuff, plus the dishwasher is on the fritz again. I can't get along without it, so get it fixed."

I pushed my resentment down to keep it from boiling over and walked into the kitchen to look at the dishwasher. It wouldn't turn on, so I checked the connections and the fuse box, all of which seemed to be working. "I think it's the motor, I'll get a new one while I'm out." I tried to speak quietly and calmly, but it was to no avail.

"Don't give me your god damned excuses, it's always something, you've always got an excuse you miserable son of a bitch." It was the way she always addressed me, and I smiled secretly as I listened to her insult herself without realizing it.

"She's been here again. Your Aunt Mary. She came last night and keeps looking in my windows. Bitch. I don't know what she's about, but I'm not letting her get to me." My mother was spitting the words out in anger, but I could see a flicker of fear in her eyes. Aunt Mary had died in this very house 20 years ago. She choked on a piece of chicken my mother gave her. It was ruled an accident, but I always wondered because my mother knew Aunt Mary was on a liquid diet following throat surgery and gave it to her anyway. My mother inherited all of Aunt Mary's estate. If a dead Aunt Mary could scare my mother, more power to her.

I looked around the house to see if anything else needed repair. This was no easy task since my mother never threw anything away. The floor was stacked with magazines and boxes of stuff, leaving little trails through the mess. She has always done this to some extent, but now her hoarding had become an obsession. I couldn't wait to throw everything out when she died. Maybe I'd burn it, that would be much more freeing. I avoided my old bedroom; I never wanted to go in there again.

"Check outside for signs of your aunt. If you find any footprints, track her down. She won't get away with terrorizing me, let me tell you," whined Mother. Now she was sounding like some petulant child.

I just looked at her. Every time I had been here over the last few weeks, my mother had told me someone was spying on her. A peeping Tom, she said. I hadn't taken her seriously; this just seemed like more evidence of her growing senility. But I dutifully went outside and examined the ruined flowerbeds under the windows. Nothing. The ground was dry and no sign of anyone was evident.

Mother is losing her mind, I thought to myself as I headed off to do the errands. I was enjoying seeing Mother upset and a little afraid. She who put me through so many years of terror and shame.

I was born when my mother was 30, the result of sleazy sex behind the bar where she worked as a cocktail waitress. She always blamed me for coming along and ruining her life. "If it weren't for you I could have married some rich guy and been taken care of. Let me tell you, I was beautiful! Lots of men wanted me until I got stuck with you, a miserable snot-nosed stupid piece of shit."

Later on the physical abuse started. She would lock me in the closet in my room for hours or, even worse, shut me in the toy box in my room. It had never contained any toys, and I came to know it simply as, The Box. No water, no food, not being allowed out for the bathroom. Sometimes I would be in there all day or overnight, lying in my own filth. And when she did let me out she would hang my soiled clothes on the front porch for everyone to see. She loved to shame me.

It's a miracle I'm not some kind of mass murderer or serial killer. But I don't feel hatred toward all women; I don't blame them for my twisted mother. I had seen plenty of kind, loving mothers when I would sneak out at night and look through windows in the neighborhood. I saw what it was supposed to be like.

Maybe I could have been branded a peeping Tom, but my motives were pure. I just wanted to see what other people's lives were like and I wanted to figure out what was wrong with mine. Was it me? Was she right? Was I the one who drove my mother to torture me? No, I figured out Mother was the sick one. I hated her for it.

As I grew older I did have some favorite windows around town. Mostly they were the windows of girls from my school. Oh, I saw some wonderful things. And the windows of their parent's rooms, where, late at night, I learned about pleasure and screaming women and I learned to stroke myself to ecstasy until I splattered myself all over their bushes. I often wondered if anyone found my seed and thought it was some disease on their plants. It's one of my favorite visions.

You might wonder why I never left. I tried. I told my teachers and the counselors at school but no one ever believed me. I never had marks on my body. Mother was a gifted actress at all those school meetings, she was the kind, suffering mother with the odd, strange child. They felt sorry for her, not for me. And punishment in The Box came fast and furious after that. No, my only option was to endure until I was old enough to take care of myself.

I managed to get a job at a local motel as a night clerk and handyman when I was 17. I got paid a little and was given a room at the motel so I could handle repairs at all hours. I put myself through school at the community college in town and got my degree in accounting. Such a nice, quiet, solitary job. It suited me perfectly.

When I finished my errands and returned to Mother's house, all was quiet. I found her asleep in her favorite chair and had a glorious fantasy of holding a pillow over her face, feeling her feeble struggles until the final beautiful peace descended. But she woke up and spoiled it.

"What the hell are you smirking about, you filthy little turd?" She was actually snarling at me. I just turned and walked into the kitchen to put away the groceries.

After I fixed the dishwasher and got ready to leave, I decided to have a little fun with Mother. "Keep your eyes open for Aunt Mary, Mother, and let me know what she wants from you." She turned to stare at me, her face had gone almost as white as her hair.

"You think she wants something from me? What, what could she want? She's dead for God's sake, she can't be wanting anything!" Mother was getting a little panicky now.

"Maybe she wants your soul," I whispered as I walked out the door.

I was enjoying this. I even thought seriously about coming back later to peer into her windows and see if I could scare her more.

But I had other windows to visit that night. Namely, the bedroom window of Margaret Slater.

Margaret was a girl from the factory where I worked. I had asked her out to dinner about a month ago, I thought things had gone pretty well. I took her to a nice steak place and we ate and talked. She talked about work and her family, I talked about Mother. She seemed interested, so I went on for quite a while, but after she went to the bathroom she told me she had an emergency call from her family and had to go. I took her home and tried to kiss her, but I guess it was too soon, she turned quickly and went into the house. Still, I thought it was a good start.

After that first date though, she would never take my phone calls. She never returned my messages and she avoided me at work. I really didn't understand why, you would think she could have told me what her problem was. So, about a week ago I decided to look in her windows to see if I could figure it out. Maybe there was another man, or worse, another woman. How else was I to learn?

Margaret's window proved to be most beguiling. Margaret likes to sleep in the nude and often came out of the shower dripping wet to dry herself off in the bedroom. Damn, she was fine looking. Big soft breasts spilling over a soft stomach and then, down below, that dark patch of hair, I get hot just thinking about her. Sometimes she even lies on the bed and fingers herself to orgasm. I stand there and clutch my stiffness, trying not to groan at the pleasure of it. Her bushes have been sprayed so much I'm surprised they haven't died yet. It's Saturday night and I might get lucky if she has a guy over. That's the best, I imagine myself as the one thrusting into wet darkness and spilling myself into her dark cave.

Maybe you think I'm a little sick, but what do you expect? I don't know how to be with people, especially women, and this is how I learn. I watch, I take part, I imagine myself to be normal. This is the man you created, Mother.

I returned home early in the morning after a very satisfying night. Margaret had brought home a man and they fucked each other's brains out for hours. I don't know why she never pulls the curtains, maybe she likes thinking someone could be watching. Maybe she even knows I am the one watching, maybe it's an extra turn on for her. I like to think so.

It was a very peaceful sleep that night, I dreamed of better things than The Box.

I woke to the telephone ringing shrilly, over and over again. I dragged myself to the phone, thinking it was work calling. Sunday morning they ran a small crew at the factory and one accountant had to be there to close out the end of day reports. But no, it was Mother.

"She was here, she was here!" Mother was screaming into the phone. "I saw her at the window again, a flash of white! I yelled at the bitch to tell me what she wanted or to get the hell away from me!"

"Did she say anything, Mother? Did she tell you what she wants?"

"No, I just saw the flash of white and all she did was hiss at me, then she was gone. I waited up all night for her to return, but she didn't. I know she's after me, I just know it, she wants revenge, revenge for..." Mother suddenly went quiet.

"Revenge for what, Mother?" I asked softly.

"Never mind," she snapped.

"Mother, I think you should call your doctor tomorrow and tell him what you are experiencing."

"No! I don't want that quack to think I'm going crazy. He might try to lock me up or put me in a home!" That was one of her darkest fears.

I had a sudden flash of brilliance. If I could convince the doctor she was going crazy, I could have her put away and everything would be mine. "Maybe I should call your doctor and let him know how you are feeling. I wouldn't want you to have a heart attack over this or anything," I spoke with my sweetest voice.

"God damn you to hell, you are just trying to get your clutches on my money You son of a bitch you won't get anything if you put me away. I had my lawyer set it up so if I was put in a home he will handle my money, not you. You won't get anything until I'm dead, you miserable fool. And that ain't happening anytime soon." She slammed down the phone.

I went into the kitchen and got a beer for breakfast. Mother had just given me an even better idea, so I sat on the couch most of Sunday thinking through my Plan. Oh, it was a good one. Fool proof.

Sunday night. I was about to embark on my Plan and earn my long awaited freedom. Fortunately it was fall and Halloween was coming up soon, that meant I could easily get my props and no one would question me. I headed out before it got dark and went to the local Wal-Mart. There were plenty of costumes available, but all I wanted was a white wig and some pale face make-up and I found those easily. I paid cash so there was no way to trace my purchase and I thought ahead and wore a baseball cap low to hide my face. I was already dressed in black, my usual window watching clothing.

Driving towards Mother's house I went over everything again, my Plan was absolutely brilliant. My own cunning scared me.

I parked several blocks away in an area where no one was outside and no lights were on in the windows. I laid down across the seats and took a nap until deep darkness had settled down on the town. When I woke up my eyes were adjusted to the dark and I put on my makeup and adjusted the wig on my head. Yes, I was very frightening when I looked in the rear view mirror.

The baseball cap helped cover the wig as I worked my way from shadow to shadow toward Mother's. I saw no one, and I was sure no one saw me. As I reached her house I pulled off the cap and sat it down near the sidewalk to recover later. Fluffing up the wig I crawled slowly up toward Mother's living room window. There she sat, watching television in her favorite chair.

"Elizzzzabeth" I hissed. "Elizzzabeth..." Over and over I whispered and called her name and I watched as she froze, wide-eyed in her chair. Slowly, slowly she rose from her chair and made her way to the window. I had my back to the window and turned to face her, it was magnificent! She leaped back, screaming and ran toward the kitchen. I ran around to the kitchen window and called her again, "Elizzzabeth!" She ran to her bedroom and I replayed the scene again, over and over at every room she ran to. Except my old room. I left her alone there. That was where I wanted her to feel safe.

It was one of the most satisfying hours of my life. I left abruptly, wanting her to keep looking in fear, waiting for me to call her again. I knew she would not sleep that night. But I went home and slept like a baby.

Monday morning dawned cold and rainy. I drank my coffee and waited impatiently until 8AM when I knew the doctor's office opened. I called at exactly 8 and asked to speak to Mother's doctor. I told them it was an emergency and he called me back within 15 minutes.

"Doctor Abernathy, I am very worried about my Mother. I know she has been seeing you for the last several years, I am not sure if you have noticed her failing mental state, but now she is seeing things and becoming very frightened." I went on to tell him about what she was experiencing and how she was reacting. I wanted to plant the thought of her senility and madness in his mind. We ended up making an appointment for the following week. An appointment for which I knew she would fail to appear.

The work day flew by; I was excited to carry on with my Plan that evening. I walked out of work with a feeling of exhilaration. Freedom, sweet freedom seemed so close; I could almost reach out and embrace it.

I returned to Mother's again that night. Later, though, when I knew she would be asleep. Creeping up to her bedroom I stayed out of sight, and called "Elizzzzabeth...". She didn't come to the window this time, but I showed my whitened face which I knew would glow behind the lace curtain and continued my hissing, whispered call.

Finally she screamed out "What do you want?! Mary, what do you want?!" This was just the opening I was looking for.

"You know what I want", I whispered. "You know what you did to me. I have come for your ssssoul..." I thought this was a little over dramatic, but, oh, the effect it had on Mother! She was sobbing and crying into her hands and pulled the covers over her head. I added one more touch, "I am coming for you, Elizzzzabeth..."

Tuesday morning was a cold but beautiful day. A perfect match for my mood. Again the workday went by quickly. I struggled to appear as I did every other day. I even complained about my mother to some of my co-workers and told them how worried I was about her. I explained that my weekly visit was coming up on Saturday and I was concerned about her failing health. Setting up the scene for the grisly discovery I would make then. I am so very clever.

Tuesday night, the culmination of my brilliant Plan. I dressed in black and spent extra time on my makeup. White face, dark circles around my eyes, the disheveled white wig. I draped a dark sheet around myself to further disguise my shape. I was ready.

As I crept up to the house I checked the windows to locate Mother. It was late and she was asleep in her room. I let myself in the backdoor with my key. Slowly, quietly I closed the door and slid into my old room. Panic almost overwhelmed me. I had sworn to never set foot in this room again, but it was crucial to my Plan. I lifted the lid of The Box, the place of my living nightmares, and backed from the room, breathing hard. In the hallway I stopped to slow my breathing and gather my thoughts and then I headed to Mother's room.

I crawled slowly up next to the bed and began hissing, "Elizzzabeth." Her eyes flew open as I rose up beside her. She screamed and flailed to get free of the bed covers. She ran from the room. Exactly as I had planned.

She ran from room to room and I chased after her. I added a limping hitch to my gait as I lurched after her; it had a most terrifying effect. Perhaps I should have been an actor. I became so lost in the moment I truly felt like I had become Aunt Mary. Finally Mother spun into my old room and I pursued her closer, pushing her forward. She turned to run and hit the edge of the chest, falling into The Box. It was beautiful.

I slammed the lid of The Box and sat down heavily on it. The tables had turned and I listened to Mother screaming and crying with a smile on my face. The oxygen in The Box was limited. I knew this from many hours there. Mother was not as clever as I. I had learned early on to stop my crying and slow my breathing to survive. She had not learned that lesson.

"Elizzzabeth, I have come for you", I continued my haunting calls to keep her breathing hard and struggling. Mother beat against the sides of The Box and sobbed and cried until she began to grow weaker and weaker, finally silence descended and I felt peace begin to surround me. I looked around the room to see what could have logically fallen onto The Box and blocked the lid from opening. I was sure she was dead, but there was no sense in taking chances. I decided on the bookcase, it stood behind The Box and could easily have been dislodged by something falling violently onto the chest. I pushed The Box up against the bookcase and toppled it over onto the lid. Perfect.

I had no fear of fingerprints, it was my room after all. But I looked around carefully to be sure there was nothing to trace my presence here on this night. I believed I had just pulled off the perfect murder. I couldn't wait to see if it worked.

The rest of the week dragged on, it was a real test of my patience to wait and try to behave normally. I didn't even go out for my usual window watching. I could not concentrate on anything.

Friday morning was gloomy and overcast. I finished work after a long and tiresome day. I got some takeout and went home to call Mother as I usually did on Friday evening to set up my Saturday visit and see what she wanted me to do. It was important that I did everything as usual; nothing must seem out of place. I called and let the phone ring several times and then I tried again. No answer, my first hurdle was crossed, she had not gotten out of the box. I planned on telling the police that I assumed she had gone to bed early that night, so I hadn't been too concerned. I did not see how they could dispute that.

Saturday morning! Time for the unveiling of my masterpiece. I ate a leisurely breakfast and called Mothers house again at 9AM. Still no answer. Now I could act like I was panicking. I ran outside to the car. Fortune was smiling on me; my neighbor was in the garage which gave me the opportunity to tell him how afraid I was for my mother, that she was not answering her phone. Another opportunity to solidify my Plan.

I pulled up in front of Mothers and ran to the front door. Again, my acting abilities were on display in case any of the neighbors were watching. Opening the front door I got my first whiff of decay. It was almost sweet.

Running from room to room I called "Mother! Mother, where are you?" I think I was loud enough for the neighbors to hear. Of course there was silence. I made my room the last to be searched. The Box stood quietly with the bookcase lying on top. "How would the police expect me to act?" I pondered this for a moment and decided they would expect me to look inside the chest. I shoved the bookcase aside and opened the lid.

Mother lay there, almost in a fetal position, hands curled and bruised from beating on the lid of the box. Her eyes were opened wide and her face was frozen in a grimace of fear. It was the most fulfilling moment of my life. Karma is a bitch, Mother, I thought to myself. Or, in this case, a son of a bitch. I stifled my smile and called 911.

The police listened to my story and took notes, but no one suspected a thing. It was indeed a brilliant Plan, and it had worked beautifully. Mother was carted away, I had her cremated to be sure she would never return, the will was in my favor and I moved into my house within the week. I immediately began to remove every trace of her.

Two months later, I had cleaned and painted the house, thrown out all her possessions and donated all her furniture to local charities. But I kept The Box, my nightmare had now become my treasure. I polished it and moved it to the living room where it now served as my coffee table. The Box and I carried on many meaningful conversations.

I felt free, so free. I had moved into Mothers room, I still couldn't go in my old room; too many memories hovered there that could not be erased. I kept the door locked and pondered ways to remodel the house so that it could be eradicated. Meanwhile I enjoyed my peace and the quiet of my home. My home.

I had 60 days of freedom. It was the two month anniversary of my new life. That evening I drank beer and watched sports and ordered my favorite pizza for dinner. I can't explain to you the overwhelming satisfaction I felt. I felt normal.

But that satisfaction did not last. I got up and went into the kitchen to get another beer. When I came back into the living room, I stopped in confusion. The lid to the box was open.

I turned to see a flash of white at the window. No. It cannot be. "Aunt Mary?" I whispered. Please, I thought, let it be Aunt Mary. I could deal with Aunt Mary.

But it wasn't Aunt Mary. I knew it in my heart. I slammed The Box shut and drove a whole box of nails into it, sealing it forever, wishing I were driving them into her skull. Now, I wait, shotgun in my lap. If she is still out there, if she shows herself, I will blast her to hell. If that doesn't work, I will turn it on myself. I will pursue you, Mother, in this life and the next, until I am finally free.

The Darkness Beyond

Keli Becker

Alayna hesitated before entering the kitchen. It was black on the other side of the large windows and the light was off. The wind had been howling all day. This morning the weather man had predicted a strong storm approaching this part of the state.

She couldn't move from the kitchen doorway. If she turned on the light, she could be seen by anyone who might be lurking around. She shivered so hard her teeth rattled.

Alayna's rock, her husband, Carl, had died just two weeks ago. It was a shock to everyone, especially Alayna. It was sudden and he had seemed such a healthy man. He had a heart attack in his sleep and according to the doctor in the emergency room, had felt no pain. Alayna hoped so. She couldn't stand the thought he might have suffered.

She missed him desperately. The love of her life, her best friend, her companion. Her lover. Her bud. He was everything she needed and loved, and now he was gone. Alayna cried blinding tears at anything that reminded her of him: a song, a phrase, a TV show he had liked, going for a walk without him. The world was desolate without him.

Her mother-in-law, Agustina, said it was Alayna's fault for working him too hard, making him do too much. Carl's mother was always on Alayna about something. She could rag and nag and complain until Alayna wanted to scream. Stick a sock in her nasty mouth. Anything to shut her up. The horrid old woman had Carl doing handyman jobs because she was too cheap to hire someone. Who was working him too hard?

Agustina looked like the hag from a Grimm's fairy tale. She had long stringy grey hair that always needed to be washed. Her face looked like it had been carved out of an apple left to dry in the sun. Her skin was wrinkled and almost the same color as her hair. She hobbled around with the help of a walker when Carl was around, but when he wasn't she could get around just fine. Agustina played frail with Carl; grabbing at the back of a chair or the couch and holding his arm when they went out. Alayna got to carry the walker and trail behind them. Carl suggested that Agustina could get around with a cane, but the old hag whined and played the poor me card. "I can't get around with a cane, but I can do alright on your arm."

Augustina was a thief, too, she stole things everywhere they went and was loud and rude about the people nearby. "Oh, she's so fat. Look at that, she's going to have that piece of cake, as fat as she is." It embarrassed Carl and Alayna terribly but they wanted to be nice to the witch.

Alayna tried to have a nice dinner ready for Carl to come home to whenever he went to Agustina's house to help because Agustina worked him hard and he would come home exhausted and grumpy. Alayna didn't go to the miserable woman's house much. She would make a small meal or cookies or cakes to take to Agustina, but there was never any appreciation. Thank yous were nonexistent and Agustina would try to manipulate Carl into taking her out to dinner without Alayna. He loved Alayna and was faithful to her, so he never went without her. He also never went because really, he couldn't stand his own mother.

Carl once made the mistake of mentioning Alayna's fear of darkness where Agustina could overhear. The old woman had the sharp hearing of a predatory animal even though she would say "What? What?" constantly when Alayna was speaking to her. Alayna gave up trying to be polite. Agustina could hear Alayna and Carl talking softly, trying to have a private conversation, from 20 feet away.

"A grown woman afraid of the dark?" Agustina shrieked in her sharp, penetrating voice, "That's ridiculous! Only children are afraid of the dark." She turned to Alayna. "Are you a child?" Alayna was reduced to tears under the lash of the old woman's constant bullying.

Alayna was lost without Carl. He had been the buffer, protecting her from Agustina. He had kept her safe. Now she wasn't safe from his mother or the darkness. Why had the building contractor put the damn light switch so far away? Her stomach rolled and her hands started to sweat. *Come on, Alayna. You're going to have to cross this kitchen and turn the light on eventually. Suck it up!*

She tentatively stepped into the kitchen. The first step was the hardest. She forced the rest and scooted along the granite island, lunging at the light switch by the sink. The light came on but Alayna now had to face the darkness beyond the big windows over the sink. Her skin crawled with dread. Who knew what might be hiding in the forest beyond the windows? Someone could come out of those trees, which were now whipping back and forth in the strong storm-bearing wind.

Carl had installed a motion sensor light outside at the corner of the house next to the kitchen, but it didn't help when she was standing at the sink. Intruders could creep around the house and Alayna would never see them. When the light came on suddenly, as it sometimes did, she would jump and her heart would race, but most of the time it was nothing more than a bunny or a tumbleweed. Once a curious coyote came close enough but was scared away by the burst of illumination. Alayna wouldn't know if there was someone out there until it was too late. The tiny hairs on the back of her neck prickled at the thought of a face at the window.

She knew where the fear of darkness came from but knowing didn't allay the terror.

When she was eleven Alayna and her brother Johnny stayed with their grandmother in a small, dark, cramped apartment in San Francisco while their mother was looking for a job (and a man). Their mother was always 'getting settled' and when that happened, the kids stayed with grandma.

Grandma's apartment was tiny. Alayna and Johnny slept in a bunk bed against a wall. Johnny was small and skinny, with thick lenses in his glasses and braces on his crooked teeth. His hair was dull and cut in a bowl shape. He was the perfect target for bullies. Alayna stood up for him as much as she could. Her methods sometimes got her into trouble. Once she had taken a swing at a bully with her book satchel and had given him a bloody mouth. When she tried to explain to the teacher, it did no good. Alayna was told to act like a lady and get a yard monitor to take care of the kids bullying Johnny. But the monitor wasn't around at that moment. She got detention for her heroism and was in trouble with Grandma when she got home. Being a hero sucked.

There was an uncomfortable foldout couch at the foot of the bunk bed. The mattress was thin and hard and Alayna couldn't figure out how her grandmother slept on it. Maybe that was why she was so crabby all of the time.

At the end and to the left of the room was a large window in a little alcove that let a little natural light into the gloomy flat during the day. A metal fire escape from the top floor made an ominous silhouette that carved what view was available into zigzaggy twos. A sewing machine occupied the little space. At night the fire escape was a skeletal and oppressive shadow. Alayna stayed away from the window at night, terrified of what might come down those stairs in the dark.

One night her grandmother went to a friend's apartment for a visit. The kids watched The Wax Museum with Vincent Price on TV, and although Johnny fell asleep before it got scary, the movie frightened Alayna more than she could say. Alayna was sure some psycho would come down the fire escape to kidnap her and her brother, and do horrible things to them. She couldn't sleep at all for several nights and was afraid of the dark ever after.

Alayna's mother soon married again, and they all moved to a house in the suburbs. Alayna was finally away from that window and the fire escape. She felt secure with her new stepfather and her mother in the house, and safe behind the curtain over the window. The land behind the house was being developed and large equipment was parked outside the window there during the night that threw strange and hulking shadows in the darkness. Alayna didn't look outside much at night.

Alayna's fear of the darkness was debilitating. She saw psychiatrists, took the pills they prescribed, did everything they thought would help, but nothing did. The fear, stronger than the help, persisted.

Alayna hadn't been happy with Carl's desire to move to the country and live in such a remote area, but she did want dogs and horses and a large garden, and this property was just right. The nearest neighbor was a half mile away and just below a slight ridge separating the two properties. Carl had wanted privacy with no other lights to mar the sky's black cover. Alayna just stayed away from dark rooms at night.

Then Carl died and Alayna had to face the darkness alone. Her depression was complete. She considered suicide so she could be with Carl again, but something always stopped her.

Alayna braved it to step up to the sink, wash her hands, and get a glass of water. She looked out the night-blackened window. Nothing but her reflection stared back at her. She peered into her reflected eyes, looking for some confidence. Her image stared back at her, distorted. Alayna drew back quickly.

She got her glass of water and thought she felt eyes boring into her back as she turned to leave the kitchen. She spun suddenly, sure there would be a face at the window, but the black glass mirrored the kitchen as before.

In the living room Alayna arranged her beading supplies on the couch and turned on the television to keep her company. Thankfully, in the living room, the tall windows had blinds over them. The depression enveloping her was overpowering. She lost herself in movies most of the day, but depression at night with the fear of darkness looming at the end of each day overwhelmed her. She kept her dogs near after dark.

She had just settled into her nest on the couch with her dogs at her feet when the lights went out. She jumped, heart thudding painfully in her chest. The TV was still on, but the kitchen light and the living room lights were out. Must be a fuse. Alayna was baffled because if this problem was with the fuses, or an overall power outage, why was the TV still on?

Alayna felt the old familiar dread. She recalled the eyes she had sensed at the kitchen window. Had someone turned the lights out on purpose?

"Now what, kids?" She always talked to the dogs to calm her nerves. "Think it might be the fuses?" Alayna figured she would have to go out to the fuse box and check. The very thought upset her stomach. She felt like she was going to puke.

She got a good, strong, long flashlight from the table next to the front door, one suitable for use as a club, and let all five dogs out into the backyard. The three big dogs growled a bit, but that was normal. Alayna stepped out of the house cautiously, and flashed the light beam around. Nobody here. She walked quickly to the end of the house where the fuse box was.

She got the box open with little difficulty and shone the flashlight inside. She reset all of the fuses, just to make sure, and shut the box. Suddenly the motion sensor came on and a shadow melted into the darkness of the car port. Alayna screamed. The big dogs now broke into full voice; barking and snarling. They lunged at the gate to get out. The gate rattled and bowed. *I've got to get them inside before the gate gives way. The lights are on but I have to get closer to that shadow, whatever it is, to be able to get in the house. At least the lights are back on. I wonder if that thing messed with my fuses so I would have to come out here. What's it going to do now?*

She bolted for the door and slipped inside as quickly as she could. She called to the dogs but they were much more interested in tearing the fence apart to get at the shadow. Alayna used the special word; "Nummies!" The dogs slowly changed their minds after several promises of treats. They were good watchdogs and she praised them for their courage. The shadow would have to get past the dogs, at least, to get to her. She finally got all the dogs in the kitchen with her and threw both of the dead bolts on both the sturdy screen door and the solid kitchen door. She ran to check and lock the other two sets of doors. She gave the dogs their nummies, but as soon as they'd gobbled them they went back to the kitchen and growled at the door.

Alayna's nerves were shot. She retrieved her little .38 revolver from behind a certain set of books and placed it next to her on the table at the end of the couch that held the remotes, a stained glass lamp, a box of tissues, her current book, and a few magazines. You never knew what could happen in the country and it paid to be prepared.

Alayna had nearly every light in the house on. Lights meant safety. She sat back down on the couch and found a light romantic comedy. She was just snuggling into her nest with one of the small dogs and was starting to relax a little when a loud BANG from the kitchen rattled her world. She almost wet herself.

The dogs charged the kitchen the door barking ferociously. Alayna's stomach was in her throat. She grabbed her gun and cautiously approached the kitchen doorway.

Another BANG made the dogs bark and snarl even louder.

Alayna crouched down and tiptoed through the kitchen. With the wind howling outside, no one could have heard her tromping across the kitchen with ski boots on but she tiptoed into position and stood up, facing the door in a stance she had seen on TV and demanded whoever was banging on her door to leave her alone. She was calling 9-1-1 as she spoke, she shouted. Belatedly, she realized she left the phone on the table next to the couch. Too late now. The gun would have to do.

Alayna placed her shaking left hand on the door lock. The adrenalin coursed through her and made her temporarily brave. She turned the dead bolt to open. She readied herself and flung open the door. The screen door was unlatched, slamming itself open and shut with the wind. Alayna hadn't locked the door after all. But she could have sworn she had thrown the deadbolt. What could have unlocked it again? She and Carl hadn't given keys to anyone.

Except her mother-in-law. In case of emergency.

But Agustina lived on the other side of town and wasn't physically able to cross the expanse of land surrounding the house. Was she? Where was her car? Alayna hadn't heard any vehicle approach. The wind was howling, the storm announcing itself even more forcefully. Alayna carefully locked the screen door and the inside door and took another tour of the house to satisfy herself she was truly locked in. She was secure in her sanctuary. She settled back in to watch her movie. The wind raged outside. Still no rain.

BANG!

Now Alayna was positive someone was trying to break in. If her mother-in-law had the only key it stood to reason Agustina was that someone. She had been able to get around pretty well when Carl wasn't in the room. Maybe she had actually made it to the kitchen door. Had Agustina given the key to someone? Hired a thug to do something to Alayna? Agustina had hated Alayna for every moment of the 35 years Alayna and Carl had been married.

Alayna grabbed the phone and dialed 9-1-1. Nothing but spotty static on the line. She yelled into the phone that someone was trying to break into her house. Cell reception was iffy out here at the best of times and now it was nonexistent. The dogs were snarling, but at the laundry room door this time. Alayna locked the flapping screen door again and propped chairs under the knobs of all the inside doors. It was then her fear turned to anger. She recalled her childhood loathing of bullies. Whoever it was would be sorry for treating her like this.

She went into the living room and resumed her movie, and she waited. She got Bruno, a mastiff and the biggest of the big dogs, leashed and ready. He was primed to go. Her .38 was in her right hand and Bruno's leash was lightly wrapped around the left.

As quietly as she could, Alayna took the chair away from the kitchen door and carefully unlocked it. She waited with her left hand on the doorknob. Bruno growled deep in his throat. Alayna tensed.

BANG! The outside screen slammed again and Alayna threw open the kitchen door. There stood her mother-in-law, ratty hair blowing around her face, her clothes dirty rags whipping around her. She had a derringer in her hand. She started to pull the trigger, but Alayna, pumped with adrenalin, pulled her trigger first.

The vision from hell gaped at her in genuine surprise. Agustina pulled her own trigger as she crumpled in the doorway, but the shot went wild. Alayna stared at the pile before her. She heard faint sirens over the wind, winding their way up the dirt road to the house.

Alayna was in shock. She didn't want to believe Agustina hated her enough to kill her. She backed into a chair at the kitchen table and sat down hard, her gun hand limp by her side. What was she going to tell the police when they arrived? That a frail old lady had managed to get to her house, terrorize her, and wanted to kill her? Spinning red and blue lights bounced up the dirt driveway and skidded to a stop, dust boiling in the gale. Uniformed officers rushed up to the gate next to the kitchen, their weapons drawn, aimed at Alayna.

"Drop your weapon." Alayna was happy to comply. The gun hit the floor. She reeled Bruno to her so he wouldn't get shot.

"It's okay, ma'am. Just take it easy." One of the officers gingerly checked Agustina for a pulse. The pile of clothes seemed to be all that was left of her. He shook his head at the other officers. Nothing there.

He didn't check carefully enough because the pile of clothes moved and a hand appeared holding the derringer. Her head came up and the vicious eyes focused on Alayna. Only one shot left and Agustina took it.

Alayna felt a hot spot on her left side, going in just above her heart and exiting out her back. When the pain came, it came hard. Alayna collapsed. Bruno blocked her fall.

The police's guns went off and turned Agustina into a smoking heap of rags as an ambulance pulled up. One of the EMTs went to Alayna while the other started checking Agustina for signs of life. Agustina was no more and the EMTs gave Alayna their full attention. The wound was not life-threatening and they were quickly able to stop the bleeding. As Alayna was being ministered to, the police told her that her call had been heard and acted upon even though no response came through.

Agustina had threatened to take Alayna's life enough times in enough public places that her impaired mental health and hatred of Alayna were well-known in the community. A couple of business owners felt Agustina's mental health was severely impaired and had called the police to warn them about it. The police found Agustina's car hidden behind a juniper tree near the house.

It took 90 minutes to straighten everything out. Agustina's body was picked up by the county coroner. The EMTs left when Alayna refused to be transported to the hospital, but only after she promised to come in to have her wounds dressed the next morning. She had to stay and take care of her dogs. The police departed and Alayna was left alone with her emotions. She was too tired and sore to think about much. She cleaned up the blood as well as she could with her arm in a sling.

When thought was eventually available to her, she realized that the darkness, while it could hide many evils, was not to be feared by itself. She had overcome one of the evils and survived. Alayna said a quiet prayer to Carl apologizing for shooting his mother but Alayna didn't think Agustina was in any place to bother him.

Photo Credit: John Fatland

FAMILY STORIES

Family stories are tasty fodder for a writer's imagination. The stories have already been polished and embellished; many have passed into legend. It is to these rich stories, the history we learn as children sitting at our family's knee, The Sacred Circle Writers have turned their attention to this week.

Dave and Keli Becker collaborate to explore the world, and voice, of one of their most interesting family members in *Marley*; Laurie Wilson Fatland takes us to the very heart of an American disaster with *From the Shadows*, and Terryl Warnock insists that even the most legendary of family stories might just contain a tiny kernel of truth in *Deadeye*.

Marley

Dave and Keli Becker

Hi! My name is. . . well, I have a lot of names. Mostly they call me "No, Marley, no!" I live with my humans, Moms and Pops, and a bunch of other dogs.

Before I got to come live with my Moms and Pops, I was in a big rock-like house in a cage. There were a lot of other dogs in cages there too. I smelled cats there, but couldn't see them. All us dogs were barking and crying, praying to get out and enjoy life I don't remember much of my life before Moms and Pops; I was pretty young when we found each other. They came to the rock house and took me outside to play ball with me. That was good fun. But then I had to go back in my cage, watching people walk past me, smiling but never stopping.

The next day I got to go for a ride to the hospital for dogs. There were dogs barking and crying there too. I was poked, prodded, picked up and turned upside down. The lights above me were very bright and annoying. I felt a prick and fell asleep. When I woke up I was back in a cage but later that same day Moms and Pops came and picked me up. I got to go in a truck and we went to a big store full of doggie goodies. It smelled so good! Like dog food, bird, and chew toys. There were happy dogs in there. Moms and Pops got the best dog food I ever tasted, and I got a squeaky toy all my own. That was music to my ears.

Then we went for another ride where I met the rest of my new family: big sister Luna, little sister Chica (I call her a chewhaha), grouchy grandma Zoey, and a short bug-eyed male, Ziggy. Me and Luna are Heeler mixes. Chica is a Chug (whatever that is) and Ziggy is a Chihuahua. When there's a horse around, Zoey doesn't know about anything else. She's horse-crazy. Sometimes she won't even eat, and that's as crazy as it gets if you ask me.

I get to run around in a big house now, and outside in a big yard and wrestle with Luna in the dirt. It's chewing heaven here. The wooden bed frame, blankets, dog toys, furniture legs, carpet, sticks, rocks, ice cubes, boxes, mail, newspapers, magazines, plants —it all winds up in my mouth. I like to chew on trees, the parts that stick out, and weeds. Pops' shoes are tasty too, especially what he calls laces. They hold his shoes on his hind paws. Moms and Pops bark at me when I chew on the laces though, and then it's out to the back yard with me.

My favorite thing to do is eat. No, my favorite thing to do is wrestle in the dirt with Luna. No, my favorite thing to do is to jump on Chica and chase her. Wait, maybe my very favorite thing to do is chew on Moms' log bed frame. It's out to the back yard with me when I do that. I have a lot of favorite things to do. Most of the things I like to do get me in trouble and then it's out to the back yard with me. I spend a lot of time in the back yard. That's me, "no Marley, no!"

Oh, I almost just caught that bug with pretty wings but it went too high for me to jump and I can jump really high. Ask any fence. My very very favorite thing to do is jump.

Moms says I have ADD, whatever that is

Oooh...one of those things that hangs off trees just blew by. Moms calls them leaves. They break when you jump on them after they turn brown though, and when you eat them, they just leave a dry yucky taste in your mouth.

Moms has a bunch of things inside the house that are sort of like little trees. She calls them plants. They live in little bowls called pots. They make a great mess to play with when I knock them over. Sometimes, when Moms is pouring water in their pots I sneak up on her and try to drink the water before it gets in the pots. That makes a great mess, too. It's out to the back yard with me when I do that. Plants taste better than leaves do, they're juicier.

Oh...a fun bug to chase with long jumpy legs! They like to jump even more than me. I get kind of dizzy when I jump with them sometimes.

My favorite thing to do is try to drink out of that long long green snake that spits water. Moms and Pops laugh when I do that. Sometimes the water gets all over me. Sometimes it gets all over them, too. I love jumping and snapping at the water! It's a game Moms and Pops and me get to play after I've been playing in the dirt. They turn on the snake and spray me. Then I shake and shake and the water flies off me and gets Moms and Pops all wet too. They should shake, too. It feels really good. I like the way my fur fluffs up and how the air feels on my skin.

Sometimes they call me "Good dog." Moms barks it differently than when she calls me "no, Marley, no." "Good dog" feels better in my ears. Moms usually rubs my head, or scratches that special spot on my butt where my tail starts. I have a big black spot right there. It feels really good because I can't scratch that spot myself no matter how hard I try.

When Moms or Pops calls me "no, Marley, no!" it's out to the back yard with me. That's okay by me, then I get to look for ways to get out and go run in the forest.

Chica is funny looking. She only has one eye. I can sneak up on her on the side where there's no eye and surprise her. She has a lot of furry skin around her head. It makes her easy to grab and drag around. Her face looks scary when she shows her teeth. She gets mad easy. If she's on Moms' lap and I jump up on the couch beside them, Chica will growl and snap at me. Sometimes she misses and bites Moms. Then we both hear "no!" and end up on the floor. At least it's not out to the back yard.

Mom has a human named Beth who comes over sometimes. I LOVE Beth! She smells really good. I just want to lick her and lay on her lap or on her shoulders from the back of the couch. She has stuff in her hair that smells really good. I could lick it all day. I'm "no Marley, no!" a lot when Beth comes over. Then it's out to the back yard with me.

Moms takes me for walks. I love my walks! There's so much to see and smell! It's hard to listen to Moms tell me to "heel" when there's so much to check out. There are places where boy dogs have marked their place in the neighborhood. I don't care; everyplace is mine when I'm out on a walk. Ooh...and then there's horse poop! Moms says "no horse poop, Marley!". But it tastes sooo good! It's all wet and grassy when it's new. It's kind of dry and dusty when it's been there awhile. I wish I could roll in it! That would be my favorite thing to do but Moms won't let me.

Horses look kinda like dogs but way bigger. Moms and Pops get on their backs and tell them what to do. I'm glad I'm not a horse; they're fun to chase, but they're so big they're kind of scary. I stay out from under their feet and just bark at them. They don't pay much attention to me. I don't care. After I get in the horse pasture I can run and run and the fence there is easy to jump. I let Luna and Zoey chase the horses.

I have lots of toys. My favorite one is a round orange ball with feet. One of the feet was really good, so we ate it. The ball is still good to chew on though. Everybody takes turns unless I'm around, then it's my ball. Sometimes Moms throws it down the hall for me to chase.

My favorite thing is to sleep on the back of the couch. Moms says I'm like a cat that way. I love to sleep on Moms and Pops' bed, too; the bed cover is good to chew on. Moms got mad about the bed cover but I only chewed a little bit of it. She says she can sew it up. She gets mad when I chew on the logs around the bed, too, but they're wood, so they're my favorite thing. Out to the back yard with me.

Luna is a heeler mix too and she looks kinda like me except she's bigger and red and speckled all over. She's really fast when she runs. I can only catch her when she's tired. She loves to dig holes. She got into a hole almost all the way one time. It was dark in that hole and smelled dry. Some animal had lived in that hole when it was still a little hole but I think the animal moved away.

Luna and Zoey are grumpy most of the time. Zoey especially. She doesn't like me much, all she wants to do is chase the horses or sleep in the house.

A cat moved into the barn. Zoey's interested in him, too. The cat stays away from us. Pops says it caught two mice. One time we got out when the cat was up by the house. What fun! We chased that cat up a tree. We tried to climb the tree like the cat did but for some reason we couldn't.

What's a mice?

When the cat was up the tree, me and Luna took off to the forest. We ran and ran! The smells of the trees, the rocks, the weeds! I almost couldn't smell it all in. Moms and Pops called us and called us, but there was too much for us to smell to pay attention to them. We ran and ran; one way then the other way.

We found a wonderful dead thing. I don't know what made it that way but it smelled like the dogs-that-aren't-dogs that sometimes come around. They cry at us when it's dark out. They want us to come out and play. We bark back at them but Moms and Pops won't let us go out. No back yard for me then. The dead thing smelled ripe. I'll bet when it was alive that it smelled like sun and wind. It still smelled a little like that. It had really long ears. There was only one, maybe two, bites left for me and Luna. We ran and ran in the forest until our tongues were hanging out. Moms and Pops were driving around calling and calling us. We finally went back home after Moms and Pops went home too. Moms made funny noises and water leaked out of her eyes. Not enough to play in, though. Pops kinda growled at us, but he let us in the house. We were so thirsty! We went right to the water bowl and drank and drank.

Ziggy's old, Mom said in human years he's 78. He's tiny and we chase him when we can, but he's slow so he's not much fun. Humans like him a lot. He likes them right back. Moms and Pops call him a "kissass." It must be a good thing, it gets him lots of treats and pets. He always stays around the house and barn and eats pigeon poop in the barn.

Sometimes Moms throws a toy for me in the back yard. I run after it and run around with it. Moms calls "here Marley, bring it here." I usually don't. I run with it and try to get Luna to chase me.

Moms doesn't throw many toys for me to chase.

Moms and Pops are the greatest. I never dreamed life would be so good outside the rock house. I wish I could tell all the dogs there not to give up. Maybe one day they'll be free and their Moms and Pops can bring them over for a play day.

That's me, "no, Marley, no!." I love my family and they love me back. My life is pretty good. I love my life. It's my favorite thing.

From the Shadows

Laurie Wilson Fatland

He was only fourteen when the shaking started. Tall and lanky, Charles lay in his narrow bed with his long legs hanging off the end, sleeping soundly in the early morning darkness. His dreams were peaceful, unaware that this day in April, 1906, would be a day written in history.

The stillness was shattered; Charles was thrown to the floor, glass breaking all around him as the pictures flew off the walls. His dresser fell over, spewing clothes from the drawers and battering him with the books that had been piled on top.

Charles covered his head with his arms, trying to protect himself from the debris. There was no way to move to a safer place as the earth churned beneath him and the old house moaned and shuddered around him. The rumbling grew to a crescendo and then began to fade, it felt like God himself had kicked the earth and it had finally rolled to a stop.

Silence descended, everyone seemed to hold their breath for a minute, and then the cries started. He heard the muffled sounds of neighbors calling out to each other and finally the soft calls of his mother from the other room.

"I'm all right, Mother!" He called back as he started brushing off the glass shards that covered his body. He got up carefully and made his way to the door to find her. She, too, came out from her bedroom, hair covered in plaster dust, eyes wide from shock.

"Charles, are you injured?" She looked him over carefully, and sighed with relief when she saw no injuries.

The old house seemed to have come through with little damage. Plaster dust had shaken loose from the ceilings and pictures and crockery were broken, but everything else had survived intact. Both of them got dressed quickly and went outside to see how the neighborhood had survived.

All the houses were standing as far as they could see. Their neighborhood in Oakland seemed to have weathered this earthquake and left its occupants unharmed. Charles ran down to the end of the block to look across the estuary and the bay wanting to see how the great city of San Francisco had fared. It was obscured by a huge cloud of dust. As he watched in horror, plumes of smoke began to rise above the dust and flames of fire were evident in the cloud.

Charles ran back to the house and began to gather buckets, sheets and anything else that could be used as bandages. His mother watched him in silence. Charles took her by the shoulders and said, "I have to go across to the city and help. Things look bad and fires are starting to spread, I can see it from the shore. You know it's what father would do if he were here." His father was away on business, a salesman who traveled often. No doubt his father would be in a panic as news of the earthquake spread; Charles knew his father would come home as soon as he could if the roads were passable.

His mother seemed to wake from a trance, nodded to him and began to help him gather what he needed. She began to pack up what food she could spare, knowing both Charles and the victims would be in need of it.

As Charles loaded things into their wheelbarrow to take down to the port, his mother stopped him and hugged him until he couldn't breathe. "I am so proud of you; you have become a man today, son."

Charles hugged her back and told her to prepare the house for victims of the earthquake. "I'll bring back who I can, tell the neighbors their spare rooms will be needed too." He kissed her on the cheek and headed off to the port to find a small boat to cross the bay.

At the port Charles found several neighbors who had the same idea. Fred Anderson and his father were fishermen and they had already started up the motor on their small fishing boat, ready to head into the city. They called out to Charles and he loaded his goods aboard the boat quickly, the boat began backing up into the estuary and turning into the bay before he even finished stowing the bags and boxes.

It was a surreal scene as they made the crossing to the city. They bay itself was as smooth as glass, not a ripple marred the surface, and the day surrounding them dawned as calm and beautiful as any April day, ripe with the promise of spring. Yet beyond the smooth waters, chaos reigned. Clouds of dust and smoke rose above the city, tinged with the red of the fires below, a hellish vision. Charles knew that many must be trapped and dying and he silently urged the boat to go faster.

They landed in the thick of it. Fred's father had steered the boat clear of the fires and landed them near the wharf. Other boats were landing around them and they quickly formed a party of men to head into the city to rescue people ahead of the flames. Charles joined them, he needed action, sitting and waiting at the wharf for them to return would have been torture for him.

Dogs, the first thing he saw were dogs, running at him from every direction. Tongues hanging, mouths frothed, they ran in terror ahead of the fires. Bulldogs, hounds, mutts of every size churned around him in panicked packs. As if they held some unfathomable knowledge, they were fleeing to the outskirts of the city, away from disaster. Charles sent up a silent prayer that they find their way to safety and could be rescued in the days to come.

Collapsed buildings lay all around him, it was impossible to figure out what street they were on as they crawled over debris and tried to find anyone left alive. None of them spoke, they listened. The men would stop on a hand signal from the man in the lead and everyone froze in their tracks, ears tuned to hear the faintest moaning. When they heard something the men moved in unison, forming a line to clear the debris piece by piece, uncovering the dead and the injured and carrying them back to the wharf.

The roar of the fires grew louder as they made their way further into the city. Survivors who could get out were streaming past them toward the bay and toward the hills, trying to find their way to safety. Shopkeepers, seeing the approaching fires, opened their doors and began distributing goods to the victims, handing them whatever they could carry, giving away any food and clothing they could save from the flames and cheating the devouring fire.

They were close to the fire now. Charles could feel the heat and breathing was getting difficult. They were standing before a fallen apartment building where moans and cries sifted their way to the surface and to the men's ears. Desperately they tried to clear timbers and plaster in time to get to those trapped under the rubble, but the fire was relentless.

Charles heard a baby crying beneath him and struggled to clear a path to the child, he tossed aside pieces of the building in a frenzy until a hand on his shoulder stilled him. One of the men held him and silently looked into his eyes. Charles saw the men begin to move as one, silent mourners who could do no more for the dying, turning back to the wharf and their boats as the fire flung itself on the building. There was nothing more to be done.

In a daze they hurried in front of the fire, hands torn and bloody, powerless to help anyone else. When they arrived at the wharf, lines of the dead filled the streets and clearings along the waterfront, injured were piled on the boats, crying from their pain and their loss.

As Charles headed toward the Anderson's boat he saw movement under a fallen beam. Two black eyes peeked at him as he bent down to see what was there. A small black spaniel huddled under its shelter, licking its lips and wagging its tail, wanting to trust him, but confused and afraid. He held out his hand and the little dog came out of the shadows and leapt into his arms. My final rescue, Charles thought as he carried the pup to the boat. "Shadow I will call you, for you came out of the shadows of hell." He smiled down at the dog, realizing that life and hope would go on.

As they crossed the bay to safety, Charles prayed for those left behind. The sun sparkled on the water, the beauty of the day almost an insult to the city in flames. He turned toward home, knowing he would return to help rebuild. The beautiful city would rise again, a Phoenix from the ashes, a memorial to the dead, a shining monument to the uncrushable spirit of mankind. Charles softly stroked Shadow, and leaned down to breathe in the dogs scent of both destruction and hope. He knew his mother was right, he had become a man that day.

Deadeye

Terryl Warnock

Dedicated to John and Tia: It's a shame neither of you remembers your Grandpa Chick. We lost him too early. He only got to be a grandpa for just the last few years of his life and he loved it. He thought the sun rose and set on you kids. He wasn't really one to gush—he was more of a stoic manly-man kind of a guy —but he melted into a puddle at your tiny feet, both of you. He cut a rifle stock down for you the day you were born, John, and couldn't wait till you were big enough he could teach you to shoot.

Dixie and Ella Mae styled themselves the 'Sycamore Canyon Widows' as newlyweds in the early 50s. Although the boys didn't spend all of their time in Sycamore Canyon, they were out in the woods more than they weren't, and the girlfriends were in agreement that their beloved young husbands were only half-tamed at best. Barely housebroken. The 'other woman' was Mother Nature but the boys were true to their wives and always came home happy—if in need of baths—with wood to heat their homes and meat for their tables. Chick and Skeeter: wild and free, growing into the respectable men they were destined to be, but ever chafing to get outside to see wild things and wild places, to be the wild things it was in their very nature to be.

~

As friends and family sat around the remains of a big Christmas or Thanksgiving dinner, my Dad, Chick, full and rosy-cheeked, would ask "Did I ever tell you about Herb Korf?"

My mother, who had applied her civilizing influence to her wild young man for a considerable number of years, and had heard the story a time or two by then, would roll her eyes a little and say "Yes."

But the rest of us, even though we might have heard the story a number of times, would all say "No!" and beg for the story. Dixie—ever a good sport—would gaze back in time in the amber depths of a brandy, and settle in for a good yarn with the rest of us.

These days corporate mergers and buy-outs are old news, but they were a new-ish thing in the early 60s, when my Dad was working his way up from rock-bottom entry level in the management program of a small Arizona bank. Some big, back East banking concern acquired Dad's little Arizona bank and used it to train their up-and-coming executives. The parent company let their fledglings make their embarrassing mistakes out here in the hinterlands so they were a polished, finished product when they returned to the 'real world' back East. My ever-responsible, ultra-competent father was frequently placed in charge of the training and orientation of these greenhorns and it was only natural for him to want to introduce them to his beloved wilds as part of their Northern Arizona indoctrination. The family got to go along on a lot of these orientation outings—there were trips to the Grand Canyon, Meteor Crater, Sunset Crater and the Petrified Forest, of course, and camping and picnics—but sometimes it was just boys day out (because of course, all the management trainees were men in those days). Enter Herb Korf.

~

Herb was a pasty white city boy from Chicago. He was invited to our house for dinner soon after his arrival, as they all were, and proved an amiable enough guest. He was a city slicker to the core with soft, manicured hands, and although he was clearly out of his element, he was also nice, open-minded, curious and helpful. He looked like he'd never been dirty in his life. My parents were gracious hosts and Herb, as he adapted to what must surely have been strange new surroundings for him—Flagstaff hadn't yet acquired its genteel veneer; it was still a rough and tumble ranching and timber town—became as much a family friend as any of the rotating fledglings ever did.

One Sunday morning, Dad announced it was time to take Herb out and get him dirty, and that they were headed out to the Kinnickinnick Lake area to scout. Dad always said he was going out to scout for wood or game, but we all knew it was just an excuse to get out in the woods and rat around; drive the dirt roads, take a lunch, stretch his legs for a few miles, shoot some cans, maybe break a hatchet handle or two trying to stick them in stumps. It didn't matter to him in the least whether he found a downed tree to come back for in wood gathering season or a saucy buck to try and track down again come fall. He just loved being out and sharing it with anyone he could talk into going with him. Herb was up. He'd been on all the pavement tours, as Dad called them, but it was time for boys day out so he packed a lunch, gassed up the old green '56' pickup, picked up Herb, and off they went.

It was a lovely and unremarkable day until they encountered the snake.

As they bounced along in the rattletrap old truck out in the way back woods, choking on dust while Herb listened politely to the big buck stories that are the equivalent of big fish stories in my family, Dad noticed a rattlesnake to the side of the road. There's a different sensibility about the sanctity of all life now, but in my Dad's day, since they ate the eggs of the wild birds (his much-loved wild turkeys in particular), it was considered a community service to kill snakes. Herb couldn't have known that. He didn't even know there was a pistol in the glove box yet. Dad stopped the truck, leaned over to Herb's side, popped the glove box open, grabbed the .38, stepped out of the truck, shot the head off the snake, walked over to the carcass, snipped the rattlers off its tail with his pocket knife, got back in the truck, tossed the rattlers to Herb, put the gun back in the glove box, put the truck in gear, and drove off, picking up his big buck story where he'd left off; all just as casual as you please.

Now, for those of you who didn't grow up in a shooting family, no one can shoot the head off a snake. It just can't be done. Dad was a nationally-ranked competitive pistol shooter and even he said it was a shot in a million—maybe ten million.

Chick said Herb was pale and quiet for the rest of the day. Those rattlers sat in his open, sweaty, shaking palm and he was reluctant to move. He was scared stiff, glued to his seat, breathing fast and shallow. Dad had to take the rattlers from him and practically push him out of the truck for lunch. Herb was jumpy and nervous the whole time they sat on their blanket to eat, and was still on high alert when Dad woke up from his 20 minute nod in the sun after lunch. They never did get around to plinking any cans or throwing any hatchets.

Herb's stories about the Wild Man of the West became legend in the banking world of Chicago after he went back East, but he often visited us on vacation and although he was no Skeeter, the two men remained friends for the rest of their lives.

~

By the mid-70s Flagstaff had lost much of its former dusty Wild West personality. Although the sawmill wouldn't shut down completely till the early 90s, the timber industry was already in decline and most of the cattle ranchers had gone into real estate, subdividing their property to sell it off piecemeal. Dad had worked his way up to a bona fide mucky-muck at the bank and although it was no longer his responsibility, he enjoyed showing people around his adored Northern Arizona, so he still took care of breaking in the fledglings. Enter Ron Hefflefinger.

Dad took Ron for boy's day out and regaled him with the Herb Korf story as they rattled around out in the toolies in the old truck, choking on dust. When Dad got to the part about the rattlesnake Ron snorted, "Yeah, right." Ron might well have been a greenhorn but he was born less naïve than Herb, and besides, he had done some shooting so he already knew no one can shoot the head off a snake.

As if on cue, a rattler slithered across the road right in front of them. Ron eyed Dad. Dad eyed Ron. Dad stopped the truck, leaned over to Ron's side, popped the glove box open, grabbed the .38 Ron knew very well was there, stepped out of the truck, casual as you please, aimed and squeezed off a shot. Missed it by a mile, of course. The snake took off. Dad took off after it. Pow! Blam! Pow, pow pow! Dad was tall and skinny—all legs. Some had described him as 'a gangly storky-legged kind of a guy,' and Ron said watching Chick's long legs eat up the countryside waving a pistol around trying to shoot that snake was like watching a cartoon of some sort of bizarre marionette. He said it was just about one of the funniest things he'd ever seen until . . .

Bang! . . . –click. The six-shooter came up empty and the snake —Dad always said he figured either it could count or they must have been close to its nest by then—turned as fast as only a snake can and started chasing *him*. And that, Ron said, was absolutely the funniest thing he'd seen in his life ever, bar none. The snake chased Chick all the way back to the truck.

Dad jumped in the truck, pale and shaking, and fumbled with the ignition because, well, the floor boards in the old '56' were no barrier to dust or snakes or anything else. He was sweating and breathing hard and drove like the Devil himself was chasing them when he finally got the old truck to turn over.

Ron and Chick remained fast friends for the rest of their lives. Evie Hefflefinger was recruited into the ranks of the Sycamore Canyon Widows and the boys bagged many a big buck together.

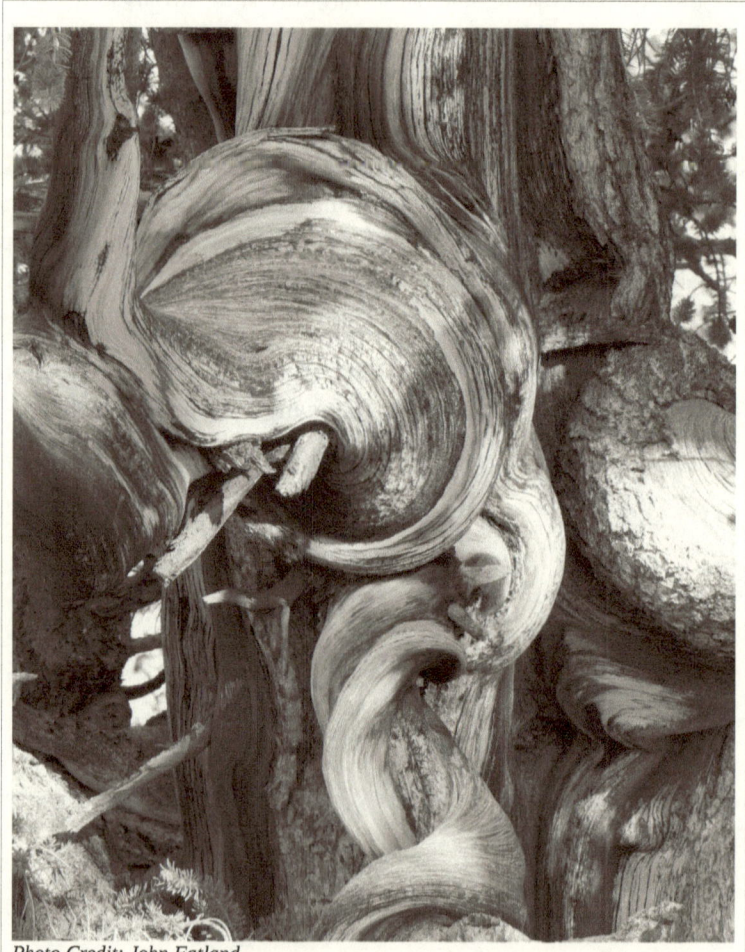
Photo Credit: John Fatland

FAERY TALES

The Sacred Circle Writers are enchanted with faeries, more correctly perhaps, by faeries. They have captured our imaginations and won't let us go. We are happy captives. It just doesn't get any better than a story with a moral at its heart spiced with a flourish of the fantastic. Some of us are working on novels featuring angels and faeries, and after the magic of the Christmas season had passed, in the dark of the year, we sought to reconnect with the magic we are certain surrounds us all the time. We thought we'd try our hand at writing a faery tale this week.

Keli Becker explores the world of the faeries as protectors in *The Well*, and as friends in the delightful *The Story of Thistledown and Tumbleweed*. Laurie Wilson Fatland's character discovers being beautiful isn't all it's cracked up to be in *Cursed*, and we all hope we might to have a *Faery Godmother* as crusty and helpful as Dave Becker's.

The Well

Keli Becker

Carly kicked any rock that was in her way with such ferocity they would have trembled to see her coming, if rocks could tremble. Her trusty companion, a chocolate Lab named Hazel, followed at a distance.

Carly was beyond pissed. She didn't care about her father's inheritance. It was the stupid money he received that had brought them here. That and this god-awful farm. Or ranch. Or whatever.

Her father, Fred, was overjoyed at his good fortune. Now he would be able to fix this place up, turn it into something to be proud of. The plans were in place to make a grand retreat out of the old ranch. Have big names come up to chill out, or have artist types in to create to their hearts' content. Get horses and have trail rides; the possibilities were endless. His wife, Carly's mother, was a little less enthused; all she saw was a lot of work, but if it would make her husband happy, she was in.

The property was stunning with pine, cedar and oak trees, open spaces, foothills, softly rolling land and two lakes. Its beauty was lost on Carly today. Black clouds overhead matched her mood. She had been ripped from her social circle, her friends, her school, her sports, and the mall. Torn from everything and everyone who meant anything to her. To become a "hill person", a hick, just so her mother and father could rub elbows and host parties for the rich and shameless. She would lose her privacy, too, with all of those strangers roaming around.

Just kicking the rocks wasn't enough. Carly began throwing them. She had a pretty good arm and started throwing them with a vengeance at an old stone well. Softball had honed her skills, she was the best short stop her high school had ever had.

She slammed softball-sized rocks at the well. Jagged pieces flew up and fell back into the mouth of the well. Carly suddenly stopped her assault and listened. Hazel cocked her head, too. She concentrated on a teeny, tiny, silvery voice she realized had been buzzing in her ears like a persistent gnat.

"Please stop. You'll hurt the baby."

Baby? What baby? Great. This stupid place was giving her hallucinations. She resumed her attack.

The tiny voice sounded in her ears again. "Please stop. You'll hurt the baby!" The tiny voice was more insistent this time.

Oh, geez. Could there actually be a baby in there? Carly didn't hear one. She thought babies made a lot of noise. And messes. If there was a baby, could it still be alive? Hazel padded to her side. Carly absentmindedly petted her. "What do you think, Hazel?" Hazel offered no opinion on the matter.

Carly stepped softly up to the well and peered inside. Her view was impeded by an iron grate that was stapled with really big staples to the opening of the well. Carly tried to lift it, to move it so she would be able to see better. No go.

"Yo! Baby, are you in there?" Hey, good name for a song. This day may not be a loss after all. Babies in Wells. Good name for a rock band.

Soft lapping sounds from the well were all she heard. Glints of light reflected on the inky black water.

"I don't see any baby," she grumbled. "Wonderful. First hallucinations and now I'm talking to myself, not to mention hearing things. Dad can turn this place into a nut farm." She smiled at her own bad joke.

She dropped a few more rocks down the well. No more "hurt the baby" voices. Maybe her blood sugar was low. She'd go back to the ol' spread and wrangle herself some chow. She would be living on a ranch; might as well start talking like it.

Carly turned to go. "Please stop. Help the baby."

Oh shit. Now what? "What baby?! There's no baby! And why am I yelling at a stupid old well? I'm going back to the house, you hallucination, you. My blood sugar must be seriously low."

"Please help the baby. She needs you. You need her. It's vitally important."

"How? How can I help this baby?" Might as well see where this figment of her imagination was going to take her.

"The baby needs you. Please help her." Carly started to wonder how she could help this baby. "The baby is hungry and cold. Please get her out. I can't get through the grate. It's iron and poisonous to me."

"What, should I throw a sandwich down to you? What's the deal?"

"Mary, the baby's mother, put her in the bucket to keep her safe. Her name is Penelope. Claudia, Mary's mother, cut the rope. The baby needs help."

This Claudia sounded like a real bitch, killing her own granddaughter. Carly and her grandma got along wonderfully. She couldn't wrap her mind around a grandmother who would kill her grandchild .

Carly suddenly became interested in the history of this place. "When did this happen?"

"When this place was younger, miners were looking for a yellow metal. One miner, Zebadiah, fell in love with a rancher's young daughter, Mary. Mary gave birth to a baby, Penelope. Mary knew she couldn't bring her infant daughter into the house, her mother would never permit it. It would make Claudia look bad to the women in town to have an illegitimate granddaughter.

"Mary was planning to go away with Zebadiah, to start a new life away from her mother. She knew her father wouldn't help her; he ignored her unless she was in trouble that made him look bad. The voluminous skirts and aprons that Mary wore hid a great deal of her pregnancy from her parents. Being ignored also helped. "Mary gave birth alone in her room one night. To keep her parents from hearing her screams, she gagged herself. She cleaned up as well as she could, planning to burn the blood-soaked sheets and blankets.

"She wrapped her new baby in a clean blanket. Penelope still had birth fluids and a waxy white substance on her. Mary fed her, wrapped her in a warm blanket and carried her down to the well. She would place the baby in the bucket and lower it just a little bit, so it couldn't be seen from the top. Zeb was coming for her the next day and she could retrieve their child then. Mary was the only one who drew water from the well for the household, so she thought it was safe to leave Penelope there for a little while.

"Claudia had secretly followed Mary to the well. Once she saw what Mary carried in her arms and guessed at her plan, she knew what she would do. Claudia snuck back to the house and grabbed a butcher's knife. Claudia crept back to the well and without a second thought, cut the rope. She heard the bucket hit the water so far below. There was one small cry, then nothing.

"Mary left the house quietly the next morning so as not to wake her parents. She hurried down to the well. When she saw the cut rope, she was inconsolable. She climbed over the stone enclosure and jumped in."

"Who are you?" Carly was moved to tears by the story, and was curious who was behind this voice?

"I am Hyacinth, the faery assigned to this baby at her conception. I was to watch over her and keep her safe, but I failed. I was unable to save her. I guard her now at her death."

"Faery. Is that like an angel?"

"Call us what you will. I am more spirit than flesh, but I can be killed. You are flesh. You can save my baby. I cannot leave this place because of the iron grate that was put over the well after

Mary's death. No one but Claudia and Mary ever knew about Penelope's murder. I would not leave the baby in any case."

Carly wondered how she would break this to her parents. "Hey, guess what? There's a baby in the well and a faery says we have to get it out!" Okaaay. Sure, that would work. So not.

"Look, little faery thing, "I've got to go get help. I hope you're not a figment of my glycemic-starved imagination. They already think I'm a nut job as it is."

"Please help the baby."

Carly ran back to the ranch house, Hazel by her side. She burst into the house and was surprised to find...nobody. "Hey, Hazel, where did everybody go?" As Carly turned, looking for some sign that people were around, the building started to shimmer. She rubbed her eyes. Carly looked over at Hazel. The dog looked like she split in two. Carly started to feel dizzy. Oh goody, she was getting sick to her stomach. No way can I hurl in here!

Carly staggered outside, past the wagging Hazel-twins. Geez, I must have a raging case of some-godawful-thing! Maybe I caught it from the well. It was probably a breeding ground for mosquitos and malaria, or polio, or ADD. Who knew?

But as little as she really knew about those maladies (she might be right about the mosquitos), she knew she had to help the tiny faery-angel. Hyacinth was depending on her! Once outside, the nausea calmed down a bit. Carly still felt as if she had come fresh off a tilt-a-whirl and was still queasy. When she stood upright, the world around her doubled, just like Hazel. Double doors had doubled again giving the two houses the look of the entrance to a stadium. Her stomach roiled again. What the hell was going on?

A powerful contraction in her uterus brought Carly to her knees in the dust.

Corral fences were reconfigured. Horses appeared where there had been no horses. The day changed to night and stars changed places in the sky. The house was dark. Carly's womb cramped, and cramped again. The worst cramps ever. She felt hot fluid gushing into a kind of diaper garment she had put together. Her period wasn't due for two more weeks and what was with the cloth bound around her? Her usual Tampax wouldn't have staunched this kind of flow, but she would have used a maxi-pad or something, not a piece of cloth wound around her waist.

Carly realized there was a minuscule wrapped bundle in her arms. The bundle kept making small noises like newborn kittens. Why would she be out here with kittens? Where had they come from? She pulled the scratchy material of the blanket away and was shocked to see a miniature baby in it. The infant still had blood on her face. It was newborn. A tiny baby girl. How Carly knew this was beyond her at the moment.

Carly had to hide her! The realization hit her like a slap. She had to hide the infant until Zebadiah came for Mary and their baby in the morning. She couldn't let her mother know she'd had the babe.

Carly had a vague recollection of a great deal of pain (whether her own or someone else's she wasn't quite sure right now), a huge gush of water and blood and body-splitting agony that had heralded her daughter's entry into the world. She knew she had given birth alone in her room. She also knew if she had told her mother, Claudia would have taken the baby and Carly would have never seen it again. Claudia had said the ladies in town would never accept an illegitimate baby. Zebadiah was coming for her and their daughter today. Only a few more hours.

Carly climbed clumsily to her feet, hampered by the long, hastily donned dress and the baby bundle. Another contraction struck and almost drove her to her knees again. Thank goodness the lantern landed upright and no oil spilled. The baby seemed to be alright, too. The tiny wrinkled face gazed at Carly and smiled. Carly-Mary's heart broke open in that moment and more love than Carly could ever have imagined poured out. Carly was sure Zebadiah would fall in love with the baby immediately. Mary wished she could show Penelope to her mother so Claudia could fall in love with the baby, too.

Mary staggered down the path to the well. If she put her new daughter in the bucket and lowered it a bit, the child would be hidden and Mary could come to check on her without raising suspicion first thing in the morning when she came to get water for the family. A teeny, tiny, silvery voice like a persistent gnat buzzed in Carly-Mary's ear. "Save the baby! Your mother has followed you and plans to cut the rope to the bucket as soon as you leave! Save the baby!"

Carly hadn't tried to force any of Mary's movements since they had joined. Carly didn't know if she could, but it was time to find out. She attempted to change Mary's direction. Instead of heading toward the well, Mary stumbled into the surrounding woods.

Whoa! What a trip! She was possessing another human being! She pointed Mary away from the well. Mary could hide Penelope and herself in the forest if she could shake Claudia. Mary didn't even know the psycho bitch was behind her.

Once in the trees, Carly let Mary lead the way. Mary knew the forest well. She had met Zebadiah in the woods in a small cave where she had also hidden from her mother. Mary didn't understand the sudden urge to go into the trees but let the urge guide her. It would be a safe haven for Penelope. Mary-Carly heard a twig snap. Her head whipped around and glimpsed a shadow slipping behind a boulder. Scared, Mary turned to run but her long skirt tangled in her legs and she stumbled, dropping the lantern. The lantern shattered, spewing flaming oil on the forest floor.

"Who are you? What do you want?!" Fear made her voice shrill. "Stop following me!" The flames gave off a hellish glow.

"That child cannot be allowed to live in this family!" Claudia screeched, "You are not supposed to have that baby! You will ruin this family's reputation and standing in this community!"

"Mother?" Mary was stupefied. She had heard her mother threaten her baby's life...but how could she?

"You disobeyed me and took up with that miner. Now you have an illegitimate child with no father. That cannot be allowed." Claudia emerged from behind the boulder with a large butcher knife in her hand. She advanced on Mary and Penelope. Her eyes flashed demonically in the flickering light of the fire.

Mary barely recognized the figure stalking her. Could this really be her mother?

A tiny spark flew up from the fire, indistinguishable from the rest until it attacked Claudia. Hyacinth struck Claudia again and again, driving her back. She was protecting the baby! Carly was too dazed to wonder how the faery escaped the well. Hyacinth rounded Claudia and backed her into the fire. Claudia swung the butcher knife but there was no way to fight the faery. Or the fire. Her skirts caught and burst into flame. Claudia was transformed into a human candle. Her screams echoed in the air. The shrieks scared Penelope and the baby began to wail. Hyacinth flitted to Mary-Carly. She lit on Penelope's blanket near her face and sang a sweet melody that calmed the baby right away. Penelope fell asleep.

Carly felt herself splitting from Mary. She had to quickly ask Hyacinth about the well. "How did you escape?"

"When you took control of Mary and guided her into the forest, even for that brief time, you changed history. Since nothing happened at the well and Mary didn't die, the iron grate was never put on. I was never caught down there with the baby. Penelope lived a very long good life. She had offspring and the family prospered. "She is your great, great, great grandmother."

"Oh wow! I saved my own grandmother's life. Mine, too!"

Hyacinth, Penelope and Mary faded back to their own histories and lives.

Carly found herself sitting on the lip of the well. She jumped off quickly. A sunset ray caught her in its light. Time to go home. She looked around at the land. This time the beauty of it struck her softly and she appreciated it.

The Story of Thistledown and Tumbleweed

Keli Becker

For Laurie

A faery tribe lived in the comfortable barn of some very nice humans. The tribe looked over the horses who resided there. The humans loved animals and had rescued many of them.

One of the animals was a cat named Tumbleweed. He was a young tomcat, full of himself and mischievous. He would twine himself around the humans' legs as they were walking and try to trip them. He was a nice cat, though, with ocean-green eyes and four lovely black rings around the end of his tail. The rest of him was a rumpled grey with a white collar of fur. He would tell fabulous stories of his exploits in the wild and could run like the wind. No one knew where Tumbleweed came from and he didn't say.

One of the faeries from the tribe bonded with Tumbleweed immediately. Her name was Thistledown. She was one of the smallest faeries in the tribe, and young compared to the rest. She was a shimmery gold and when she flew, she left a tiny trail of golden dust that could only be seen if that was what you were looking for.

Before Tumbleweed came to the faery kingdom, Thistledown had only had weasels and porcupines and prairie dogs to ride. The weasels and prairies dogs were very short rides and they tended to run into their holes without warning. The porcupines, while nice, were slow and uncomfortable. She didn't care to ride the horses from her barn as they were mainly pasture ornaments and content to stand in the sun or eat.

But Thistledown loved Tumbleweed. He would take her for exciting rides through the pastures. He knew how to avoid the stickery bushes that tore at Thistledown's lacy golden wings. He ventured into the forest sometimes, but it was extremely dangerous and he didn't take Thistledown there very often. He was, in his own way, a practical cat. He would race rabbits (who had shown a remarkable lack of interest in letting a faery ride with them), flew as far in a jump as he could to play with the birds, and played hide-and-seek with the prairie dogs. (Thistledown didn't know that Tumbleweed's motives were far from pure when it came to the birds and prairie dogs.)

Tumbleweed's heart was of the land and he took Thistledown everywhere. She soon stopped flying herself, she preferred the wildness of Tumbleweed's chase of life. Thistledown started to forget her own life's chase. The other faeries feared for her.

"He's too dangerous!" they cried. "He'll lead you into trouble!" they shrilled.

Thistledown ignored them. They were much older than she and didn't do much of anything anymore except flitter around the barn and pasture, and perch on the horses while they lazed in the sun. And the older faeries complained. Oh, could they complain.

Thistledown was terrified when two big dogs chased Tumbleweed up a tree because he dared to come too close to their enclosure to taunt them. "I'm free and you're not," he had boasted to the dogs. "I can run anywhere and anytime I want. I am not at any human's beck and call," he said as he strolled pridefully in front of their fence with Thistledown on his back.

Thistledown was a bit upset, because he was hers wasn't he? Her pretty voice sounded like the twitter of birds and the squeaking of the tiny field mice. Tumbleweed always came running when he heard her voice calling him. Thistledown thought it was her lovely song that drew him. The older faeries knew the truth: Thistledown's song sounded like food to Tumbleweed. "It's only a matter of time," they mumbled and grumbled to each other.

Tumbleweed so infuriated the dogs in the enclosure, they managed to jump their fence and give him a righteous run for his beautiful tail! He climbed a tree to save himself and couldn't get down. The human male got a ladder and got Tumbleweed down. Thistledown hid herself deep in Tumbleweed's fur so she wouldn't be seen. The whole incident was quite scary. Thistledown hoped nothing like that would ever happen again.

One day, Thistledown came out of her seed pod bed, nestled in one of the barn nooks, to find Tumbleweed gone. Disappeared. Just like that. He usually slept on the tractor seat where the male human had made a bed for him. She called and called for him but he didn't return. She sang her songs for him.

The other faeries nodded their heads together. THEY knew why he didn't come. He must have found another faery to be with, one who sang better or knew more exciting places to go. He was a young tomcat, after all. He was like a tumbleweed, he'd just go anywhere the wind blew him.

Thistledown was overwrought. Where could her beautiful Tumbleweed be? She decided to stretch her lacy golden wings and look for him. Thistledown had not flown since Tumbleweed had appeared in her life and found she had quite forgotten how.

She started with short flights among the stalls in the barn. She progressed to the pinion pine tree. They weren't great distances but surely Tumbleweed could not be far. Some other evil faery must have ensorcelled him. Maybe a faery had him bound with an iron chain. Maybe he was in an iron cage! How would she ever save him then? Iron was poison for faeries.

Thistledown flew a short distance in the direction of the pasture. Nothing there but dozing horses and complaining faeries. She tried another way. Nothing that way but weeds and bushes and prairie dog holes.

As a last resort, Thistledown tried in the direction of different humans. A couple of her tribe had ventured over the pastures there, mostly in the summer when the flitterbirds came for the nectar that was put out for them. The flitterbirds only came in the warm summer. The other faeries told her they were a very wild ride. The flitterbirds could do things other birds absolutely could not! The faeries that rode the flitterbirds were older than Thistledown by a couple of hundred years or so, and had much more experience. They thought riding a cat was too boring. The flitterbirds were exciting with their aerial antics.

Thistledown flew cautiously toward the other humans' house. She had heard the older faeries talk about the sorceress who lived there. These other humans had a huge black cat they called "Hoss." Thistledown's tribe called him "Ferocious." No sweet names for him. He caught and ate prairie dogs, mice, even flitterbirds from time to time when they were drunk from the nectar and flying stupidly.

The other faeries avoided Ferocious and didn't ride any animals who were silly enough to ignore their warnings about him. It was said a faery could (and sometimes did!) get eaten over there!

Thistledown was desperate. She needed her Tumbleweed! She knew the sorceress could ensorcell animals and make them do her will. She made horses carry her. Had she ensorcelled Tumbleweed, too? Thistledown had to find out if he was there. If he was, she had to save him! Who knew what horrors he could be going through!

This thought strengthened her resolve. She made her way to the sorceress's domain. She heard cat sounds, terrible cat sounds, of fighting, spitting and hissing. She came upon a scene from her worst nightmare (if she ever had a nightmare; faeries tended toward sweet dreams). Ferocious and Tumbleweed were squared off, both furred out; with ears flat back, and tails that twitched and lashed angrily. They slowly circled each other, growling. Their eyes sparked with fire.

Thistledown was afraid to enter the area but she had to save Tumbleweed, her best friend.

She hovered over their circle of furious energy, reluctant to go any closer. But she must! For Tumbleweed!

Thistledown darted at Ferocious and plucked a hair from his rump. Ferocious didn't even blink. Tumbleweed saw the little golden spark and renewed his attack on Ferocious.

Thistledown cried out her song, to encourage Tumbleweed by freeing him from the bad energy. Tumbleweed lunged at Ferocious and landed a swipe of claws on Ferocious. All Tumbleweed got was a pawfull of long black fur. Ferocious, though, decided he had had enough. With one final hiss at Tumbleweed, Ferocious leaped into the field and disappeared.

Tumbleweed straightened up, shook himself to settle his fur and glared at Thistledown. "I could have won that fight if you hadn't interfered. What are you doing here?"

Thistledown was taken aback. "I came to look for you, to bring you back home so we can go on adventures together again. I miss you and our travels so. Then when I got here, I saw you needed help so I did what I could for you. Maybe I saved your life."

Tumbleweed growled at her. "You didn't save my life, you silly faery! I was doing fine. In fact, I was winning!" His ocean-green eyes sparkled angrily. "And maybe I don't want to go on rides or adventures with you anymore," he said, with much less confidence. Tumbleweed could not meet her eyes.

"I'm staying here. I won't go back with you," he said with what sounded like genuine regret. "I used to like our adventures but the humans over there were talking about taking my..." Here he paused, then stood up and turned far enough for Thistledown to see his impressive malehood.

Thistledown was amazed. She had heard of such things but never connected Tumbleweed with them. "How could they do that to you?! You're magnificent...if you'll excuse me for saying so." She blushed furiously.

"Oh, no problem." Tumbleweed was pleased with what she said. He felt very proud of his malehood. "I just wish there were some female cats around."

"Come back, please Tumbleweed, please! We'll go for a ride and find you some females. I miss you so!"

"I...I...I can't. I don't know how or why, but when I try to get back something just keeps me from crossing the pasture. I mean, I can disappear for a couple of days when the humans talk about... altering...me. But I just can't make it over there. Wait, I know! You could move over here!" Tumbleweed was overjoyed with his solution. It answered all of his problems he thought.

Thistledown was heartbroken. "How can I leave my tribe? I can't, I just can't!" Thistledown was so distraught, she answered herself. "I need them. They are my family, my life. We just do not leave our tribe. Oh, how can I explain to you? You are so wild and free and have no ties to anyone or anything. I am not like that." Thistledown felt a golden tear escape her eye.

Tumbleweed watched the brilliant particle drop from Thistledown's face, like a falling star across the flawless morning sky.

"I don't know...wait! I hear the human from this place," said Tumbleweed. "Let's hide. Quickly, get on!" But as Thistledown snuggled into Tumbleweed's fur, she felt something was not quite right, and as Tumbleweed crept farther into Ferocious's old barn domain, Thistledown felt the wrongness even more clearly.

"Tumbleweed, please let's go somewhere, anywhere, just away from here," whispered Thistledown urgently. Never had she been so upset.

Too late! A beautiful woman entered the barn where her magical steeds resided. Thistledown recognized her from stories the older faeries of her tribe had told. This was the sorceress, Lori-lay, she of the long, shining, golden-yellow hair and deep green eyes. Her silver hooped earrings sparkled and shone against her cheeks in the filtered sunlight. Her flowing top and skirt had spangles on them and shot sun rays to every corner of the murky barn.

"Here you are, Barney," cooed Lori-lay. "I've been looking for you."

"You let her name you BARNEY?!" Thistledown was aghast. She shot off Tumbleweed/Barney as Lori-lay bent in a smooth move to pick up the now ensorcelled cat.

"We're going to the doctor's office and take care of your unnecessary parts. You don't need them and once they're gone, maybe you'll stay around here more. That is if you can get along with Hoss."

"I can get along, I can get along, just watch me," Tumbleweed meowed plaintively. "And what do you mean by 'unnecessary' parts? All of my parts are extremely necessary!"

Sorceress Lori-lay pretended she didn't understand Catish as she stuffed the now spitting and hissing Tumbleweed into a portable animal carrier. There were other animal smells in it: dog, cat and possibly one other creature Tumbleweed just couldn't figure out. The image of a grey bird entered his head, but none like he had ever seen before. "Tarzan" came to his mind like an old echo. Tarzan was Lori-lay's talking bird, something Tumbleweed had never encountered. All of the previous animals had been okay when they had gone into the carrier but had come back hurting. Now HE was in it!

"Thistledown, Thistledown, help me! I'll do anything you want if you'll only get me out of this thing!" Tumbleweed meowed so pitifully that Thistledown's heart was close to breaking. But she could do nothing to free her friend. The carrier was loaded into the big truck Lori-lay drove. The sorceress backed up from where she parked and left Thistledown, a tiny golden mote in the air, to cry her tiny golden tears for Tumbleweed.

Two days later, Tumbleweed came back, a vastly changed cat. As Lori-lay opened the animal carrier, Tumbleweed slunk out with his rear end close to the ground. He no longer strutted pridefully to show off his malehood. He didn't have it anymore.

Thistledown had gone to the sorceress's domain every day to see if Tumbleweed had returned. When she heard through KFEY, the faery grapevine, that he had just arrived, she flew over to the sorceress's barn as fast as she could. When she saw him brought so low, she felt the start of tears begin. But the tears were also tears of joy at having him home again.

Thistledown realized that she loved Tumbleweed not just for all of the adventures they had on their wild rides, she also loved him for himself. She loved all of the silly cat jokes he told her to make her laugh; the conversations they had had laying on the hay in a warm sunbeam in her barn; the excursions into (but not too far into) the wild woods where wild faeries lived. Thistledown and Tumbleweed were especially careful, none of her tribe knew very much about these woodland faeries and fearful stories had been told about them. Stories without much truth to them, as is usually the case with the unknown.

Thistledown settled next to Tumbleweed's lowered head and stroked it gently. "I missed you so and was terribly afraid you were never coming back again. Are you still ensorcelled? It feels different around here."

Tumbleweed raised his head and tested the air. "I do think you're right, Thistledown. The enchantment seems to be gone. That means—when I'm feeling a little better, mind you—I can come over to your tribe's territory, if it's okay with them that is, and we can go for a ride."

"Oh, that will be so wonderful!" trilled Thistledown, happy beyond any more words.

She planted a tiny golden kiss on the tip of Tumbleweed's nose and all was right with the world again.

Postscript: Tumbleweed soon realized he could travel between Lori-lay's territory and Thistledown's tribe any time he wanted and for as long as he wanted, but he no longer had the desire to roam as he used to. He was content to stay in his own little area and be a friend to Thistledown. Besides, the food was better at Lori-lay's.

Cursed

Laurie Wilson Fatland

Analisa sat on a rock in the forest, chin in hand, filled with so much anger she was almost steaming. How dare her mother treat her like this! Early this morning Analisa had done her chores and then asked her mother to buy her that beautiful new dress she had seen in town. It was a simple request and she deserved it, after all. Papa would have bought it for her, but Papa was no more. When he died last year, Analisa knew things would change, she had always been his pet, but Mama had become an angry monster since he died, who did not appreciate all the hard work Analisa did for her. Her soft hands were now raw and chaffed; Papa would never have allowed it.

Analisa had been born with a curse. The curse was beauty. Analisa was extraordinarily beautiful; she had dark hair with gentle curls, bright blue eyes, soft lips that carried their own pink color. Hers was the kind of beauty that women distrusted and men could not get enough of. And so she grew up spoiled by her father and coddled by every man she met. Her heart grew hard and small with selfishness.

Her mother's harsh expectations had sent her fleeing into the woods that morning, angry that she would not spoil her as her father had done. Now she was lost. The ground was too dry to follow her own footsteps back and there was no trail that she could see. So, she sat on the rock and fumed.

Eventually the light was beginning to fade and she was growing hungry. "I must find some shelter before dark," she thought. "If I can stay safe and dry, Mama will be sick with worry when I don't come home. Maybe she will begin to appreciate me more." So Analisa decided to climb a tree and look for a path that might cut through the forest.

A tall oak stood nearby with heavy branches she could climb. She scaled the tree in no time. Since she was only 16 her childhood skills were not far behind her. There was nothing to be gained, however, the trees went on for miles and she could see no opening to indicate a path. But wait! Not far to the east she could just make out a thin trail of smoke snaking its way into the darkening sky. Where there is smoke there must be fire and where there is fire there must be people! Analisa hurried down from the tree and ran toward the smoke.

Soon she caught a glimpse of a cabin in the woods. There was no road to it, and no obvious path. This did not look like a welcoming cabin. The fence around it was made of bones and the cabin itself was dark and covered in moss. Still, Analisa trusted her beauty and charm, so she walked up to the door and boldly knocked

It took a long time for someone to come to the door. She heard a shuffling and creaking coming from inside until finally the door opened just a crack. "Who is there?" a deep voice croaked.

"Why, my name is Analisa, I come from the village but have lost my way in the woods" Analisa said brightly. "I am seeking shelter and food for the night, will you help me?"

The door opened wider and an ugly old woman with warts all over her face appeared. She began to chuckle and looked Analisa up and down. Analisa was used to this however, and smiled prettily at the woman. "My, you are a pretty one", croaked the woman, "Come in, come in."

Analisa sat at the table in the dingy cabin while the old woman brought her a bowl of stew that was simmering over the fire. She did not see the old woman put a drop of potion into the bowl as she was ladling it out. Analisa ate hungrily as she babbled on about the village and how badly her mother treated her, but soon she grew drowsy and moved to the chair by the fire where she fell deeply asleep.

Such a gift, thought the old woman. Normally I would roast you and eat you my little lady, but no, you, I think I can use for something much more interesting. And she began to concoct a new potion which took her most of the night.

Analisa had stumbled upon the cabin of Mabayarga, the Witch of the Woods. She was feared by all the villagers about because those who became lost in these woods rarely returned. Now Mabayarga had decided to expand her evil influence and through Analisa she had found a way.

When Analisa awoke the next morning, stiff and sore from sleeping in the chair, she looked around the shabby cabin and at the old crone watching her; it seemed a good time to leave. "Can you point me in the direction of the village?" Analisa asked sweetly.

The old woman just smiled a toothless smile. "Well, I'll be going." Analisa said, things were getting very uncomfortable with the old woman refusing to speak. "Thank you for your help, I'll find my own way", Analisa said and headed for the door of the cabin. Surely there was a path leading from the cabin that she could follow.

However, when Analisa reached for the door her hand would not obey her. It refused to take the door knob; it refused to open the door. Analisa stood there, dumbfounded. The old witch began to cackle.

"It seems you will be my guest a little longer," the witch laughed. "You and I have some things to do first." The old woman made a gesture and Analisa began to clean the cabin, she could not help herself.

After hours and hours of sweeping, washing and scrubbing, the witch allowed Analisa to collapse in the corner of the stone floor on an old blanket. Analisa lay there in complete exhaustion. After a time, the old witch told her "Stay here, I will return," and she left Analisa alone. Analisa tried to rise and flee, but her body would not obey her.

The witch returned late in the day, mumbling to herself and grinning. She gave Analisa a bowl of stew and told her, "Sleep, my pretty. Tomorrow I need you rested."

After eating the stew, Analisa fell into a deep sleep and knew nothing until the next day dawned.

Early the next morning, the witch shook Analisa awake. She made her wash her face and comb her long silky hair while the witch rummaged in an old chest. Finally the witch pulled out a beautiful embroidered gown and had Analisa put it on. It was blue, like the gown she had wanted in town, and even more beautiful as it was embroidered all over with silver thread. Analisa's dark curls and blue eyes were stunning in the dress. When Analisa saw herself in the mirror, she could not help but smile. Surely, the old lady had some great plan for her!

The witch took Analisa by the hand and led her to a clearing in the woods. A cloth was laid out on the grass and a feast of bread, roast meats and a flagon of wine tainted with the potion, were set out upon it. The witch bade Analisa sit down and wait and she was told that she should offer the wine to anyone that should appear. Meanwhile Mabayarga ambled off into the woods.

Soon a giant deer with towering antlers ran into the clearing, staring at Analisa. Analisa began pouring the wine to offer the deer. Suddenly it turned and ran and a handsome young man came riding into the clearing, his horse stomping and prancing. When he caught sight of Analisa, he froze.

"Who are you?" he demanded, for he was the young prince out hunting from the nearby castle and he was used to demanding things. But the witch did not allow Analisa to speak, only to smile and offer the wine.

The prince dismounted and came over to Analisa. He was very hungry, so he sat and began to eat, for princes are used to taking whatever they needed. "Can't you speak?" he asked Analisa.

Sadly, she shook her head and held out the flagon of wine. The prince took it and drank deeply, handing it back to her with thanks. He gazed at Analisa and took in her beauty and the beauty of the fine gown she wore. Surely she was in need of his help, so without another word he swept her up in his arms and rode with her back to the castle.

The old witch watched from the woods, laughing with pleasure for now, both the prince and Analisa were under her spell, just as she had planned; for she had found where the prince was hunting and placed Analisa in his path for just this dark purpose.

When they arrived at the castle, the prince presented Analisa to his parents, the king and queen. They, of course, were enchanted by her beauty and silence and were delighted when the prince announced he would marry her.

Meanwhile the witch began to use her evil influence over them. She made the prince bring money and treasures to Analisa every day, and every night the witch would visit and take them from her. Soon there was very little left in the treasury, but the king and queen were too busy with the wedding plans to notice.

Then the prince began to issue strange decrees: All witches were to be released from the prisons; the villagers were not allowed to leave their homes; all families must give their oldest child to serve the castle and many of them were taken by the witch, never to be seen again. The people grumbled, but the prince was not in control.

One thing happened though. Analisa's body was controlled by the witch, but her thoughts were her own. She watched the prince and knew she had put him under the witches spell. She began to feel sorrow and she began to love him. The hard crust that had formed around her heart began to crack and break apart. Her heart grew and softened and she regretted how she had treated her mother.

The potion began to wear off of Analisa, for she had never taken much of it. One night when the witch came, instead of handing the treasure to her, Analisa threw it out the window. The witch jumped after it in her hunger for gold and fell to her death. The spells were broken.

The prince retrieved all of the gold of the kingdom and reversed his evil decrees. Analisa stayed at the castle and took care of the king and queen and the young prince and they all grew to love her mightily for her good heart. Analisa brought her mother to the castle and cared for her too.

And so, Analisa's curse was also broken; for though she remained beautiful, it was no longer her curse, but an ornament to her good heart.

Faery Godmother

Dave Becker

I know my Faery Godmother was there when I was born and that slap on the fanny was her.

I know my Faery Godmother was there when I got a Charlie horse in my calf just before I ran off the curb on my new 3-wheel trike and I hit the pavement.

I know my Faery Godmother was there when something told me to get on the other side of the guardrail while I was changing a flat tire just before a car rear-ended me on the freeway.

I know my Faery Godmother was with me when my pen passed over the right answers on my written driving test.

I know my Faery Godmother was with me when the pen again passed over the right answers on my college final exam.

I know my Faery Godmother was with me when the pen mysteriously passed over the winning lottery numbers.

I know my Faery Godmother was with me when I got a tickle in my groin the night my wife got pregnant.

I know my Faery Godmother was with me the night I heard my newborn scream, knowing he got the same slap on the fanny I did.

I think I was the only one in the delivery room laughing because I know it wasn't his good lungs, it was my Faery Godmother slapping my newborn on the fanny.

Hopefully I won't need her again till she jumps on my chest to draw my last breath so I can say goodbye to my loved ones.

GRAND CANYON CAVERNS
17 miles

Photo Credit: John Fatland

TRAVEL

Constrained by neither time nor space, the imagination is a powerful and versatile vehicle for travel. It was the dark of the year, the sparkle and fun of the holidays was far behind us. We had cabin fever. This week the Sacred Circle Writers let their imaginations wander. Come vacation with us.

Keli Becker hones her descriptive craft with powerful, fun imagery to take us on a tour of Flagstaff Arizona's funky old downtown area one enchanted night in *Tripping the Backstreets,* and Laurie Wilson Fatland's dream vacation turns nightmarish in *Luberon.*

Tripping the Backstreets

Keli Becker

Come with me on a little trip. A little trip on the backstreets. Do you dare? Travel inside your mind. You will find treasures beyond belief.

Come along. I'm not so scary. I am clothed in flowing robes of shadows. I am a creature of the night. But trust me. You'll see. Sights and sounds. Scents and flavors. Textures. All like you've never experienced before. Let your heart open to new vistas. To new adventures. To things never seen before, tasted before, heard before, felt before. To new-old backstreets, back doors. To many, they are just alleys, but they are always changing. Hidden. Secrets. Nighttime is the best time to travel the backstreets. For only at night will some things let themselves be seen. Or heard. Or felt.

Backstreets hide in darkness and sometimes behind trash. Unlucky humans often loiter in backstreets, lost and abandoned like the animals who roam the backstreets with them. Without the garbage the backstreets would have the dirty-spice smell of licorice.

Backstreets are not for the faint of heart. It is only by getting past the ugly that you can arrive at the beauty. Like a grain of sand that becomes a pearl. Like a cluster of cells that becomes a human. Like a dirty little bulb that becomes a gorgeous flower.

Snow never seems to melt back here. Puddles never dry up. There is always loose asphalt to sprain the ankle of the unwary.

Overhead, phone and electric wires form a net to keep the wild magic from escaping. Backstreets and alleys stitch the city together from one end to the other, side to side. They are shortcuts and shadows. The Sun doesn't show his face but the Moon is always welcome here.

Backstreets can hide many things: lovers, lost books of magic, gods and goddesses in disguise, murals only half glimpsed, faeries dancing from moonbeam to moonbeam, stardust, a golden ring.

Follow me. I may only be a shadow among shadows, but that is so you can allow your senses to take over.

And if you feel the need to stay in a place, stay. But don't lose your way home. It's easy to become lost. The marvels of these streets can be enchanting.

I'll be your guide. Come. Follow me.

~

We'll start off at a small speakeasy whose front door opens on this backstreet. The close smells of old smoke and old whiskey welcome you. You can almost get a contact buzz. Some of the longtime patrons have taken on the patina of the ancient mahogany bar that stretches from one wall to the other in this small windowless room. This is their place. The walls are painted with nicotine, dirty brown-yellow. The inebriating spirits hail from another era when men's and women's pleasures had to be taken on the sly and never spoken of in the daylight. Only a secret word would allow admission to this hallowed place.

Here, have a shot of this bracing elixir; it will strengthen you on your trip. Ahh, do you feel the sting on the tongue and the heat going down to your belly? You are ready to move on.

Next we come to the back entrance of a restaurant, offering up savory scents. Come in, come in! Taste their corned beef and cabbage, arguably the best in town. Mmm...salty and thirst-inducing. Quick, drink this quenching dark beer down. They go well together, don't you agree? Dart boards on the walls, TV, foosball in one corner of the room, pinball in the other. Buxom young waitresses; modern sirens to lure unwary men away from their money. Sprites hiding behind decorative plates on the walls. Careful! They'll steal the money from your pants too. Time to go!

An herb store is next on our backstreet trip. Which herb catches your fancy? Sage for smudging and cooking? Chamomile for calming? Ginger for your stomach? Cinnamon and cloves for mulling wine on cold nights? Dandelions for a spring tonic? Yerba

Maté tea for energizing yourself? What is your malady? What calls to you? The shop owner favors a different herb; you can see it in her eyes. Don't judge her; she suffers from arthritis and fibromyalgia. She will share some with you if you like. She's very generous. Oh, two of you are staying. No problem. Enjoy your time here. The rest of us will journey on. Farewell!

Watch your step. The stairs are old and rickety.

We're coming to a music shop. Some discordant notes hang in the air from someone dreaming of rock star fame, but sadly, for now, lacks the skills. In the pauses you can hear phantoms sing haunting songs of loss. Spritely unicorn melodies fill the air, and the nighttime stars sing arias to the Moon. Here you can find sheet music for faery songs; but be careful; their songs can lead to eternal dancing. Ahh, the beginner has stopped and skilled hands now stroke lutes and strum guitars creating heavenly sounds.

What's your pleasure? A green tambourine? A shiny red harmonica? Heartbeat pounding drums? Heartbreaking violins? A sexy sax? An angel harp? All this and more can be yours, if you want. To make music that can move the stars.

Ahh...so you do want to hear more songs and arias, sir and madam? Please enjoy. You can always catch up later. If you're lucky.

We'll just move on.

Turn to your right and we'll stop at a coffee shop. Oh, watch out for that icy slush. It's very slippery. You can skate to our next destination if you please. Exhilarating, is it not? You are ready to enter the caffeine palace. Coffee and teas available for any mood that takes your fancy. The aroma beckons you nearer. You can't ignore it.

There's a coffee that will keep you up all night but won't leave you tired the next day. A tea that can help you see music notes in the air. Another coffee that can help you to see beyond this reality and into others. No one knows where this coffee comes from. It's a mystery how it's roasted, but it has helped a few people find their truest selves. Very powerful, so sip it with caution.

This store is said to have the best coffees ever tasted. I think I must agree. It fills your mouth with warmth and a slightly bitter taste mellowed with wonderful roasts. It's balanced smoothly. It doesn't give you the dreaded "coffee breath." College students in this town love this place.

I see a few of you have decided to throw caution to the wind and give the reality-changing coffee a try. Good luck and I hope you find what you are seeking.

Step carefully in this backstreet. Loose asphalt can cause ankle sprains and you never know when a black cat may cross your path in this enveloping darkness.

You can smell our next destination. It's a powerful smell and brings you visions of a hearth and warming fire. The store is open and brightly lit. Breads and pastries are displayed in the glass counter. They melt in your mouth with flaky crusts and real fruit centers. The scents fill your being. The bread has come out of the oven and is ready to eat. The golden crust is perfect, slightly hard, and crunchy. Inside, the soft white, precious manna. Take a slice; cover it with fresh butter and feel it melt into doughy goodness in your mouth. Crunchy and soft combine in buttery splendor!

I see some of you hurrying to buy loaves of this miraculous bread. Don't forget a couple of cookies, for energy and pure home-like pleasure, on our trip. They will go well with the coffee you brought.

Watch the stairs; they are steep.

Our next destination is a bookstore and magic shop.. Not just any bookstore, but a magic one. It contains books of a similar ilk, like cookbooks, but of two kinds. Regular cookbooks and grimoires, or Books of Shadows, which are magical cookbooks; ancient wisdom enhanced with current knowledge. Those are very, very special. Anyone can use them, but they should only be used carefully. Spells, curses, good luck charms, and potions. There are Voodoo books, but they are risky indeed for the novice to use.

But enough of that. Explore! Enjoy! Oh, look! A book on gargoyles! We don't often get to see gargoyles in the backstreets, but you must look up. That can be perilous if you're not watching out for objects in the streets.

I have always loved gargoyles. They can fly, but ponderously. These narrow streets hinder their wings. Occasionally, they will take to the ground and walk, but it just makes more holes in the asphalt. Most gargoyles in this town live on the sides of a church, to protect, and to remind humans of their sins. One took off and never came back. You can still see his empty perch.

This is also a magic shop where you can take classes if you're new to the Craft. You might even be invited to join a Circle. Lessons last a year and a day. Then you might become a priestess or priest. It is your choice. You can learn many, many things.

You can learn about herbs, plants and potions used in spells and magic. Interpreting dreams. The Tarot cards. Pendulums. How to look into a crystal ball and tell the future. How to make charms for almost anything: luck, love, prosperity, healing, and more. There are crystals and incense. Oracle cards and angel cards. Beautiful jewelry with stones of power. Lovely fountains to fill the air of your living space with the sound of running water, which is very healthy and helpful for meditation.

There is clothing for rites. Cloaks like mine, but cloth, not shadows. Feel them, soft and slick. Sabbats, esbats. The year is full of celebrations. It is a joyful Craft.

I could stay in this store all night. My vibrations connect with it. But I have more wonderful places to show you if you follow me. Stay if you wish. Both decisions can be right. Come, come and take in as much as you can. You will be glad you did.

Oops, we interrupted two lovers. Please excuse us, we'll be gone in a minute.

These streets also draw beauty. All love is beautiful when pointed in the right direction.

We're going to a jewelry store next.

Here it is. This is not just any jewelry, it feels like magic. Beautiful jewelry with wonderful powers. Sometimes you can feel the pull of the energy of the pieces in your belly. Listen to your instincts. You will know which stones are calling to you. Pick one and see where it takes you. You like the agate. Are you in need of a calming crystal? Agate may be able to help you. Blue lace agate can be used on the throat in chakra cleansing. This is your truth center. Red jasper can be helpful for the base chakra, your creative and sexual center. Light green colors aventurine at the spleen chakra. Low on energy? This may help. There are so many crystals to choose from. They are as individual as you are. You don't need help picking one. The right stone will call to you. You will be drawn to it.

We will go to a bead store now. Here you will be able to make your own magical jewelry. Infuse it with your own personality and power. It will be one of a kind tuned only to your vibrations. Others may wear it, but it will always only truly be yours. See the beads. What a wonderland of colors and sizes and textures. What calls to you? There are classes to be sure, and from them you can wander through the doors of endless wonder.

String them, wrap them with wire, and hang them in the light of a sunny window so their prisms can cast rainbows on your world. Make bracelets to adorn your wrists, necklaces to grace your neck. Create sparkling wonders. Infuse them with your own power. Make patterns with symbols only you know. There are vials you can string on a chain to hold your potions or essential oils. There are lockets for pictures of your loved ones, or a lock of their hair. Are you inspired? Are you moved to create? Purchase your beads and we will go to the next site.

Here is a crossroads in our backstreet journey. A powerful goddess, Hecate, looks over crossroads. We will acquire an offering and our passage will be blessed. Maybe She will accept a Hawaiian BBQ dish. She is not without a sense of humor.

Kitty-corner from us is a Psychic. Does anyone want to know their future? Have their Tarot cards read? Oops, she has a client. We can save this for another time.

We have more places to explore but I feel you tiring. Are you up for one more adventure? It's right around this corner. Let's go. This is a place where many tales are told. Some amazing, some sad, some joyful. Open your minds and hearts and you will hear tales of lives lived. An antique shop can hold many wonders. Every piece in here has a story to tell if you let it. Just touch the pieces and listen.

This small table belonged to an elderly lady who was estranged from her granddaughter, her only living relative. The granddaughter went to her grandmother's deathbed right next to where this little nightstand table was stationed. They reconciled and the old lady died in peace.

That davenport was in a large, happy family. They came from Ireland to make their fortunes, and succeeded in spectacular fashion. The family owns the restaurant where you had the corned beef and cabbage. They also brew the dark beer that complimented the meal.

Are you hearing the stories? Do they move you? This furniture can serve you well. Add your stories to theirs.

Our trip through the backstreets is done. Oh, look! The sun is just starting to brighten the eastern sky. Its rays will not penetrate most of the shadows. I must return to those shadows until my next trip.

Come join me again sometime. The backstreets are always changing. They will always welcome you back for your next adventure.

Whatever you do, wherever you go, safe journeys to you until we are together again!

Luberon

Laurie Wilson Fatland

Emma ran her fingers over the stones, warm from the Provence sun. She felt the touch of other hands who had left their presence here nine hundred years before. Some raw peasant had built this little house long centuries ago, and he built it to last.

She had checked in at the office in the large stone house standing across the lane. The *"mas"* as they called the big stone homes of Provence. This week would be the highlight of their trip to France; seven days in a rented, restored farmhouse in the Luberon Mountains of Provence. The owner had redone all the buildings on his farm with modern kitchens and bathrooms, but left the charm and history intact.

Her company had offered a prize, a one week trip to Paris, for the salesperson with the largest increase in sales for the year. Emma won it hands down. And she'd worked her butt off for it. Selling medical supplies for a living was not the most glamorous job, but it took a lot of knowledge and a lot of skill. She was proud of all she'd accomplished. And here she was, in France!

When she and her daughter Annie learned they had won, they decided to extend the trip for a week to explore the South of France. Paris was a magical city, but they wanted some quiet time to be together, just mother and daughter. Emma found this house on an international rental website and it looked perfect; a historic stone farmhouse sitting on a horse farm in Provence. Both of them were avid horseback riders. Annie competed on the local show jumping circuit and at age 11 had made quite a name for herself. Emma rode for fun and leased a horse at the same stable where Annie rode. It was one of the things that bonded them so deeply.

The description of the property said you would be assigned your own horse for the week and could ride whenever you wanted. When she had called for the reservation, the man asked about their riding ability and told them he had the perfect horses for them. Annie was thrilled.

While she waited for the owner to bring the key and fresh linens, Emma explored the outside of the house. Annie had already run up to the stable to see the horses. The old house stood in a row with similar buildings on a narrow lane of cobblestones. It must have been housing for the farm workers who planted and harvested for the owners of the large *mas*. An arched doorway with an old plank door was the main entrance. The upper floors had shuttered windows with flower boxes that were charmingly overgrown. Around the back of the house she saw the modern addition that included the kitchen and a small patio that overlooked the valley down below. It was everything she had hoped for!

She heard Monsieur Bertillion call from the front of the house "Miss Webster!" Rushing back around the house she bumped in to a stone spout coming out of the wall, and almost fell.

"Here I am", she called back and dusted off her jeans.

"This is your key," Monsieur Bertillion spoke with a heavy French accent. He handed her an old brass key and showed her how to open the ancient lock. They stepped in to a low-ceilinged room, made of chiseled rock and timbers. It was cool and scented with smoke from the large stone fireplace. Emma could have walked into the fireplace without ducking. The room was simply furnished with a couch, a chair and an antique rug on the stone floor. "This is the oldest part of the house." He pointed to a set of stairs to left, worn down from centuries of footsteps. "The bedrooms are up there, and you will find the kitchen and sitting room through here." He led them through a glass-paned door into a modern room lined with bookshelves and large windows opening to the view of the valley.

The kitchen was small, but had all they would need. They were on vacation, and Emma didn't plan on doing much cooking anyway, but the patio off the kitchen was charming and the view stunning. She was going to enjoy this.

Putting the linens down on a chair, Monsieur Bertillion suggested they go and meet the horses. "Yes, I'd love that", Emma agreed, "Annie, my daughter, is already up there."

They walked down the lane and up a small hill to the barn. Annie was leaning on the fence petting a sweet Halflinger mare that nuzzled her gently. "I see you have already made friends! She is the one I chose for you! That is Miel, which means Honey. Now follow me and I will show you where the tack is." Monsieur Bertillion led them into the barn. Soft straw covered the floor and the walls were lined with saddles and bridles for the horses. "They are labeled for the horses, here are the halters. You can just tie them to the wall to tack them up for riding. You be the only ones here this week, so make yourselves at home. Now Madame, I will introduce you to your horse."

Emma followed him out into the pen and he led her to a fine looking chestnut. "This is Rodrigo. He is a Selle Francais gelding. Very nice horse. He will be yours for the week."

The elegant French breed was a cross between native French horses and thoroughbreds, they were known for their abilities in both dressage and jumping; Emma was excited to be able to ride him. "Thank you! He's gorgeous!"

After a few instructions on how to find the trails into the National Forest, Emma and Annie made their way back to their little house to unpack. "Mama, this house is so cute! I feel like I've gone back in time!" Annie was buzzing with so much excitement she could hardly get herself settled in.

They explored all the nooks and crannies of the old house, even finding an ancient stone sink in the front room wall that drained through an opening in the wall. It was the same spout Emma had crashed into outside. The front room was dark as the only window was small and shuttered but it kept the room cool, almost cold. Emma shivered as she walked through it to the big open room with the view.

"Let's go into the village, Annie, and get some supplies for dinner and breakfast. Then we can go for an evening ride before we eat. What do you think?"

"OK, let's go!" Annie wanted to go riding more than anything, but whatever her mother decided was fine, as long as riding the horses happened soon.

They spent a long time at the market, examining all the strange food and drink. They came away with a roast chicken, salad, some paté and, of course, fresh baguettes for dinner. Croissants and jam would be their breakfast. A local beer for Emma and lemonade for Annie finished off their purchases.

They put the groceries away quickly and changed into riding clothes, eager to ride before evening fell. The warmth and clear sunshine of Provence slowed their pace as they walked up the hill to the barn. Mr. Berthillion was penning up his sheep for the night, the soft baaing and shuffling of the herd was a lovely background to the job of saddling the horses. As they rode off, Mr. Berthillion raised a hand in farewell.

The path into the Luberon forest led up a steep hill behind the horse pen and then leveled off in the woods, shaded by the thick trees. The path was wide; soft dirt cushioned the horses hooves and the silence made them quiet their own voices to enjoy the peace.

After winding up to the top of the mountain, the path lay before them straight and smooth. Annie took her horse into a fast trot, Emma following, and then they eased into a gentle gallop. The partnership between rider and horse thrilled them both as they harnessed the muscle beneath them and raced ahead. There was an opening in the trees and Annie slowed to a walk to look at the view below.

An ancient town clung to the side of the mountain. Huddled together, the ocher buildings with their red-tiled roofs looked as if they were gathered together in fear of what might come upon them. Emma remembered the history of the area and the armies that could have risen against the little village. No doubt there had been many tragedies here. Even with the echoes of past violence the scene was a pretty one, fields of mustard glowed yellow in the early evening light and the rows of lavender shadowed soft blue in the valley. No wonder so many famous painters flocked to this area, the whole landscape looked like a painting. Emma felt herself relax for the first time in ages. Together she and her daughter rode slowly back to the farm in easy conversation.

After dinner they unpacked and chose their rooms. Emma picked a small bedroom with shuttered windows that looked over the cobblestone lane. Annie was drawn to a balcony that hung out over the large modern living room, a bridge between the old house and the new. It had a small bed surrounded by books and allowed her to see the landscape that was like a painted masterpiece outside the big windows. They both chose not to watch television. It seemed wrong to disturb the peace of the old house with the noise of the modern world.

The week strolled by, easy and peaceful. Days spent exploring the local villages, exquisite lunches in cafes that stood the test of time, and early morning and sunset rides in the forest filled their days. The silent countryside let them sleep deeply and dreamlessly through the cool nights.

The little stone house surrounded them with the past, weaving the days and nights together into a tapestry of time. There were only two nights left and they were already sad to leave. They never spent time in the front room of the house, though. Its dark chill seemed to suck the warmth from the day the moment they entered.

Sleep came easy that night as darkness fell over the landscape. But it didn't last. Emma woke with a start, listening intensely for what had shocked her from sleep. She could hear nothing, and kept still, feeling the deep smothering darkness that lay over the house. She rose from bed and walked softly across the hall to check on Annie, who was breathing peacefully.

Thirsty, Emma went down the stairs to get a drink of water from the kitchen. She stepped into the cold room, the icy stone floor chilling her bare feet. Reaching for the glass door, she heard the sound of ragged breathing behind her. She spun, but strong arms slammed her into the stone wall. Desperately she reached for the door handle, but someone fought her, grabbing and wrestling her for the door, pulling her back into the dark recesses of the room. Emma pushed against the force, but there was no body to push against, only an inky black cold. She broke free of the darkness and grabbed the door again. Finally pulling the door closed as she leaped into the modern part of the house.

She stood listening. Silence. Only the sound of her own ragged breaths. She was shaking, trying very hard to convince herself she had been dreaming. Emma stumbled into the kitchen, relieved to see the modern appliances. She splashed her face with cold water to be sure she was awake, and turned on the lights. Standing quietly she tried to sense if someone was in the house, she could hear nothing, but she felt it. A brooding presence that seemed to lurk in the darkness of the past.

A new wave of terror flooded through her. Her baby, Annie, lay on the other side of that door with nothing protecting her from the angry being she had just fought with. Still praying it was all just a dream, she tore open the door and bounded across the room to the stairs, running to Annie.

Annie was sleeping; she seemed peaceful and unaware of her mother's fear. Emma began to breathe easier. It must have been a dream. She sat for awhile and convinced herself to go back to bed.

As she sat down on the edge of the bed, a book was thrown to the floor, hard, with a loud slam. She ran back to Annie's bedside as the sounds of more books being thrown grew around her. Annie still slept, unbelievably, but all around her the crashing of pottery and pans and books heaved in anger to the stone floor rose and filled the house. The sounds came from below, from the cold ancient room and from the modern part of the house. Not wanting to wake Annie, she curled next to Annie, holding her close, and put her hands over her ears to drown out the furious violence below.

Somehow she must have drowsed off for she woke to an eerie quiet in the early dawn. Emma rose and peeked over the balcony to see the ruin of the angry wave that buffeted the house last night. Nothing had been moved. All the books were on their shelves and all the dishes and pottery stood whole and undamaged in their cabinets. Maybe it had been a dream, but she still felt the anger. Something in this house did not want them here any longer. She had an overwhelming desire to get out.

Quickly she packed Annie's things and then her own. She dragged their suitcases down the stairs, hesitating in fear before crossing the cold main room and flinging open the door. She propped the door open as she loaded the car to allow the warming rays of sun in, hoping to banish that lurking anger to the shadows. The key to the door had been flung across the room and lay against the stone wall. It had not been a dream.

It was still there. An angry being watching her. She felt its desire to beat her and damage her and destroy her. She ran up the stairs and shook Annie awake. "Let's go, honey, something has come up and we have to leave early."

Annie rubbed the sleep from her eyes and followed her mother down the stairs and into the car. Gravel spun beneath the tires as Emma sped off, Annie watching her curiously. "Mamma, what's wrong? Are we leaving because of the ghost?"

Emma pulled the car over and looked at her daughter. "Did you see a ghost, honey?"

"No, I never saw him, but I heard him breathing at night. He was under my bed."

Chills ran through Emma. "Did he hurt you?" she whispered.

"If I stayed in bed, he breathed like he was asleep. But if I put my foot on the ground his breathing got angry and loud. I tried to keep him calm."

"Why didn't you tell me?" Emma sighed, shaking her head, hating to think of the fear her daughter had kept hidden.

"He told me not to. I was afraid. And I didn't think you would believe me." Annie began to cry.

"I'm so sorry, baby, I would have gotten us out of there sooner, if I'd known."

"Mamma, why do think he was so angry? I think he hurt someone there."

Emma had no answer and told Annie so. She thought about the immense anger that filled the house last night, an anger so wild and intense that it lasted centuries. An anger that created its own force and was strong enough to touch the present. She shuddered in sympathy for whoever had experienced its full force in the beginning. May they have found peace.

They drove away in silence, one eye on the rearview mirror, watching the past trail behind them.

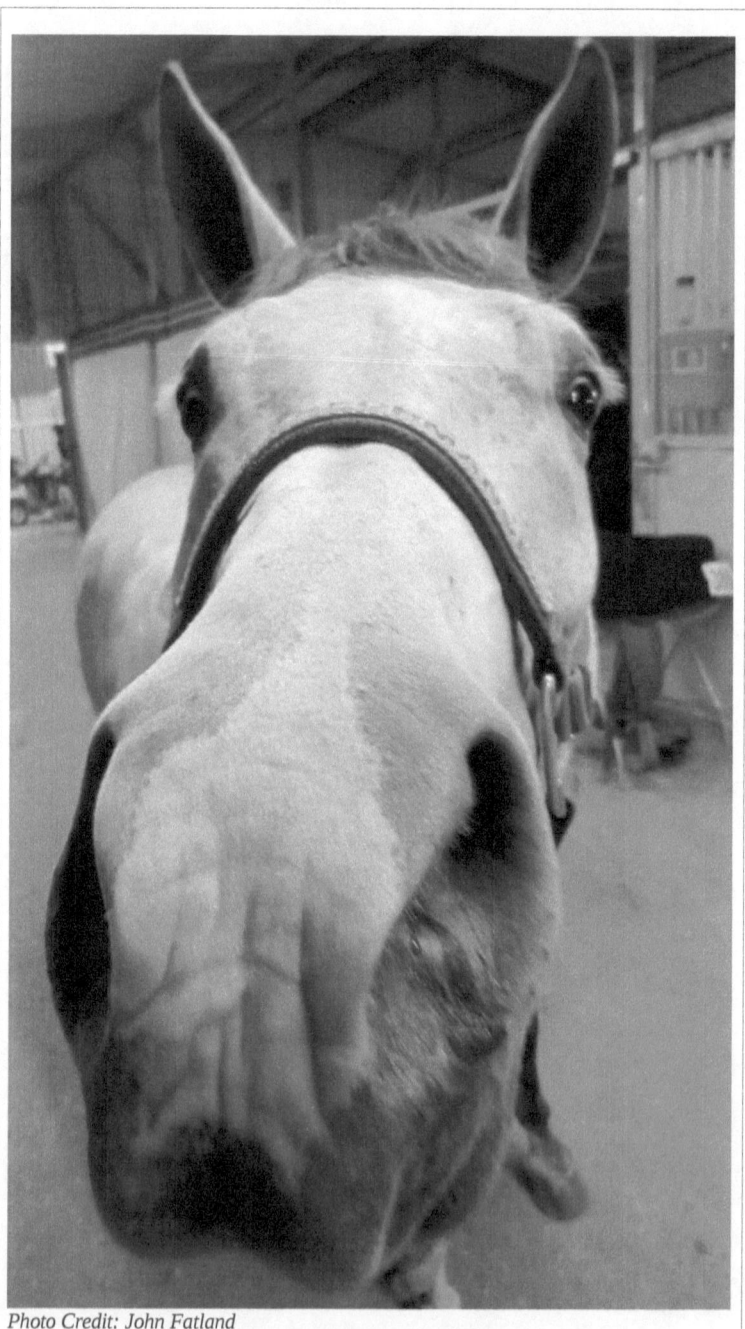

Photo Credit: John Fatland

HUMOR

Most everyone in the Sacred Circle Writers aspires to be a serious writer, but that doesn't mean we're morose. We're all lighthearted by nature and love to laugh. The prompt this week was to give our readers a smile, to write something humorous or the back story to a joke.

Katarina Karjala lingers with the best kind of childhood memories; those that are bittersweet, fun, and ultimately teach us life's greatest and most important lessons in ways we'll never forget with *Wrestling Time*. Dave Becker lets his ever-sardonic sense of humor have free rein in *Bear.* Laurie Fatland finds poetic justice through the retelling of an old Navajo joke in *He No Look Good*; and her character eventually finds true love in *Desperate Measures*, just not where she thought she would.

Wrestling Times

Katarina Karjala

Everything was set up. The wrestling ring was well lit by three sets of neon lights, Polacek and Kubovic in the middle, slightly hopping, in a lower squat, with their hands ready in front of their chests. The audience was divided almost equally into two groups, and the wrestlers were ardently looking at me. As a referee I gave a signal to start. Most girls cheered for the muscular Kubovic, who resembled Silvester Stallone; the boys rallied behind Polacek, well known for his coarse personality. A vigorous fight escalated with increasing decibels of the high-pitched voices of supporters. Kubovic was proud of obtaining scratch marks on his face and Polacek's left cheek showed a not really healthy strawberry color. After Polacek landed a strong punch into Kubovic's stomach, Andrea, most athletic from all girls, didn't wait a second. She jumped into the ring because she was openly in love with Stallone and secretly with Kubovic. My protests as a referee were overheard and even though my arms waved in a fan-like movement, nobody paid attention. The whole audience one by one mingled in an array of colorful sweaters. They fought each other with honest ferocity: the boys, who slightly outnumbered the girls, screamed their lungs out. Nobody noticed when a teacher came in the classroom and, with a strong disciplinary tone, gave an order to follow him. At that moment everybody was back in reality, in the 6th grade classroom of 6B. Now, all of us, including me, a referee, were moving behind the teacher in a formation of quacking ducks to the principal's office. Just because our classroom was conveniently located at the farthest end, we had enough time to discuss further tactics on the way there. The main corridor and oversized staircase, able to take river of rushing students, now appeared to be unnecessarily spacious.

The principal, a tall former partisan of World War II, was sitting behind an L-shaped desk in his office. Contrary to his height the office would classify for an economy size, therefore it hardly accomodated thirty students. He was reasonably angry and we were solidly united. His welcome speech began with: "Oh, infamous 6B."

Wearing eyeglasses gave me a serious and trustful look so for that reason I thought, perhaps as an elected referee, I qualified for a self-elected spokeswoman.

"Mr. Principal, may I say something?" My classmates made a corridor so I could stand in front of his desk. First I took a deep breath. "I want to apologize for our behavior but we think that staying all day in the classroom has an impact on our learning abilities. You know, we all get the wiggles after forty five minutes of sitting, especially now, in the winter. This is why we wrestled."

The principal stood up in the towering fullness of his six point three feet height, and looked down at the sardine-packed configuration of students in his office. I resembled a penguin, holding my arms tightly next to my body. With a slight smirk on his face he said, "I am not going to call your parents, but I don't want to see this kind of behavior again."

Our fear of punishment evaporated with the speed of camphor. We were young and full of energy, we had to utilize the "wrestling ring," in the front of our classroom, framed by the first row of wooden desks, the teacher's table on one side and an oversized green chalk board on the wall. The available space and the fact that we stayed in the same classroom the whole day, was an invitation for mischief. The two-sided board opened like a book and was sometimes used as a banger to play Laurel and Hardy, although frail kids like me were not invited.

Two weeks later the opportunity came during the long break when teachers had a meeting. In no time we were divided in two teams and I as a referee took my post standing on the middle desk in the front row. Kids, feeling superman powers, were punching around, sometimes their own team members. It didn't matter. Weaker fighters were pulling each other's shirts or hair. Enthusiasm was unanimous and demonstrated itself by a pungent smell of sweat. Nobody thought even for a second to open windows, it could be a fatal mistake because people on the street might hear our roaring. When I saw signs of fatigue, as a referee, I gave a signal and wrestlers crept back to their desks to devour a quick snack, to clean bloody noses and cover bruises. My duty was to collect all tangible evidence of the activity; ripped buttons, torn out bunches of hair. Nobody detected us this time, so we commemorated our victory. The teacher, who came to teach, found a classroom full of students obeying all the rules, sitting quietly at their place, ready for education. Such angels.

The very next day the school's intercom system was playing music when we entered the classroom. After the teacher came in, we all heard a familiar, cracking sound coming from an amplifier the size of a dinner plate. A voice said: "Attention, please, attention please. 6B to the principal's office." In 6B you could hear the water dripping from the faucet to the sink. We felt in our bones that a punishment for last wrestling would be eventually issued. Quietly and as slowly as possible we followed the teacher. The same way we crowded again into the principle's office. Principal was standing with his table-like back toward the door, looking out of the window which was barely allowing sun light in. The window was blocked by a mature oak tree.

When he turned around his mouth was closed in a tight line. "Good morning 6B." He looked at us with a reproach and we were ready for an avalanche of complaints. Instead he calmly continued. "You know that during the war I was fighting fascists in our mountains. I was a partisan."

'Not again!' thought many of us, tired of listening to the same stories over and over.

"Do you remember the underground bunker or as we called it with a Russian word *zemlianka*? You went there, to the deep forest, last spring. During the war we had to reside in that wooden structure with no windows, just dirt on the floor, for over two years." His face was displaying all the pain he went through as he told the story. "To dig out the fire wood covered by four feet of snow, sometimes without mittens, and winter boots, was hard work for hungry men." He stopped for a while staring at us, calculating the impact of his words. An uneasy feeling overwhelmed me and looking around I saw embarrassed faces of my classmates.

"We were dreaming about warm summer days and fresh bread. There were twenty-nine men of different nationalities with me. Thirty, the same number of students in your classroom." The sound of rustling leaves intruded through the open window as if the aged oak tree knew something.

Most of us were familiar with the story. One fall day his father, who was in the mountains with him, went to the village to bring some food. A local fascist group caught and tortured him for about a week. When his body gave up they threw him in the nearby forest. No clothes on him, he wore just his bloody wounds. He didn't reveal the location of the group.

For a moment the principal looked down at his shoes as if there were some kind of memories hidden in them. Maybe he was thinking of his father. He lifted his head and looked at us, standing there stiff as ice cycles. Then a light smile rose on his face. Relief could be sensed on our side. "So, the teachers and I decided," he made a little pause, his eyes fixed at us, "that we are going to teach you during P.E. how to wrestle and also how to box. I already ordered sets of boxing gloves. You will practice, learn rules, and in the fall we are going to have a school tournament in both disciplines."

We couldn't believe our ears.

The principal was an impressive man. Not just his size, but his charisma, self-discipline and deep understanding of his students naturally evoked respect.

Bear

Dave Becker

It was a cold, dark, dreary night. Snow piled up high on the ground and made moving throughout the village cumbersome.

Inside the one and only bar in town, the fireplace was blazing, and the room was comfortable. Moose, Elk, Deer, and Humans drank excessively, but responsibly. A few Bears had avoided entering their dens that year to put on weight. Drinking added calories, and whiskey did the trick.

Dirty Mary sat at her usual spot at the end of the bar waiting for a trick who had money, and would treat her like the lady she thought she should be.

All of a sudden the front door of the bar blew open and the frigid air stoked the fire in the fireplace for a second. The flames flared up, and the chill outside was now inside, but only for an instant.

Nobody paid attention to the tall Black Bear who entered the bar and sat on an empty bar stool which was all alone in the middle of the bar.

The bartender noticed the lonely bear now sitting at the bar out of the corner of his eye, but refused to acknowledge him in hopes he would leave.

Before the bear said anything, the bartender had already made up his mind that he wasn't going to serve the bear anything.

Bears usually drank a whole bottle of whiskey. They got belligerent when they got drunk, never paid their bill, and were lousy tippers, if they tipped at all.

The bear caught the attention of the bartender, and ordered a fifth of whiskey. The bartender ignored him for a second, then quoted the bar's policy "We don't serve Bears."

The bear, taken back by the statement, thought for a minute, and noticed Dirty Mary sitting at the end of the bar by herself. Dirty Mary looked like easy prey, so the bear threatened to eat her if the bartender didn't serve him.

The bartender restated the policy "We don't serve Bears."

After a small skirmish the girl was consumed and the bear again ordered a fifth of whiskey.

The bartender then stated the second policy "WE DON'T SERVE BEARS ON DRUGS."

The bear, confused, questioned the policy and asked why the bartender said that they don't serve Bears on drugs.

~

The bartender stated the obvious, "The girl was a 'bar bitch you ate.'"

He No Look Good

Laurie Wilson Fatland

The Joke

An Indian rode up to a trading post leading a beautiful appaloosa stallion.

The white man who ran the trading post fell in love with it the moment he saw it.

"How much for the horse?" he asked.

"Him not for sale" said the Indian. "He no look good."

"What, are you crazy?" said the white man. "He's the best looking horse I've ever seen!"

"No, he no look good." replied the Indian.

"I'll give you $1,000", said the white man. The Indian just shook his head.

"OK, $2,000, that's the most I've ever paid for a horse."

The Indian just stared at him and shrugged. "OK." The Indian nodded his head, "but remember I tell you he no look good." The Indian took his money and left the beautiful horse with the white man.

The following week when the Indian returned to the trading post, the white man came out screaming and yelling, "You stupid Indian, you sold me a blind horse!"

The Indian smiled and nodded, "I told you, he no look good!"

The Story

It was a grey and stormy day, which matched his mood perfectly. Sam Whitehorse finished saddling his old, reliable chestnut and put a halter on a beautiful leopard appaloosa stallion that stood waiting in his corral. Gleaming silver, with a spattering of brown spots, this stallion was the best horse he had ever raised. Big, muscled body, strong legs and a long curved neck that ended in a perfectly formed head, Sam never tired of looking at this horse.

But the spirits, with their ironic sense of humor, had played another trick on him. Sam knew he would never ride this one into town, swelling with pride at what he had accomplished. The best thing to do with this stallion would be to turn him out with the mares on his father's land and hope for another perfect foal to come along next year. Raising horses was always a gamble, and it took years to know if you'd won or lost. If he could get another foal this good, the gamble might just turn out to be a draw. Sam sighed and mounted up, leading the stallion behind him.

Sam hated Fridays. Every Friday he had to ride into the nearest trading post and stock up on supplies for the week. The land his father held was about a mile past the trading post, since Sam was taking the stallion to his father's place to run with their mares, this time it would be an overnight trip. His pretty, chubby wife Rose had given him a list of what she needed at the trading post; she stood in the door of their house and watched him ride away as he lifted his hand in farewell.

It was always so humiliating to do business with the white man. Mr. Spencer was the white man who ran the Smoking Tree Trading Post which was named for the large lightning-struck tree that stood next to it. The trading post was the closest place for Sam to get what he needed but it was still a good five mile ride from their house. Mr. Spencer treated Sam as if he were a naughty child who could not be trusted. He spoke in a loud voice, slowly, like Sam could not understand English. He watched every move Sam made, making it obvious he thought Sam was a 'thieving Indian.'

Sam had watched Mr. Spencer carefully over the years; he knew how Mr. Spencer overcharged the Indians while charging a much lower price to the white men who came in. Mr. Spencer never gave a fair price to the Indian women who came in looking to trade their handmade blankets and baskets for food, either. The good looking ones certainly got his attention though, and he would leer at the women and flirt with them in the most shameful ways. Some of them, Sam knew, even sold themselves to Mr. Spencer for food. Sam spit on the ground, wishing it was Mr. Spencer's face.

As Sam rode up to the trading post, Mr. Spencer walked outside zipping his pants up. He looked up to see Sam and the horses and was obviously struck by the appaloosa stallion. He watched them approach, looking at the stallion with an appraising eye. "That's a nice looking horse you got there, Sam," he said.

Sam just shook his head as he dismounted from his chestnut. "He no look good," Sam said, in broken English.

Mr. Spencer gave a glance at Sam and went over to inspect the stallion more closely. He ran his hands over the horse's legs, picked up his feet and looked in his mouth. "About 3 years old, I'm thinking", Mr. Spencer said. "Pretty nice. What are you asking for him?"

"No, not for sale," Sam shook his head again.

"C'mon, Sam, this horse is too good to be hanging around on the reservation." Mr. Spencer smiled at him. "Tell you what, I'm feeling mighty generous today, I'll give you a thousand dollars for him."

Sam looked Mr. Spencer in the eye and repeated "No, not for sale. He no look good."

Now, Mr. Spencer was starting to get angry. He was not used to Indians defying him. "Don't be a stupid Indian, Sam, I'm offering good money for this animal." Mr. Spencer gave Sam an appraising look and said, "OK, you got me. I'll give you two thousand for him. That's the most I ever paid for a horse, and its more money that you and your family ever had at one time. That's my final offer."

Just then a movement behind the store caught Sam's eye. It was his little sister Annie, sneaking out the back and pulling her clothes together as she crouched down and ran. Sam realized what had happened and rage rose up in his heart. He struggled to keep his features calm so that Mr. Spencer did not know what he had seen.

Sam looked at Mr. Spencer with narrowed eyes. "OK, I sell him. But I tell you again, he no look good."

"Fine, fine," Mr. Spencer smiled. "Come on in and I'll get you your money."

Sam followed him into the store and handed him the list from Rose. "Here what I need. Take from money. I be back." Sam turned and left the store, he needed to find Annie.

Sam found Annie huddled behind the nearby barn. Her pretty face was red from crying, the tears still wet on her cheeks. Black braids framed her face and dark eyes gazed up at him as she blushed in shame.

"What are you doing, little sister?" Sam spoke to her in their native tongue. "How dare you dishonor us like this!" Sam's anger could not be concealed.

Annie stood up, tears still falling, and stared at him in defiance. "What am I to do? Our family needs money. I have no talent weaving rugs or making baskets. I cannot help them any other way."

Sam could not believe his ears. "You let him shame you, shame all of us? Why did you not come to me? I will always help our family, you know this!"

"I, too, have to find my way, Sam. I, too, have to help." Annie turned and walked away. Gathering her pride around her, she walked tall.

Sam returned to the trading post, loaded his supplies and took the remaining money from Mr. Spencer without a word. Sam ran a soft hand down the stallion's neck, saying a gentle goodbye. He mounted up and rode off. Still seething in anger, Sam was unsure where to go. He was not ready to face his father knowing what Annie had done, and was not ready to return home to Rose.

Following the creek that ran beside the trading post, Sam rode on for a few miles and decided to camp out in a grassy clearing. He sat for long hours staring up at the starlit sky contemplating the meaning of honor and pride and the history of his ancestors. When he finally slept, Sam dreamed a warrior's dreams, of victory and loss, of standing up for what was right and just. When he awoke with the dawn, Sam knew what he would do. He had a plan.

Knowing Mr. Spencer would not be able to resist riding the appaloosa stallion, Sam rode back along the creek to Mr. Spencer's home, which stood beside the trading post. There was no one around, it was too early for the store to open, but sure enough, Mr. Spencer was outside in the corral with the stallion.

When he saw Sam, Mr. Spencer began yelling, "You stupid Indian, you thieving son of a bitch, you sold me a blind horse!" He screamed, "I want my money back, now!"

Sam smiled and said "I told you he no look good." He stared at Mr. Spencer and said, "But he good horse, well trained. I show you how to ride him. Get on."

"He better be, you dirty redskin," Mr. Spencer snarled. But he mounted up and rode the stallion over to Sam.

Sam immediately rode off at a brisk trot, not giving Mr. Spencer time to say anything. The appaloosa stallion followed obediently, listening to the other horse's footsteps and following his scent. The stallion kept pace as Sam urged his horse into a smooth gallop.

Sam stayed far enough ahead to prevent any conversation, increasing their speed until both horses were in a full run. He could hear Mr. Spencer screaming at him from behind, but he never turned his head and he never slowed his pace.

They were fast approaching the edge of a cliff that overlooked a deep canyon and the creek below, but still Sam never slowed his horse. He could hear the pounding hooves of the appaloosa following him. Just yards from the edge, Sam picked up the reins and slid his horse to a sudden stop, the appaloosa barreling past him, Mr. Spencer pulling on the reins with all his might. The stallion had braced himself against the bit and was determined to run, ignoring all of Mr. Spencer's efforts to stop him.

At the last second, Sam let out a shrill whistle, the stallion stopped and slid, his hind legs underneath him, spinning toward the sound. Mr. Spencer went flying off over the stallion's head, rolling to the edge of the cliff. The stallion struggled for footing and managed to gather himself up and leap toward Sam. Mr. Spencer was not so lucky.

As Mr. Spencer rolled and tried to stop himself, fingers scrabbling for purchase at the cliff's edge, Sam yelled to him "See, him very well trained!" And he watched Mr. Spencer roll off into empty space, falling to the bottom of the cliff.

Sam did not even wait to see how he landed or if he were killed outright, he turned and rode off with the blind stallion following. They followed old paths up into the hills, Sam watching and listening for the band of mares that roamed there. The stallion sensed them first, snorting and pawing the earth. Sam spoke to him with soft words, calming the horse as he dismounted his quiet chestnut and removed the saddle and bridle from the appaloosa.

With a smack on the butt, Sam shooed the beautiful horse and sent him running to join the mares. Whinnies and low nickering came rolling back to him; Sam knew the stallion was being accepted. Now, the wait begins. Surely one of those good mares would produce a fine foal. Sam smiled to himself as he rode towards home.

Tomorrow he and Rose would ride to his father's place and give him half the money from the stallion. It would keep them well for a least a year. He thought of Annie and knew it was time to find her a husband. Sam had heard of a well respected young man on the other side of the reservation that might be looking for a wife. Perhaps it was far enough away that Annie's past would not trouble her.

Sam looked to the heavens, hoping he had satisfied the spirits this day. He prayed they would leave him alone for the next few years, their troubling sense of humor directed toward some other family. He felt a sense of peace; he had made his bets this day, good bets, the gambler inside him sure that this time he would win.

Desperate Measures

Laurie Wilson Fatland

Ellen needed a man. Now. This wasn't about sex, that was easy to get, this was about something more, something long-lasting. All of her friends were married and having children. Damn it, she was 29, time was running out.

She stood in front of the mirror like she did every morning, inspecting what she had to offer. Decent-looking face, shoulder length brown hair, pretty honey-colored eyes. And great boobs, she had really great boobs. Why couldn't she find someone? Here she was, almost half-way through life and all she had to show for it was a sucky job, a crappy apartment and a shit-box car. Time for action.

Early morning, it was her scheduled hour for a run in the park. Ellen had always stayed in great shape, for her it was a necessary part of the package. She put on a tight spandex shirt and leggings to show off the goods, tied her running shoes and headed out the door. Today she would inspect what was out there and come up with a plan to snag the right guy.

As she jogged around the park trails, she passed the usual prospects: the plain looking cop who always nodded a greeting; the old men on the park benches reading their papers; the fathers walking their kids; the gay guys checking each other out. Nothing, there was nothing. And then she saw him.

Gorgeous. Tall with light brown hair and soft blue eyes. A good dresser, he was in well-fitted jeans, not too tight, not too baggy, and a cream colored pullover. He was walking a dog, a Great Dane who was as big as a horse. As she approached, she slowed her pace and smiled at him, "Hey! Beautiful dog!" That was all she could think of to say. He just smiled at her, but, oh what a smile! White teeth, dimples, this guy was really fine.

Cutting across the park she changed her route so she could pass by him again, planning her strategy to get his attention. This time, as she came up on him she acted like she tripped and bent over to retie her shoes. Ellen made sure her full cleavage was on display. She had great boobs and she wasn't afraid to use them.

When she looked up, he asked "Are you OK?"

Ellen batted her eyes at him and smiled "I think so!" she was about to say something else, but he walked away.

Shit! That didn't work. She would have to figure out another way to get his attention. She ran on, taking a different short cut to pass him again, but he was gone! She ran the entire perimeter of the park, but there was no sign of him. Ellen wasn't giving up, though. This guy was the solution to her problems. This guy was the one. Well, tomorrow was another day.

The next morning she headed out early with her hair up in a ponytail, make-up just right, and wearing a low cut tank top that really set off her eyes. Today she decided not to run so she would have more time to engage him as she walked past. Nodding at the cop as usual, she walked briskly on the path around the park until she saw him up ahead, the huge dog at his side.

This time he would have to notice her. She picked up her pace to a very fast walk and when she was maybe 10 feet in front of him she pretended to twist her ankle and fell, almost literally at his feet. He had no choice but to stop. She looked up with the sweetest, saddest look she could muster into his blue eyes. Both of them were staring down at her, him with concern and the dog in complete surprise. "I'm so sorry, I could have tripped you!" She held her ankle with both hands.

"Are you alright?" He asked with a concerned look on his face, holding out his hand to help her up.

"I, I think so", Ellen stuttered. But as she got up she acted like she could not put weight on her ankle. "Ow!" He had no choice but to put his arm around her and support her as she hopped to the nearest bench. "Thank you so much. Oh, I'm Ellen by the way." She smiled up at him while the dog nuzzled at her hand.

"I'm Dave, I've seen you here before, I think. Are you going to be all right? Maybe I should call you cab, we aren't too far off the street, and they can get you home."

Just then the cop came running over. "What happened? Are you OK?" He looked suspiciously at the big dog.

"Oh, I just tripped," Ellen assured him, "This kind gentleman was going to help me get home." Ellen smiled at Dave.

"Well, Officer, now that you're here, I'll let you take over. You'll know the best way to help out." Dave smiled at Ellen and the cop, waved goodbye to them and headed off into the park.

Damn! Ellen couldn't believe how easily he had passed her off. Now, how to get out of this situation with the cop so he didn't know she was faking it. She watched Dave disappear into the trees while she rubbed her ankle before turning to the cop. "I think it's better, it just stung for awhile."

He sat down beside her on the bench and took her foot into his hand, checking out her ankle. "It doesn't look swollen, and there is no heat in the joint. But I noticed you weren't running today when you came to the park, like you usually are. Maybe it was bothering you a little before you fell?" The cop seemed genuinely concerned.

Ellen turned to him, looking at him for the first time. He was actually kind of cute in a cop sort of way. Crew cut hair, nice brown eyes and a sweet smile. Not her type at all, but OK-looking. "Thanks. I think I'm going to be fine. She put her "injured" foot on the ground and pretended to test it out. "Yes. I'll be OK, I can walk on it." Ellen began to walk around with a slight limp. "I'll be on my way." She smiled at the cop and walked off slowly.

"Be careful out there," he called after her. "See you tomorrow."

Ellen waved at him and once she was out of sight walked normally again. Time to go home; it wouldn't do for Dave to see her walking around like she was just fine. This whole morning was a disappointment. She would have to think up something foolproof to get Dave's attention. Desperate times called for desperate measures.

After arriving home, Ellen got out her laptop and searched Great Danes For Sale. Yes. Not far from the city was a breeder with dogs for sale. If she had her own Great Dane, Dave would be intrigued. He'd have to. Ellen called and found out that the breeder had puppies available. "Um, do you have something that's housebroken? I don't really have time to train one."

Amen. They had a 1 year old dog that someone had returned when they had to move into a retirement home. "I'll be out there in an hour to get him." Ellen got into her rusted old car and made the drive out to the country.

His name was Brutus, and he was immense. He weighed 120 pounds and had some more growing to do. Ellen had never owned a dog. She wasn't sure she should. But if things worked out between her and Dave, then he would know how to take care of Brutus. She stuffed the dog into her backseat and made the drive home.

The dog explored the apartment and then lay down by her feet. There was something very comforting about having this big beast next to her. Brutus laid his huge head in her lap and stared up at her with his deep brown eyes. Ellen found herself stroking his head and admired his beauty. He had a coat of brown and honey streaks, what did they call it? Brindle. Actually, his coloring kind of matched her own. They would look good together.

Brutus slept next to her bed and Ellen was amazed at how safe she felt. Not that she had ever been afraid. But maybe she had been and didn't know it. Anyway, she was really enjoying this dog.

The next morning she dressed and they headed to the park. And there was Dave. He noticed her! "Hey, I didn't know you had a dog!" He was smiling at her as he came up. Or really, he was smiling at Brutus.

"I just got him. You inspired me." Ellen stood, petting her dog, who was greeting Dave's dog too. They had a nice conversation about Great Danes and Ellen thought she was getting somewhere. Then, out of nowhere came the cop. He stopped to stroke Brutus and Brutus wagged his tail and licked him, they really seemed to like each other.

The cop waved goodbye to them and walked off down the path. Dave turned to watch him go. "Damn, he has a really nice ass." Dave sighed. "But he never seems to notice me."

Shit! Ellen couldn't believe it, Dave was gay! And after all she had gone through, even burdening herself with this dog. Damn. She just tugged at Brutus and headed home. What a waste.

The next few days Ellen spent at home with Brutus. They took their walks in a different park so she wouldn't have to see Dave or the cop. Everywhere she went she got lots of attention because of Brutus. Kids loved him. She had children following her around the park, and men and women always stopped to talk to her. It was kind of awesome.

Ellen started to love her dog, who was quiet and faithful, who stared at her with adoring eyes and made her feel safe. Ellen began to feel satisfied with life. Hey, she thought, what did I want a man for anyway? To be my companion, to make me feel safe and loved. Well, Brutus brought me all of that! And as for children, I can have all the interaction I want with kids, I just have to walk Brutus. All the anxiety left Ellen and she realized she was happy, really happy, for the first time in her life.

Ellen didn't need a man. She just needed her dog. And with that she gave up looking and went back to walking Brutus in the old park. She saw Dave and waved at him from afar. No hard feelings.

When the cop saw her, he waved and came over. "Do you mind if I walk along with you?" He looked at her with his nice eyes and smiled his nice smile. Ellen pulled her tank top a little lower and thought, why not?

Photo Credit: John Fatland

A SPIRITUAL EXPERIENCE

The sudden, unexpected and untimely loss of our beloved Dave this spring turned our thoughts and discussions deeply inward. The Sacred Circle's creative attention wandered to Other Worlds with him. We are all convinced there are other dimensions and ways of being we cannot begin to see or comprehend from This World, from the narrow scope and view of a human lifetime. We wish Dave well on the next leg of his grand adventure and although we cannot tag along until our time, we let our literary imaginations follow in his wake. Godspeed, Dave, we know you're a million miles away from here with wings on. We also know we will see you again, someday, somehow, somewhere.

Laurie Wilson Fatland's always creative imagination wandered first to the religious beliefs of other cultures in *Epiphany*, and then even further, to the cosmos in *Andromeda*. Katarina Karjala contemplates the briefest of moments that can change entire lives in *The Kiss*.

Epiphany

Laurie Wilson Fatland

The smoke rose in wispy tendrils and tickled my nostrils with the sharp smell of burning cedar. It was a welcome respite from the heavy stink of sheep that lay over the entire camp. I wasn't sure if it would ever wash out of my clothes.

My pale skin was burning in the heat of the day as we sat around the fire. I was the honored guest of my dear friend, Dan Manygoats. His family offered me *'ach-ii*: fat-stuffed sheep intestines cooked over the open fire; then the eyeballs and tongue from the freshly roasted head. They smiled and laughed at my expressions as I tasted the delicacies and the children waited to snatch whatever I did not finish. I did my best, not wanting to offend, but my stomach was roiling and burbling from the unaccustomed meat.

I had met Dan early that spring. We were at the local swap meet, searching among the dusty tables for treasures, when we both stopped to examine a Navajo rug woven in the Thunderstorm pattern. It was beautifully done in dull reds, sharp black and the creamy white of natural wool. The intricate pattern left a small opening for Spider Woman, the weaver's guide, to escape if she chose to. Dan was an older man, his skin weathered from years in the harsh sun, his thick black hair was cut short, and he wore creased jeans with worn old cowboy boots instead of the traditional dress of a Navajo elder.

The first story Dan told me was of the history of weaving and how his people had been taught by Spider Woman to create beautiful patterns in wool. He showed me why this was a particularly special rug, perfect in its symmetry. I bought it and we struck up a conversation about why I was living on the reservation. I began to talk about Jesus and he began to question me. It was the start of our deep friendship.

Of course, I didn't tell him my real feelings. I had come to the Navajo, the *Din-eh'* as they call themselves, to save them. I came to bring them into the light. It was clear to me that this ancient people, with their dark and fearful religion, needed saving. The Beauty Way they called their religion, but I saw its ugliness.

They lived in constant fear. Fear of crossing the coyote's path. Fear of speaking the name of the dead. Fear of skin walkers, the mysterious shape changers that stalked their worst nightmares. They feared offending the spirits who would bring trouble to the ones they loved. The medicine man ruled them all, he was the only one who could cleanse away those fears and heal the fearful. He alone could restore harmony. He held the ultimate power.

I took the rug home and hung it on the wall of my small trailer. It was a lovely piece of art, but it was also a reminder of the traditions I had come to destroy. My little white trailer, which stood behind the local hotel, wasn't much of a home, but it was enough. The rug took my focus off the dirty wood walls. I felt the presence of Spider Woman, she had never left this rug; she glared back at me all the while I sat and contemplated it.

The next morning I awoke to the crunch of gravel outside my trailer. Peeking out the window I saw a beat up old Chevy pickup parked outside. Navajos never come straight up to the door. With few phones out here to announce your arrival, it's considered rude to just walk up and knock. You wait, giving the people inside time to make themselves presentable.

It was Dan. He got out of the truck as I came outside. "I would like to show you something," he said. I got into the rusted truck and we drove off down the dusty roads. It was the first of many days we spent together.

Dan took me under his wing. We drove everywhere, and he showed me the sacred lands. He took me to Spider Woman's rock, to see the Three Sisters; he told me the legends and the stories of his people. And he questioned me closely in return. His questions stirred and excited me, they were deep and appreciative. I knew in my heart he would be my first convert. I would save him. I would walk him into the light. He was well respected in town and looked up to, if he converted to Christianity, others would follow. Dan was a man who stood firmly in his traditions but who had opened his mind to understanding the white man's world. He would ensure the success of my calling.

We spent days driving the dirt roads of the reservation, dust plumes billowing in our wake. Dan showed me the ruins of the Anasazi. He showed me petroglyphs and shards of ancient pottery. And during these expeditions he began to tell me his own story, it was not told like a white man would tell it, direct, to the point and in one sitting. He told it in bits and pieces that seemed to spiral around the climax, leaving me pondering what each piece of the story meant. His telling left me anticipating the end until he wove it all together, complete, like one of Spider Woman's designs.

Dan Manygoats had always been inclined toward the spiritual. As a child he stood in awe of the medicine man who had the power to heal the broken and bring a family back into harmony. When something bad happened to a Navajo family, an illness, a death, a troubled youth, it was understood someone had drifted from the Beauty Way. Someone had strayed off the path whether they knew it or not. The only way to fix the problem and restore the family was to pay the medicine man to come and perform a ceremony. It was also an occasion to bring the family together and feast on a freshly butchered sheep. Family is the very core of Navajo tradition. Dan grew up thinking a man could make a good living singing families back into peace and be fulfilled himself.

He told me that he began to learn as a young man. Studious and serious by nature, he pursued his studies and apprenticed with the local medicine man. He sang, he dreamed, he collected the herbs and crafted his own drums and rattles. He learned the intricate sand paintings and the secrets of their power. He was gifted.

The final step, though, had yet to be revealed. His teacher took him on a long walk, in silence, across towering Black Mesa, to the very edge, where a one thousand foot drop opened beneath them. They sat at the precipice in silence, drinking in the vastness and subtle colors of the Navajo lands, tasting the powerful medicine of its mystery.

"You are ready, son." the medicine man said at last, "It is time for the final test. One last thing is required before the full power of a medicine man will descend upon you. You must kill someone you love. Not with your hand, of course, but with your will. You must will it. You must curse them. You must cause it to happen with your medicine. When it is done, you must sleep on their grave for 7 nights. Only then will you control the spirits and come into your full power."

Dan was rocked by this to the very core of his being. He had never heard of this requirement and did not know it would be asked of him. He hung his head and did not answer. For many days he searched his soul. He had tasted the power; he did not want to let it go. He weighed the price he was asked to pay against the benefits he could offer his people. In his mind he searched through all of those he loved for a victim he would be willing to sacrifice. His lovely wife? His beautiful daughter? He found he could not, he would not, pay this price for this powerful vocation.

The story frightened me. After our feast with his family, with my stomach still queasy from mutton and fry bread, we sat alone in Dan's hogan, the round mud hut he used when staying on the mesa. We were far from any sign of the modern world; his family had left for town. Dan had finished his story, the weaving was complete. We sat in silence; both of us watching the final pattern emerge before us. It was a dark religion. It held a dark power. I didn't believe it was true, I wanted to show him it held no power over me. I was leaving for my home in Chicago the next day. My father was ill and I had been called home. This was my last chance.

"When you called these spirits, Dan, how did you do it? What made them come?" I asked. I wanted to see his primitive tools. I wanted to convince him they were not real, that they held no real power and could no longer influence him. I wanted him to discover that the power of Christ had freed him. I wanted the white man's smug satisfaction that we were superior.

Dan looked at me and, without a word, went to a chest against the wall. He pulled out a wrapped parcel. It held a rattle made from an eagle's claw and a small drum. He closed his eyes and shook the rattle. He began to beat a strange rhythm, uneven but compelling. He beat the drum softly at first, growing louder as the rhythm intensified. He closed his eyes and began to chant.

I felt it come. A strong, cold wind burst into the windowless hogan, something invisible and of immense power entered. Every hair on my body stood on end. A sense of darkness and of intelligent evil filled the room. I began to pray. My god was surely more powerful, light would prevail against darkness. He chanted, I prayed. I prayed until I could no longer breathe.

"Stop! Stop, Dan!" I was gasping for air and normality.

Dan stopped and the dark presence diminished, flowing from the room. I swear I felt its amusement. It had overpowered me; it had humiliated me and my god.

"They wait for me," he said. "They wait for me to fulfill my calling."

I sat there, chilled and frightened. Dan watched me. We did not speak of what happened, but when we parted Dan held my hand gently, smiled slowly and said "I have grown to love you."

I left with the very foundations of my faith shattered. My religion did not hold all the answers. My god was not almighty, not all powerful. There were other ancient powers out there, dark and stronger. Still, I cling to my religion. It is all I have. It is the piece of driftwood I hang on to in the tumultuous sea of life. But I have had my epiphany. I have learned to fear the darkness. I fear the power. Now I sit in my home, a bottle of whiskey in my hand, and stare at the Navajo rug and Spider Woman. She mocks me. I have terminal cancer. They say I have less than six months to live.

I cling to my sliver of faith, floundering. He won. I earned the love of Dan Manygoats and it cost me my life. In six months I will be gone and Dan will have earned his power. I wonder how he will find my grave. Perhaps Spider Woman, with her intricate webs will guide him. She watches, she waits, and the darkness hovers near. I feel it.

The Kiss

Katarina Karjala

That summer day was not a normal one in the central European town. Extra crews of volunteers painted fences and polished the whole municipality. Flowers were planted and the streets were swept. Women ironed their best dresses and their husband's Sunday pants and white shirts. Some went to a hair stylist and some went to the store to buy a new hat and white gloves. The whole town, nestled under the protective hills, was upside down because of the arrival of unusual guests. They were young and they were royalty. Prince Norodom Sihanouk of Cambodia and his wife wished to see first-hand the modern aluminum plant and the small hospital with its special surgical unit designed to save the lives of workers who had been burned by sizzling molten aluminum.

The welcoming citizens were carrying flowers of all colors which competed with the women's radiant dresses. The spotless blue sky was a witness. Anarchists were out of fashion in all of Europe, everybody worshiped the government now. Stalin was already in his dark chamber, underground, terrorists and drones were unknown. Everybody was happy.

I saw a plethora of black aerodynamic cockroach-shaped cars coming. These were the finest cars of the communist production, Tatra, as I learned later, available only for the affluent. Men who looked like carbon copies, all dressed in black suits and white shirts, choked by ties, drying their foreheads with handkerchiefs, poured out of the cars.

"Where are they? Where are they?" people whispered.

"Papa, did the princess arrive?" I asked my father.

"You have to be patient," he said gently, and I noticed that his forehead was sprinkled by sweat as well. Suddenly there was excitement and the crowd was moving like a field of golden grain ready for harvest. The people were all looking one direction and they were smiling.

This must be it, I thought. First the cockroach men, perhaps security, also called "gorillas," passed by me, politicians followed, and then I spotted them.

Angelically charming, the princess' delicate body looked very fragile to me. I had never in my short life seen such black hair and dark almond-shaped eyes. As a matter of fact, at that time I had never seen anybody who was Asian. I was not sure if a real princess would have such a spotless olive-colored complexion. The princess was not dressed up like the princesses I saw in the pictures of my fairytale books. She didn't wear a tiara, but rather a small hat, white as snow, partly covered her hair. Moving with the grace of a royalty, she was more elegant than anybody I had ever known. Her right hand, covered by a silky white glove, was gently moving like a pendulum in front of her. I wanted to ask my father if she was a real princess, but I already saw him moving downwards in a slight bow. From my short, child's perspective I saw the couple walking straight toward my father and me.

Then something unexpected happened. The princess stopped her husband, picked me up, kissed my chubby cheeks and stroked my fine straw colored hair as if she could organize those unruly curls. Everybody stared at me and I was like a marble statue, frozen, afraid to move; worried that the slightest motion of mine would take away the magic moment. The crowd stopped breathing for a second in awe, perhaps from envy, or simply because such a personal act was unexpected. The tiny me was enchanted, it felt as if a silk butterfly landed on my face. To protect my treasure I held my hand over that spot. I was kissed by a real princess.

Nobody took a picture, so I have only the very formal black and white photos taken by the government's photographer. Years later, people kept telling me: "You were lucky, kissed by a real princess." I didn't feel lucky, it just happened.

Time went by and I got a sibling and much more work. Mother needed help with my little sister, father an extra pair of hands to work in the garden, then in the house and in the orchard. Parents of mine emphasized hard work and the importance of education, so my childhood snuck away from me under a load of duties. People stopped telling me how lucky I was.

My freedom returned when I left the town and went to university. Entering adulthood was like opening a secret chamber of life and knowledge, where time swirled in circles of friends. Then a husband came to my life, a first child and a second child. I settled down. A daily routine overruled everything; running between work and family until one day everything shattered. The father of my children came home and told me that he was in love with another woman. I found myself holding my cheek, asking: "Am I a lucky girl?"

For two weeks I lived in a blur. A stranger looked back at me from the mirror. The son we had was only nine months old and our daughter not quite four. I couldn't see them through my tears. That sister of mine, eight years younger, not little any more, came to hold my hands and change diapers. I teased her that she was paying me back for all the care I gave her when she was a small girl. One morning I woke up feeling resurrected, like the ancient bird Phoenix rising from ashes, standing strong on both of my feet, feeling the stream of energy coming from the earth. I stroked the heads of my children and held hand over my cheek for a moment. Was I a lucky girl?

There were more of those darker times in my life caused by a collapse of communist society. The Year 1989 and The Velvet Revolution brought many hopes, among them a free market of plenty, but there was not a foundation built for it. Party members and their friends were the fortunate ones who bought factories for $1. Others had to feed their children; the government was not subsidizing costs of food anymore. The free market guaranteed skyrocketing of prices while paychecks were on hold; there was no free labor market. Most of the new capitalists didn't want to work hard; they dreamed about the promised paradise. For the same reason they sold equipment of their plants to our Western friends, who had a free labor market and who also welcomed inexpensive and skilled workers. I recognized that in a new society I have to find a right yardstick to measure. Many lamented but I saw an opportunity. I went back to a university. Numerous people asked me: "Why did you go back to school? You already had your degrees." It was unknown at that time for people with university degrees to go back to a college. I put my own life on hold for four years, working, going to school and breathing. No self-doubt was allowed, neither bogus hope. My children were the main navigating tool and because of them I wanted to avert tragedies others were facing. Many of those confronted by a new society were playing blind to any adaptation. Disillusion was not my master. That was me who was kissed by a real princess.

As soon as I was done with the school, I was a lucky girl once more, committed to my work and it paid off. I allowed myself to enjoy my existence again. A man came to my life. He promised to protect me and carry me on his wings, so I took the flight and left everything behind except my children. However those wings were just like those of Icarus who flew too high, too close to the sun.

The little angel, that butterfly-like kiss has been with me through all my life, telling me: "Keep going, malfunctioning elements or those not bringing any positive feelings to our lives are predestined to be replaced." I kept going and I kept smiling. What happened to the little girl? My straw-like hair turned grey. The white waters of my life with many tributaries grew into the serenity of an immense river. I have been a lucky girl.

Andromeda

Laurie Wilson Fatland

She had an otherworldly walk. She moved with grace and elegance, skimming the earth as if it had no hold on her. It was the first thing that struck me about her.

I met her in the park, early on a Sunday morning. I had been for my usual run and was resting on a bench afterward. To my surprise she came toward me with a smile and sat down on the bench next to me. Most people in New York avoid each other. They avoid speaking, they even avoid eye contact. We don't have enough space as it is, so we have carefully constructed boundaries and unspoken rules of conduct. This act broke all of them.

I could have walked away, but instead I smiled back and looked her in the eye. They were beautiful eyes. Almond shaped and an almost glittery blue. I found myself completely taken in. She had long blonde hair, silky and so light it was a glowing white, her features were pleasant, but it was her eyes that drew you in.

"I am Andromeda." She spoke in a musical voice, soothing and soft.

"Nice to meet you, I'm Nathan." My smile must have looked ridiculous I was so intrigued by her.

"Why are you here?" It seemed an odd question, but genuine. The notes of her voice rang in my ears, a strange kind of melody.

"I was running. I just sat down to rest."

"What are you running from?"

I laughed. "I am just running for exercise. To stay in shape." I was thinking she must be foreign.

"Ah." She smiled. "You must be healthy."

"I am! I've always thought it is important to take care of myself." This line of thinking made me drag my eyes away from hers and look her over. She was on the thin side, but nicely put together.

"Would you like to eat something? Together?" She touched my hand; it was a cool but exhilarating touch.

"Well, sure. There is a nice coffee shop just around the block." We stood together and she took my arm, as if we were a long married couple. I found it charming.

When I asked what she would like to eat and drink, she seemed confused. I pointed at the menu. She looked at it for awhile and then told me "You choose. I trust you." She made me feel like a man. Like the old definition of a man, the protector, the breadwinner, the one in charge. I liked it.

I ordered both of us a bagel with lox and cream cheese and a latte. When it came to the table she stared at it strangely. "What is this?"

"You've never had a bagel before?" I was astounded. I showed her how to put the cream cheese on the bagel along with a slice of the lox. I took a bite.

She copied me exactly. "Wonderful!" A slow smile lit up her face.

I was fascinated. I could not take my eyes off her. Every gesture, every expression was something new and different. I felt like I was in the presence of an exotic animal no one had ever seen before.

We left the coffee shop and walked around the city for hours. I showed her all my favorite places, I was the tour guide and she was the tourist, asking me endless questions about the city, the people, the food and the history. I had never felt so important.

"May I see where you live?" She gazed up at me with innocence, but it was an obvious invitation. We walked to my apartment near Central Park and rode the elevator to my floor in companionable silence.

As I opened the door, she walked in behind me, running her hand over objects and caressing them. It was as though she had never been in an American home before. I followed her around, noting which things she seemed most fascinated with. The books, the television, the microwave. Some of them she laughed at, other things she examined carefully and thoughtfully.

When we came to the bedroom, she felt the softness of the bed and sat down. "This is where you sleep?" She met my eyes and smiled.

"Yes. And other things." I sat beside her and took her face in my hands. I kissed her. The coolness surprised me, but left me with tingling warmth.

She hesitated, but kissed me back. Then she ran her hands over my body and slowly began to remove my clothing. It was the most sensuous thing I had ever experienced. She examined every part of me with her eyes, her touch and her lips. I was in ecstasy.

I pushed her back on the bed and began to do the same to her. Her body was cool but held a vibration, as if every cell were electrified. She kept her eyes open and locked on mine. Her eyes grew wide as I ran my fingers between her legs. The warm wetness growing there seemed to surprise her and she ran her tongue over parted lips, softly moaning.

I could not stand it any longer and entered her suddenly. The electrical sensation intensified, her eyes grew even wider and then closed halfway as we rocked in rhythm. We came together, throbbing stars in my eyes and her soft cries melted together. We held each other, relishing the touch of skin on skin and eased into relaxed exhaustion.

I did not want to let her go. I had found something precious. I would crave this sensation; I knew I could never get enough of that cool electrical current running through her and into me. It was like drinking cool water which never quenched your thirst. We spent the rest of the day together, resting, making love, touching every inch of each other; it was exploration of the most fulfilling kind. She would not let me use protection; she insisted I come inside her, over and over again. I had never felt so free, so desired.

As night fell, she rose and dressed slowly while I watched her. "I must go home, Nathan."

"Where is your home, Andromeda? I must find you again."

"You would call it Centaurus. It is too far for you, Nathan. I fear we will not meet again."

"No! Don't leave me, please! I can't live without you." I was addicted. I could not lose her now.

She smiled at my desperation. "I have what I came for." She ran her hands over her belly. "We have created something, you and I. We have created a new world." She turned and opened my bedroom window, leaning out and breathing the air.

She turned back to me. "Thank you." With a final smile, she leaned back and fell out of the window.

I screamed. I ran to the window. "Andromeda, no!" I leaned out to look below, but she was gone. I called the police and the paramedics, not sure where she had fallen. I ran down to the sidewalk to find her.

I found nothing. When the police arrived, they checked the building, the sidewalk, neighboring patios and balconies. Nothing. She was gone, disappeared into thin air. The police were angry with me for wasting their time. There was no evidence that she had ever been there.

When I returned to my apartment, I could smell her scent. It was nothing I had ever smelled before; it held something of ice and roses. There was nothing else. She was gone. I was left with a terrible sense of loss.

I have thought about this encounter every day for months. Who was she? Where was she from? I looked up Andromeda. I looked up Centaurus. They were galaxies of stars.

I have become convinced she was an alien. A star dropped from the heavens. She had sought me out to impregnate her. Was she searching for me, or was it a chance encounter where any healthy human male would have served her purpose? I don't know. I want to believe I meant something to her, that the magic of our coupling created more than life within her. I'll never know. Perhaps this was just an experiment of her people, but I sensed a relief in her when she left me, as if we had accomplished something momentous between us, as if we had saved the world. I long to see our child, I am convinced it is beautiful. Does it have special powers, special wisdom? I have to believe so.

She has left me ruined, in a dark void of space. I will never be satisfied with life on this planet again. I will never be satisfied with another woman. I am strung out, sleepless and lost; my addiction has left me empty. It is an unobtainable fire that will devour me in the end. I stare up at the night sky, trying to see the stars. I long to follow her. I would take that leap tonight if I was sure to find her. Perhaps I shall. It would be a leap of faith, but I have nothing to lose. For I am no longer of this earth. It has no hold on me.

Photo Credit: John Fatland

ELEMENTALS

As the reluctant spring of 02015 gradually won over a stubborn winter, the Sacred Circle's thoughts waxed pensive and far-ranging. We found ourselves looking inward, foundationally, to the elements that make up everything that is: Earth, Air, Fire and Water. At the same time we looked outward; outside ourselves to contemplate the Circle of connectedness that binds it all—us all—together. The prompt was to write from an Elemental point of view.

Laurie Fatland's fiery *Boss Mare* would impart a taste for Element of Earth to any foolhardy enough to try to tame her, and Terryl Warnock explores the antagonistic, yet mutually dependent, relationship between Element of Fire and Element of Air in *If Only*.

Boss Mare

Laurie Wilson Fatland

They call it eatin' dirt, that moment when you've been bested by a dumb beast and find yourself face down, suckin' the teat of Mother Earth.

Dumb beast may not be quite right; some of them are downright smart. I've ridden many of 'em in my time, from broncs to gentle ponies, but there is one I never could come to terms with.

She was a mare. Figures, now that I think of it, females of every sort of creature are the hardest to get along with. Ain't no tellin' what goes on inside their heads.

This one, she was somethin' else. Damn good to look at, well-muscled, solid legs and a pretty face. She was a brown and white pinto with a long, thick, black mane and tail, real flashy. She looked like the kind of horse that ran through a young girl's dreams. She was a horse a man could be proud to ride.

She had other ideas, though. She didn't want to be anybody's saddle horse. She wanted to be in control. This mare was a born Boss Mare, in a wild herd she would've been the leader and God help any stallion or mare who thought diff'rent. She was born to lead, not follow, and a good saddle horse has to be a follower.

It shoulda been different, but it was her misfortune to be born on a ranch, not out on the plains. Her destiny was to be a saddle horse. That's why she was born and bred.

Over the years, I'd become a well-known horse breaker, had a magic touch with 'em, if I do say so myself. They brought her to me to be broken out. They said she'd been taught all the basics. She was halter-broke, knew how to stand tied and would pick up her feet for trimmin'. They didn't tell me much else.

She was a damn pretty mare; I liked the look of her. But the Devil was in her eyes. She took the measure of me, lookin' me over and wonderin' how difficult I would be. I took the measure of her, too, I knew she'd be a tough one just from the knowin' way she looked me over, almost smug like.

I left her alone for the first few days, hoping she would settle in. She was just bidin' her time, though, waitin' for me to make the first move. She had some things down, like they said. She liked to be groomed, she would pick up her feet for cleanin', but always kept one eye on me. One day while I was brushin' her I tripped over my own spur and landed smack under her belly. I didn't move for a minute, lookin' up at her to gage if she was goin' to stomp me. I swear I saw a flicker of a smile in those eyes, like she was thinkin' she should crush me now and save us both a lot of trouble later. But she didn't. She let me crawl outta there thinkin' she was maybe a sweet mare after all.

It was time to get to work, so I led her out to the roundpen one day. Just like it says, it's a pen with no corners for a horse to get stuck in. This was where we would begin to fight. I snapped a long line to her halter and shooed her out to the fence. It's an old cowboy trick to get control of a horse early on. You make 'em run and you make 'em turn and stop, steppin' in front and raisin' your arms to make 'em go the other way. Not this mare. To her it was a game, a game where she would come as close as she could, scarin' me or blowin' past me. She would cut into the center and send a kick my way, just missin' my leg or my head. I got scared, I admit it, but then I got angry and chased her off, making her run faster and faster. I wasn't goin' to let her quit until I said so. She turned on me, though; she blasted across the center of the pen, knocking me to the ground, giving me that first taste of dirt. It turned into a whole meal as she pulled me around the pen, slammin' me into the wall. She won. I limped out of the pen and left her there 'til she was good and thirsty before I put her up and went to lick my wounds and work out a new plan.

I was gettin' desperate. I figured I would try tyin' her down. It's another old cowboy trick, tie up their legs so they have to lay there. Horses don't like to be layin' there helpless, it goes against their natural instincts to run. Next time in the pen I used the rope to take her legs out from under her and laid her down, tyin' up her legs so she couldn't get up. I left her there for awhile, 'til she quit strugglin' and learned her lesson. She quit strugglin' alright, but when I came back in she was watching me, wary, angry, like she was stewin' in her juices the whole time. I ran my hands over her, makin' sweet talk, thinkin' we'd be friends when I let her up.

Hell no. That mare took me down in the flash of an eye, I was eatin' dirt again.

The next few times in the pen weren't much better. I think she was getting bored, though, 'cause one day she started to lope nice and easy around the pen and would turn and watch me when I said whoa. I thought I was gettin' somewhere, but there was always that look in her eye, like she was just playin' with me.

I decided she was ready for the saddle and spent a day sackin' her out, rubbing her all over with the saddle blanket before I threw it over her back. Faster than lightenin' she swung her butt into me, knockin' me to the ground and giving me another servin' of dirt.

After a while she quit fightin' and I was able to get a saddle on and cinch it up tight. She got to kinda enjoy wearin' that saddle around, like a lady wearin' a new hat. Things were startin' to go well, I thought. Until I tried puttin' a leg over. I had dirt for breakfast lunch and dinner for a week or so. But I finally got on and put some basic steerin' on that mare.

She got real good at some things. If she was int'rested. Some days she would let me work cows off her or open gates and fix fence. If she got bored though, or she thought you was askin' too much, watch out. You'd be dished up another plate of dirt.

I rode her out a lot; thinkin' open range would tire her out and make her more willin'. She never tired, though, and it was me that was fightin' to turn her around and head back home at the end of the day.

When the ranch owner came to pick her up, I had to be honest. I told him this was no saddle horse. I told him she couldn't be trusted, that she was dangerous and someday she was goin' to hurt somebody real bad. I told him I would do him a favor and put a bullet in her head, right here, right now.

He didn't take me up on it, though. He thought about it, studyin' that mare as she stood there, sweet and calm as could be. I saw her laughin' at me, she was too damn smart.

The ranchman said she was just so good lookin', he wasn't ready to give up on her yet. If she wasn't safe to ride, he'd make her a broodmare and have her turn out some fine babies. I tried to talk him out of this, she'd probly pass on that nasty temper of hers and he'd have a herd of good-lookin' worthless saddle stock.

He just laughed, I think he was kinda proud that his horse got the better of me. I watched 'em drive off, that mare turned and looked at me from the trailer she was loaded in. If she coulda I think she woulda give me the finger in farewell.

I don't eat dirt anymore. I never did develop a taste for it and I got more careful in my old age. I never forgot that mare, though. I've puzzled on her over the years. Could I have done somethin' different? Moved slower? Showed her more respect? I can't figure out what woulda made things easier. She was just smarter and more determined than me.

I ran into that ranch owner the other day. I asked him what happened to that pretty pinto mare of his. He was shakin' his head, tellin' me she came to a sad end. I guess after she got turned out with the other mares, she took over; she became the Boss Mare, fightin' and intimidatin' the others until she was leader. One day the ranch owner made the mistake of turnin' his herd of mares out in a pasture that bordered on his stallion pens. That pinto mare kicked her way through the fence seperatin' her from the stallions, the splintered wood tore through an artery in her leg and she bled to death in minutes.

When they found her, she was all that was seperatin' those mares from the stallions. The mares stood around her, lost without their leader. The stallions were afraid to cross over her body, they all knew she was the Boss Mare. She was still controllin' things from the other side.

I don't know if she died tryin' to get in with 'em, or just tryin' to kick the living daylights out of those stallions to teach 'em a lesson. But I take some pleasure knowing that she died livin' the life God meant her to live, the life she was born to. She's buried in that pasture now, gone back to the earth she so loved shovin' my face into. I'm not far off joinin' her. It's fittin', really, that we'll both be eatin' dirt in the end.

If Only

Terryl Warnock

The word faery, is derived from the word fae (fey), meaning visionary or marked by an Otherworldly air or attitude. Faeries are minor Thisworldly manifestations of the sacred Elements of Earth, Air, Fire, and Water. They can be willful little sprites. The tales faeries spin lure the trusting and naive to a surreal time and place; a nice enough place to visit, typically very nearly idyllic, but an Otherworldly place, untrue and out of time. They're mischievous tricksters, hurtfully so on occasion. Their tutelage will, if necessary, keep the enchanted stuck for as long as it takes to learn what they need to learn. Then, and only then, will the Faeries release the now wiser and more wary to return to the real world.

~

Salamander's stretch started at his frilly neck, moving sensually and slowly down the length of his serpentine spine, deliciously extending at last his new-grown leg and tail with lazy, impudent arrogance. He shuddered with the sheer carnal delight of it. "Ahhh," hissed Salamander, Element of Fire, exulting in his fierce strength, "I am as beautiful as I am indestructible," he said, "they simmer and simper in my presence and they cannot hurt me no matter how they try. I need no one. It is I who lights and warms the world and as well they should grovel in my presence."

Faery, Element of Air, now polluted and spent from stoking the Fire to restore Salamander after his dreadful injury, was pushed up and away without a thought by Salamander's heat. Faery wondered momentarily if Element of Fire even knew she was there, or cared how much she'd spent of herself to fan the flames that revived Salamander so spectacularly. She was too tired, too sick, and too dirty to wonder long though, or care overmuch. She let go her tenuous hold on Earth and surrendered, letting Salamander's vanity push her up and up, out into the darkness where she could cleanse herself, and where the winds of Mother Earth Herself, spinning through the vast, churning cosmos, regenerated her. "Ahhh," Faery sighed, "I am remade and renewed. I am as eternal and enduring as the wind. I am the very breath of life, and they are nothing without me, any of them. I shall stay here, with my own kind, where it is safe and clean. Let Salamander fend for himself. He doesn't need me and I don't need him, he only makes me dirty and uses me up and pushes me away." Element of Air exulted in her freedom. She sparkled and danced, making music with the tops of the trees, winking at the stars, and cavorting with the clouds.

"If only," said Faery, "it wasn't so cold, everything would be perfect." She was drawn, inexorably, earthward again, descending with the cold as was her nature. As she came to Earth she saw Salamander was surrounded and injured. Again. Salamander was angry and shouting. Again. Salamander was always at war. He was jealous and judgmental and impatient and because he always sought war, he always got it.

Element of Fire looked heavenward and said "If only it wasn't so still, with just a kiss of breeze I could regain my strength and fight the good fight. I'd win at last and everything would be perfect."

"Don't worry, Salamander," said Faery, "I'm here. I will never leave you. It's so icy and gloomy without you." Faery rushed to lift up Element of Fire, who had fallen of his battlefield wounds to naught but beautiful, smoldering, glowing embers, warm and comforting and alluring, but dying. Faery wanted nothing so much as to embrace Salamander, to be warm and wanted again.

The flames leapt. "If only Faery wasn't so flighty and overwhelmed," Element of Fire roared, "Salamander could stay strong and win the battle once and for all. Justice would prevail."

"If only Salamander wasn't so impatient and angry all the time," chimed Element of Air, "Faery wouldn't be exhausted before the day is won."

Salamander's stretch started at his frilly neck, moving sensually and slowly down the length of his serpentine spine, deliciously extending at last his new-grown leg and tail with lazy, impudent arrogance. . . .

~

Life without the challenge presented by pain and confusion is a Faery tale to seduce the unwitting into the belief that painlessness is an achievable goal. A goal that might be realized if only . . . If only there were more money . . . If only there were more time . . . If only I could quit . . . If only it were perfect . . . If only he understood . . . If only she realized . . . If only I could lose weight . . . If only I could sleep . . . If only it didn't hurt so much . . . If only I worked harder . . . If only I gave more . . . If only I got more . . . If only . . .

We owe the Faeries our gratitude for tricking us with their tales, lest we forget the blessings of learning and growing, and that doing so without unnecessary pain is the best we can hope for.

> **Grant me the serenity to accept the things I cannot change**
>
> **The courage to change the things I can**
>
> **And the wisdom to know the difference.**

Photo Credit: John Fatland

POETRY OF THE SACRED CIRCLE

As much as telling stories, poetry paints vivid pictures with words. Poetry tends succinct and powerful where prose tends lengthy and subtle; the poet accomplishes in a line or two what the writer of prose may take pages to develop. A poem can leave the reader with a powerful vision or distilled emotion; perhaps even a deeper understanding of humanity. There is magical power in words, and nowhere is it more manifest than in poetry. The Sacred Circle is deeply infused with such magical power and so, unsurprisingly, also embraces the rhythm and power of poetry.

The Gargoyle's Lament

Keli Becker

Do not look up at me and cringe
I am of your making
From the depths of your guilty souls

I am only stone
I do no harm
I was created to protect and remind

To protect your structures
From the ravaging power of the rain
To remind you of your Deadly sins

It is a heavy load to bear
For one such as I
Not for humans to carry
You would surely crumble

I only cry my rainy tears
And watch you in your pain
Sitting here upon my stone perch
Bound for all eternity.

Just One More Day

Keli Becker

One more day
I need you
Just one more day
To hold you
To be held by you
Just one more day

One more day
To hear you laugh
One more day
That we are one
To tell you I love you
Just one more day

One more day
To see you smile
One more day
To hear your heart beat
To feel your heat
Just one more day

One more day
To hear your voice
I had no choice
I don't have
Just one more day

The Lawman

Dave Becker

There once was a lawman who roamed the old west

He brought law and order and tried to make the west
its very best

He traveled thru rain, dust, and snow

And where he'll reign justice nobody knows

He traveled the deserts enduring the vengeful heat

He traveled thru mountains not knowing what he'd
meet

One day he cut thru a canyon

A short cut that he knew

But danger lurked ahead

High in the rocks a man laid askew

In less than a minute a bullet removed him from his
horse

He hit the ground among the rocks

And took cover there of course

The bullet hit his shoulder tearing his favorite vest

Now it was time to find this man

And give him his very best

He scanned the wide horizon dissecting every rock

Just waiting to see a movement

He could answer with a rifle cock

His patience paid off two-fold

When a crow gave up the man

He leveled his ol' carbine

And laid him out in the sand

He made his way across the canyon

To identify the man

He saw him on a poster

He was a wanted man

He loaded him on his saddle

And took him into town

There he got his just reward

And had a good night on the town

He drank a fifth of whiskey

And had a good night's sleep

Now it's time to hit the road

And find another creep.

The Lawman II

Dave Becker

The Lawman rode in frail

After two months on the trail.

He needed a bath, so did his horse.

He needed a drink, so did his horse.

He needed a meal, so did his horse.

He needed a woman, so did his horse.

The whiskey went down smooth

And the bed was for real.

The meal for twenty-five cents was a steal.

The bath made him feel real.

And the woman...well, you know.

He took to the bar

And saw a card game from afar.

It would be fun to win a few bucks,

Because life on the trail really sucks.

There was room for one more

Me and my .44.

He scanned the table

And everyone was able.

He took off his hat

And sat down at the table.

There was Jake the Snake

Every hand was fake.

There was Louie the Lizard

Who always bet screwy

There was Peg Leg Dave

Who seemed to have eyes in his back.

And there was Sam

Whose card playing was no scam

The game was boring

Till whiskey started pouring

Pairs and three of a kind were normal

But he wasn't here for normal.

Jack turned over two aces

And Louie turned over three aces.

Everyone jumped from their places

Jake became bugeyed and pulled his .38.

Dave swung his leg out and hit Sam

Louie grabbed his money and ran

And Sam slammed down his hand

And his derringer went off in his hand.

I pulled out my .44

And the game was no more.

The Lawman III

Dave Becker

It's time to get out of this town,

So I can lose this frown.

Time to get back in the trees,

Where my mind can be free.

I can go to the pines,

Where the weather will be fine.

I can go to the cottonwoods,

Where life would be good.

I can go to the oaks,

Where there are friendly folks.

I can go to the aspens,

Where nothing happens.

I'll camp out under the stars,

Where there are no bars.

I can sleep all day and all night,

Without the worry of a fight.

I can brew coffee all day long,

Knowing it'll be nice and strong.

I'll keep my fire stoked,

And my beans hot and cooked.

I'll listen to the coyotes all night,

Knowing that my .44 and I will be alright.

I can watch the eagles soar,

And reminisce about their stories of lore.

I can listen to the crows "clack,"

And the pigeons fight back.

I can watch the lizards, bugs, and birds scurry,

Knowing I'm not the one in a hurry.

I can listen to the wind in the trees.

I can watch the clouds move with the breeze.

I can drink from fresh mountain springs.

And I can be one with what nature brings

Life is good for this lone Lawman,

My whiskey, my .44, and my horse is all I need.

Yes all I need.

The Lawman IV

Dave Becker

I came into town for supplies,
But the local sheriff had for me
A big surprise.

Some rustlers were working north of town,
And the sheriff wanted to know if
I would help take them down.

He didn't know how many,
And he didn't know how few.
But as soon as I found out,
He would help me round up
The rustling crew.

Since I was camped in the area,
I could scout during the day,
And when I found them,
We could plan the next day.

After 9 or 10 days of short trips from camp,

I came upon a canyon that was dreary and damp.

There up the canyon were 50 or so strays,

But I couldn't see the rustlers because of the haze.

I contacted the sheriff,

And said I found their camp.

He got together the posse,

Then we surrounded the canyon for a look-see.

We got there at dawn,

And made our presence known.

We arrested all the rustlers without a fight,

And had them all in jail by that night.

Now it's time to head back into the trees,

Coddle my bottle, and put my mind at ease.

The Lawman V

Dave Becker

Got word the sheriff was shot dead,

A bullet right in the head.

He was a strong public servant,

Who didn't deserve to be cut down.

I picked up my camp,

Got a room in town,

Swore off whiskey,

Till I put the shooter down.

I knew all the posse, and the deputy too.

We were all in agreement to right this aggrievement.

We checked wanted posters.

We checked hotel rosters.

We talked to tourists,

And we talked to area purists.

We went to farmers and landowners,

North, South, East, and West.

Then a kid, playing in the street, confessed,

A man in a black vest,

With two silver guns,

Went East two days ago,

With a holster low on his buns.

As the posse and I got ready to go,

A wanted poster came thru,

That was our man,

With a reward of ten grand.

The next town was forty miles,

We'll have to ride hard,

There'll be no smiles.

I telegraphed the sheriff ahead,

Beware of this man,

He wants you dead.

We rode into town a couple at a time,

So we could surprise him,

One last time.

We checked every saloon,

And we checked every stable,

Wouldn't you know

We found him at a craps table.

We snuck into the saloon,

A couple at a time,

And surrounded him as

He lost his last dime.

His guns were all shiny,

And his black vest new.

We threw him in jail,

To wait till his neck went askew.

I split the ten thousand,

With posse and friends,

And headed north

To land's end.

The Lawman VI

Dave Becker

The Lawman was about a mile from town,

When a group of townspeople come up over a crown.

They said they needed a sheriff,

And would he be interested if

He got a steady wage,

A hotel room that was always made,

Daily meals to keep his zeal,

And a stable for his horse to seal the deal.

He said he had business in Big Creek, to see his son Zeek,

But he would be back in a week.

The mountains were windy.

The desert was sandy.

The thought of getting off the trail

And being in one place sounded dandy.

He rode into Big Creek,

Looking for a store named Zeek's.

He found the store,

And thought working there would be a bore.

I snuck into the store,

But Rufus the bloodhound,

Let out a bellowed roar.

Zeek spun around, and I tripped on the hound.

We made plans for dinner,

Two big steaks would be a winner,

We talked and talked ,and when we were done,

Deciding to retire sounded like fun.

I moved in with Zeek,

A large house not for the meek.

I worked at the store,

Which turned out not to be a bore.

The Lawman VII

Dave Becker

After months in the store,

It was Rufus I adored.

He slept in my room,

And did nothing but snore.

I did the deliveries,

And Zeek ran the store.

One day I was down the street delivering meat,

When I heard a shot.

A shot I never forgot.

I came back to the store,

Where there was a crowd galore.

There on the floor laid my son, shot with a .44

Rufus was licking his face,

Trying to bring him back from grace.

I hugged, and hugged, and hugged him some more,

Till the rage inside me came thru my pores.

I locked the store door,

And went in the back to get my .44

I filled a sack full of supplies,

And Rufus and I went on a mission of vengeful lies.

The eyewitness accounts were consistent,

I was looking for a man that was law resistant.

Rufus and I rode the country outside of town,

Looking for a campfire, smoke, tracks,

Anything that would help me track this man down.

We camped high on a mountain,

With a hundred mile vista.

And just before dawn,

A morning campfire found our eye.

The light was about five miles away.

I said to Rufus we better get movin',

We can get him today,

And if we're quick we can remove him.

We did better than we thought,

He was as good as caught.

We approached his campfire at dawn,

Before his .44 was drawn.

But Rufus caught his scent,

And launched himself from a rock without relent.

He snapped his neck,

And won my respect.

We left him for the buzzards,

Til his innards turned to custard.

We waived the burial,

And left him to Gabriel.

We headed home and back to the store.

So I could restart my life just as before.

I removed the guns from the case,

And Rufus assumed his place at the front door.

The whole town showed up at the funeral,

Which for me was admirable.

Rufus laid at my side,

And we cried, and cried, and cried.

Mojave: Beneath the Arid Skin

Laurie Wilson Fatland

Stark white, it slaps the eye,
A visual swear word.
Like old women's wrinkles protrude
Until thoughtful eyes find beauty
In shape and angled bone.
Art of a vicious creator.

Stabbing shades of faded green,
Hard-shelled venom poisons
The unwary. Still poets with time
Await cooling sky, creeping life
While wind notes play lonely songs.

The land stings the vision yet
Time strokes with soft fingers.
Dreams of ghost-like tumbleweeds
Lumber across footprints of the lost
Sucked into changing drifts, bold
Strokes of a mad artist.

Ground Hog's Day

Laurie Wilson Fatland

Ground Hog's Day, rodents with dead grass fur,
Reincarnated small weathermen
Peering from earthy portholes, sniffing
With wrinkled noses for Spring's flowered perfume.
If she's not near, back to herbal dreams,
Nestled in hungry sleep in cold ground
To await the green dance of rebirth.

My mother was born on Ground Hog's Day
And now she slumbers in cold, dark earth.
Nestled in her hollowed den, dreaming,
Her secret stash of kernels not shared.
I long to taste those hidden riddles,
To know of her enigma essence.
But Spring calls now, it's my turn to dance.

Siren Sounds

Laurie Wilson Fatland

Catgut and rosined horsehair sing,
while elephant teeth chew notes,
spitting them into a harmonious soup,
fine cuisine for gourmands of sound.

Drink deep the spicy melodies
Warmth creeps through old veins
Trumpeting forth youth recaptured,
Reborn in forgotten burial grounds.

Luscious reincarnated kisses
Taste of siren sounds from the sea.
To drown in this fantasia broth
Sounds a heavenly death to me

Time and Time Again

Laurie Wilson Fatland

Time turned his back on us,
That thief of days and years we lost,
Withered leaves blown from fingers,
Swept much too far away.

I've dreamt in reverie,
Old women in flowing dresses
Who stroll empty beaches, lost
In soulful communion.

Minds agile as in youth
Faces weathered with age, we laugh
In endless conversation
And turn our backs on time.

We will find each other
I know, on some far away shore
Where all final answers lie
And we'll laugh at time.

EDITOR'S PICKS

The Sacred Circle Writers don't confine themselves to **just** writing in response to prompts. These miscellanea were just too good to be left out although they don't fit neatly into any particular category. Katarina Karjala gives us fascinating insight—from the unique insider's perspective of an idealistic young woman—into a stunning moment in history with *Why People In Czechoslovakia Didn't Like Russian Tanks*. The somber mood of the seriousness in Eastern Europe behind the Iron Curtain is lightened with some comic relief by the ever-irreverent Dave Backer with *The Detective*, and Laurie Wilson Fatland's *The Key to Fear* explores a very satisfying outcome to a very scary situation.

Why People in Czechoslovakia Didn't Like Russian Tanks

Katarina Karjala

Czechoslovakia, August 21, 1968.

The early morning sun was trying to break through the brown blinds on the window of the bedroom Sasha shared with her eight years younger sister Hanna.

"Get up!" An order came from the other bed and a good size pillow zoomed over Sasha's head. Not ready for a fight, she grabbed it and stuck her head underneath it. Sixteen years old Sasha was desperately trying to get more sleep before the demanding school year. Before long, the other bed squeaked under the weight of Hanna's jumping body. Hanna's internal clock was on a different timer than Sasha's. The only problem Hanna faced was how to get her sister to join her play.

"Stop it, Hanna!" shrieked Sasha, but it was too late to restore her desired sleep. Her right hand, dangling from the bed, fumbled around to find the transistor radio stationed next to the bed's base, hit the metal frame and hurt her knuckle. The radio she had gotten as a Christmas present last year was the main artery connecting Sasha through the medium of music to the outside world. At that time her interest in the news from the officially banned station Radio Free Europe[1], was limited. Most kids her age at that time didn't fully understand the real purpose of the station. That morning, after the sound of the click turning the radio on, instead of her beloved music Sasha heard a gravelly voice announcing: "Czechoslovakia has been invaded by the armies of the Warsaw Pact."[2] It was a bolt from the blue.

---

[1] Radio Free Europe was a US broadcasting station for the communist bloc, operating in 1949-95 from Munich, Germany, and funded by Central Intelligence Agency

[2] Warsaw Pact a collective defense treaty among the communist states of Europe, 1955-91,suppressed the revolution in Hungary in 1956 and Czechoslovakia 1968

Sasha leapt out of her bed and rushed to the kitchen where her mother was making crepes for breakfast. Hanna was little bit surprised by her sister's action, but continued to amuse herself by jumping on the bed.

"Mom, mom! Turn on the radio! We have been invaded!" cried Sasha, holding her breath in the hope it was some kind of black humor. The aroma of the thin Slovakian crepes tickled her nose. Not able to resist, she snatched one, burned her fingers and dropped it back on the plate. Mother and daughter rushed to the stand where the radio sat, fitted in the corner of their modest kitchen, to turn it on. From the large box, framed in high polished mahogany wood, a solemn male voice was repeating the same message; that Soviet, Polish, Hungarian and Bulgarian armies had crossed the Czechoslovakian border during the night of August 20.

Sasha's mother Petra had a foreboding feeling in her gut that something like this would happen sooner or later. A gradual shifting in the political scene had been apparent from the mid-sixties. Alexander Dubcek[3] sharply criticized his predecessor and in in January 1968, was approved by Moscow to the position of the First Secretary of the Communist Party of Czechoslovakia.[4] Soviets soon realized he was a wolf in sheep's clothing who had outgrown the old doctrine they were pursuing. His main targets were political freedoms in his country, aiming to loosen Moscow's grip. As his approval grew among his own Czechoslovakian people, the Soviets had become increasingly impatient with him and also the whole political scene in Czechoslovakia. Sasha witnessed the rise of popularity of Dubcek but didn't put any weight to it, so the invasion was a bit of shock for her.

"Are we at war now?" Sasha asked, the voice on the radio still echoing in her mind. It brought back unpleasant memories of raw war pictures from the Russian movies they were obligated to watch as part of their education.

---

[3] At that time the head of Communist Party of Slovakia
[4] The most important political position in communist Czechoslovakia

"Wait, wait. I have to call your father," gasped her mother. It was Wednesday and her husband, an early bird, was already in his mayoral office. His working habits were written in stone – he was the first one there and the last to leave. The staccato of the phone line conveyed a clear message. After about half an hour of desperate trying, they heard the front door slam. Sasha's father, his face as pale as the walls in their apartment, hurried into the kitchen.

"Hi girls", he said with a forced smile. Hanna, still wearing her pajamas, sobbed quietly crouching in the kitchen corner, holding a plain crepe in her hand as if its vanilla fragrance would comfort her.

"I have a meeting in Bratislava[5] and must leave right now," her father said. "Sasha, could you please take Hanna to your room? I have to talk to your mother. And close the door. Please." Sasha was eager to listen but she complied when she saw his frown. Afterward, her father came to their room leaving the door ajar; allowing Sasha to see that her mother was wiping her eyes with the bottom hem of the colorful apron tied to her waist.

"Dad, when are you coming back? What if the Soviets block the roads?" Sasha didn't want to let go of his bear hug.

"Don't you worry; if the roads are blocked then all our hiking will come in handy. We know the Slovakian mountains, don't we? I will find my way back. Help your mom and Hanna." He whispered in her ear. She heard the familiar softness there.

"Now, a flight for Hanna." He grabbed his younger daughter under her slim arms and spun her around until she laughed out loud. Then he embraced his wife, almost a full head shorter than he was, and looked sadly in her eyes. They were two deep blue lakes holding secrets. Hurriedly he took the small suitcase she had packed on short notice, and said gently, "I will be back I just don't know when. Stay tuned to the radio, they will broadcast as much as

---

[5] Bratislava, a center, later the Capitol of Slovakia, in Czechoslovak Federation (from October 27, 1968).

they are allowed." He offered his contagious smile and left. From the window they saw him leave in a large black government car that was already full of other passengers. At that time Sasha didn't know how influential her father, Viktor, was. In public he appeared reserved and pragmatic and had an intuitive ability to find a right solution to any problem. Very few had experienced him as a fierce arguer, able to stand up for his people's interests.

To Sasha the whole situation didn't make much sense, so she turned to her mother for help. "Mom, I know that dad is working for the opposition, but was it necessary for him to go?"

Petra looked at her daughters, holding back her tears. "The opposition is forming a new government and your dad is playing an important role in it," she said quietly, as if she was in danger that somebody unwanted was listening. "They are having an assembly to decide what kind of passive resistance the nation should adopt." she exhaled deeply. "Nobody wants war. Nobody wants to see blood on the streets."

The voice from the radio was repeatedly appealing to the citizens to stay calm, to carry on with their daily lives, to go to work as if nothing was happening and to buy only limited food supplies. Sasha appreciated the fact that her mother was a teacher and still enjoyed the summer break. Regretting that she didn't have time to tell her father about her involvement in the underground Literary Club, she thought she could unfold the story to her mother.

"Mom, I want to talk to you," she said, wondering if this was the right time.

"No, not now, Sasha. I have to run to the store, we don't have much food here. Check in with me in about an hour, I will need a hand to carry the shopping bags." Both girls looked from the window and saw that the line in front of the store, located under their apartment in the same building, was snaking up all the way up to the road. Sasha's mother, as fast a thinker as her husband, was devoted to her family and was ready to protect her girls. As she joined the line at the store she contemplated if this was the right time to introduce Sasha to the changes in the country, and lead her through the political perils of domestic and international affairs.

There were many things in politics before the invasion that Sasha, like any other teenage girl, didn't pay much attention to, although people everywhere, including her Literary Club, were talking about the changes that needed to be made. With lots of questions going through her mind now, Sasha suppressed her shyness and decided to call George. He was two years her senior, had already been accepted to the College of Journalism, and went to the same high school as Sasha. She had barely noticed him before she had been introduced to him at the Literary Club last year. For Sasha, the slim, tall boy, reminding her of her father, was an open book of knowledge. Slowly she felt more than friendship toward George and to her surprise, he reciprocated. At this moment of fear and uncertainty she passionately desired to hold his hand, and feel his soft lips on hers; the gentle touch she wanted to last forever. These warm feelings were spoiled when nobody picked up the phone at his family's house. Acting on hunch, Sasha looked resentfully at Hanna and said frankly, "We have to go check if Mom needs help and then I will see my friend Sylvia, so I will drop you at Aunt Elena's house. You can take what you want, I will carry it." Hanna said nothing.

A few minutes later Sasha said "Are you ready?" Hanna gladly nodded, excited to see her cousin, born in the same year.

In front of the store the line was long and stagnant. Their mother was deep in conversation with another woman, so Sasha just gestured, showing that she would be right back. Her original plan was to dash out of her own apartment to check George's house but there was Hanna she had to take care of first. Hanna, who was much shorter than Sasha and barely able to keep up with her older sister, walked one step behind her. They reached their Aunt and Uncle's house, where Sasha simply waved, once she saw Aunt Elena open the door. Sasha left. Feeling free she galloped through the town to check the house of George's parents. On the way she had to cross the medieval square. The minute she stepped on the uneven surface of the cobblestones, she regretted not taking her bicycle. Sasha didn't want to slow down but gable stones dictated her speed now. She was familiar with the neighborhood of George's house because close by was the house of Helena's parents, where her Literary Club had meetings. She passed the local bakery, located in a respectful cube-shaped building. Not able to resist the deliciously scented air she promised herself to buy a freshly baked apple strudel once back in the center of town. The one story house of George's parents was like a small mushroom surrounded by large, tall houses. There was an unexpected solace just being in their front yard, but even after she repeatedly rang the doorbell, the door remained shut. She examined his bedroom window but there was not a glimpse of a movement. Two bird feeders placed in the front garden and always full of seeds, were empty now.

Sasha wished she would calm down, especially once she rejoined her mother, who had progressed in the line and was already at the front door of the store. But she was not able escape her mother's eagle eyes.

"Did you drop Hanna at Aunt Elena's house?"

"Yes."

"What's going on? Is your friend Sylvia in town?" Mother continued, feeling that something was not right with her older daughter.

"No." Sasha didn't want to reveal her secret about George. She didn't realize that in a small town, like theirs, even birds sitting on electrical lines knew everything.

As a young man, Sasha's uncle Rudolf longed for a medical career. His brother Viktor, Sasha's father, preferred teaching and had hoped to enter the world of politics. They both found their life partners while attending college. Rudolf fell for the dark haired, tall Elena and Victor for short Petra with the temperament of her strawberry-colored hair. Both women worked as teachers and both families were carefully planned so the children would not be born too far apart. That fact predetermined the free time the families spent together. A family practitioner, jovial Rudolf was apolitical. He made it clear he just wanted to serve good people who were sick and was not interested in their political affiliation.

On August 21, like at any average day, Rudolf took care of his patients, listened to their complaints and didn't have time to follow the news. It was his wife, Elena, who called him during his short lunch break, explaining that the Soviets planned a four days surprise invasion, and that all Czechoslovakian citizens were asked to form a nonviolent resistance movement to slow them down. The government requested people to change direction of the street and road signs so the invading armies would be routed into deep forests or back where they came from.

"So don't be surprised to see your patients coming with small injuries like hammered fingers or paint in their eyes," Elena tried to lift the mood of her husband.

"I don't see those injuries here. But it could easily happen to me," he said jokingly. "By the way, keep the kids in the house, especially Lucas. I am afraid that his teenage brain might underestimate this situation."

"I will do my best. Hanna is staying with us now. Emotions are running high in their apartment after Victor left," said Elena with concern.

The nation was on the move, resembling a large anthill. People supplied themselves with paint and brushes, hammers and shovels. They painted and displaced signs, or removed them. The maps the Soviets were equipped with suddenly became misleading. Radio stations repeatedly called upon the people not to react violently. All the hopes and expectations of Czechoslovakians were turned to the West.

Not Sasha's. The day of August 21, 1968 was a long one; her father didn't call, and neither did George. Sasha and her mother spent most of the day running between the radio, a black and white TV and neighbors and friends. At midnight, bone-tired Petra thought it would be better to get some sleep and she asked her daughter to go to her room. Sasha went to her bed and was listening to the songs of burping frogs coming through the open window unsuccessfully trying to force her mind to shut down, when the phone in the hallway rang. Always faster than her mother, she grabbed the phone.

"Dad, dad, where are you? Are you on the way home? Did you see Russian tanks?" Her mother was holding her tight around the shoulders.

"Sasha, I miss you all terribly, in all conscience I would love to talk to you, but I need to talk to your mom now," her father said, "There is only one phone available for private calls for many people here." Sasha handed the phone to her mother, but tried to pick up words as her mother listened to her husband whispering, short and fast. Looking at her mother with questions in her eyes, Sasha sensed that something had gone wrong.

"He has to go to Prague[6], and also he said Austria and West Germany have opened their borders for our people who want to emigrate. All they need is a valid passport," mother repeated what she just had learned.

Sasha looked at her, "Are we going to emigrate, Mom?"

"No." Petra answered quickly, but not very convincingly.

Viktor had called his family to relieve their feelings and fears but the result was just the opposite. Knowing where her parents kept the passports, Sasha took them out and counted. She couldn't believe her eyes, her father's was missing. Confusion overwhelmed her. She thought, this is not possible; he would never leave his family. Sasha's mother was standing behind her, looking at the passports.

---

[6] Prague was the capitol of Czechoslovakia

"Honey, you know your dad, right? He would leave the country, only if his life were in danger."

"Mom, but he doesn't know the Czech mountains.[7]"

"Don't you worry; there are many good people over there who would help him."

The next day, August 22, first thing in the early morning, Sasha raced down the stairs from their second floor apartment, to the mail boxes located inside in the hallway at the building's entrance. The metal box was empty; perhaps the mailman hadn't brought any mail yet. Through the glass doors she saw people lined up at the news-stand to buy a newspaper. Anxious, she checked the mail box a couple of hours later. It was still empty. Unsettled, she decided to go to George's. Thinking about what she was going to say to his parents when they opened the door, she grabbed a sweater and her bicycle, and pedaled to their house. A neighbor, a gray haired lady, who lived across the street, was sitting in a rocking chair in the sun in front of her house. She got up, supporting herself with a worn wooden walking stick and she gestured Sasha to come closer to the gate.

"They left," the old woman said, "the whole family, carrying small suitcases. I have no idea where they went."

Father's words about open borders resonated in Sasha's ears and a wave of disillusion overwhelmed her. She had just seen George two days ago, and still felt his arm around her shoulders. She hurried back home to grapple with her feelings.

Back in their apartment the radio announced that Russian tanks had entered the city of Prague the night before, and seized the airport and other strategic places. Russian military cargo planes roared from the sky the whole night causing sleeplessness for many. There was the sound of shooting in the background of the radio report, intensifying Sasha's fears. She turned on the TV.

---

[7] Czechs live in the western part of Czechoslovakia, Slovaks in the eastern part

"Mom, mom, come here, you have to see this!" she shouted. But at that time, her mother was not at home. She was standing in the long line at the butcher shop to get the meat and eggs a local farm had supplied, fresh, during the night. Astonished, Sasha saw the streets of Prague and Bratislava on the TV, full of tanks and people, some of them carrying Czechoslovakian flags, some sitting on the outside of closed tanks. Those people spontaneously and fearlessly or, she asked herself, maybe recklessly, had gone out into the streets to protest. Sasha saw a burning Russian tank, heard the sound of automatic gunfire, and saw another Russian tank with the large words in white: "Wehrmacht 1944,"[8] painted by Slovaks on it. Tears were running down her cheeks.

In the meantime, American actress, Shirley Temple[9] found herself in the middle of the invasion. She was helping with the evacuation of the American Embassy in Prague. Soviet soldiers, some apparently confused, were shooting into the air causing bullets to fly close to the windows of the Czech radio station. Accidents, or a way to harass the journalists spreading uncensored news? Nobody knew. Warsaw Pact soldiers were told that it was important to help Czechoslovakian people to suppress the counterrevolution but instead of flowers and welcoming speeches they saw anger, they saw fists and citizens yelling to them in Russian to go back home.

Sasha preferred to listen to the radio because of its greater mobility than the TV. Every hour the radio reported the exact position of the Warsaw Pact armies and they were still far from Sasha's town. As the animosity of the Czechs and Slovaks against the Soviets grew, the nation was more and more unified. Sasha found the newspaper on the kitchen table; the bold headlines encouraged people to maintain peace, deliberation and dignity.

---

[8] Wehrmacht- the armed forces of the Nazi Germany, World War II
[9] Shirley Temple, one of the founders of the International Federation of Multiple Sclerosis made a trip to Prague on August 17. She was coming from a conference in Vienna to invite Czechoslovakia to join the organization

That afternoon Petra asked Sasha to help her make an apple pie. They were preparing the ingredients when Sasha heard a vehement voice from the radio. She couldn't believe her ears; the voice was that of George. He must be in Bratislava then, she thought, But where is his family? Why didn't he call me? Georgie, I wish you were here. At the thought of him, a happy smile broke out on her face for the first time since the invasion. She touched her long hair, the color of ripe grain, imagining her hand was George's.

That day Sasha's father didn't call. Some people in their small town were packing, ready to abandon their home and head to the West, to an unknown future. Three days later an announcement came over the radio that the entire invading army from Poland was routed back to their country after wandering the countryside, thanks to the people who had painted over and turned street and road signs. The citizens of Czechoslovakia cheered only for a short time. Then, a report about casualties came like an ice-cold shower.

The night brought Sasha some sleep and a sweet dream about George. They were walking through their town, holding hands and talking about something she couldn't understand. The next morning the mail box rewarded her with a postcard that had a picture of Bratislava on it. Simple words written in a hurry with a shaky hand said "I love you, George."

A strange roar of engines was coming from outside. Sasha opened the door of their apartment building and heard a man screaming: "Russians! Russians are in the town!"

Czechoslovakia 1967.

Fourteen years after the death of Stalin, strong feelings of disillusion were still present in the Czechoslovakian society. A glimpse of hope for independence was gaining ground. The Iron Curtain between the Western countries and Czechoslovakia had started to melt at last. This was partly because the older "brother"[10] in Moscow had been aging, giving the impression of getting wiser or perhaps senile, with his hands steadily losing their grip and allowing some breathing space. There was a sense of transformation in the political system of the Czechoslovak Socialistic Republic, a satellite state of the Eastern Block. Little streams of new ideas grew gradually into a river.

Sasha was born to the parents, Viktor and Petra, just few months short of Stalin's death[11]. She was too young to have experienced the Stalinist purges in the fifties, but old enough to sense the shift in society in sixties. More freedom meant more western music played by the Radio Free Europe. Her politically active parents, involved in the opposition movement of sixties, thought carefully how to bring some light of knowledge about the political reality of their communist society into the life of their fifteen year-old daughter without jeopardizing her safety. Freedom of speech was still limited in the Czechoslovakian radio stations so they decided to take a more diplomatic step. At Christmas 1967 Sasha got her own transistor radio, tuned to the banned station, Radio Free Europe. The first English words she learned were 'Radio Free Europe.'

On an early June 1967 morning, Sasha and a group of her friends were on the way to high school. Newly installed street lamps ensured the safety of pedestrians crossing two busy roads; one led into the medieval town center, the other away from it. The city gardeners were planting flowers and grass in the median dividing the roads. Sasha liked the design of the slim street lamps reaching up to the sky; placed in the middle of the median, their two arms stretched out to the opposite sides of the main pole. The new road replaced a centuries-old cemetery that now hosted its dwellers and visitors on a hill overlooking town. During the day Sasha walked to their family's apartment building using the sidewalk alongside the cemetery. Not at night, it was creepy, so she ran.

---

[10] USSR was called an older brother
[11] Stalin passed way in 1953, March 5

The group of girls clowned around as they walked through the medieval town plaza, which was framed by fragrant linden trees, the soles of their shoes clicking against the worn, cobblestoned sidewalk. Before heading uphill to the school they stopped at a two-hundred years old baroque column, a memorial for plague victims. "We should recite verses of Jacques Prevert love poetry to them." Laughing, they formed a small choir and recited it in front of the monument as if it would help the thousands who didn't make it during the Black Death. People were opening their windows to welcome a warm early summer sun, and were surprised by the group of already well-tanned youngsters.

A woman stuck out her head from an open window and said "Girls, you are running late!" Laughter and heavy backpacks mercilessly hitting their spines didn't help them run up the slope to the school.

During a break Sylvia, a classmate of Sasha's, came to her and whispered. "Follow me." Sylvia navigated between groups of talking students to a quiet corner and handed Sasha a small piece of paper with an address, murmuring softly "A Literary Club wants you to join them. Don't tell anybody. Remember absolutely nobody."

"Why? What do they do?" asked confused Sasha as Nora, a chunky teenager dressed in a flowered jump suit matching her rosy cheeks, approached them.

"Talking boys?" Nora asked, "Are you hiding from others?" Sylvia gave Sasha a long look. The school bell announcing a new section rescued Sasha and Sylvia from Nora. Sasha was not sure what to make of it all and looked around for Sylvia after school but instead made eye contact with Nora, who sensed something was going on like a woodpecker senses a bug in a tree. While scanning the hallway for Sylvia, Sasha tried to get rid of Nora. Sylvia was gone. Sasha hustled down the endless, wide travertine stairs, stopped in front of the building and looked around. The familiar chatter of her friends came from around the corner.

"Did you see Sylvia?" she asked them.

Ela pointed at a car leaving. "Her father just picked her up. The rest of this week she is at the Conservatory in Bratislava." Sasha knew what it meant. Sylvia was a prodigy of the local piano virtuoso, who was blown into their small town by some mistake. The virtuoso recommended that Sylvia study simultaneously at two high schools. This being Wednesday, Sasha knew her friend would not be back in town until Sunday morning. The piece of paper, burning in her hands, said the Literary Club meets on Saturday. She tried hard to keep her composure and was considering if she should talk about it to her father, the newly elected mayor of their town, in spite of Sylvia's request not to talk about the invitation to anybody. She waited for the right moment but it didn't come because he worked very long hours.

When Saturday arrived, Sasha grabbed the leather bag that she had named the "black hole" bag because things disappeared in the deep space of it. She mumbled to her parents some reason for leaving the apartment and, not sure what to expect, walked in the direction she thought the listed address should be. She found it in the vicinity of the local bakery, which quietly advertised itself with the smell of freshly baked bread.

The owner of the house where the meeting was taking place was a local architect and so Sasha naively expected to find the most exquisite house in the neighborhood. A colorful garden welcomed her after she opened the short metal gate and followed a narrow brick walkway to the door. Her hand was hot and trembling slightly as she pressed her palm against the cold metal frame of a cast iron doorbell. Before long she heard the steps of somebody approaching from inside. Something ran at her very fast as soon as the door opened and she was pinned to the gate by a large grey dog. His paws were on her shoulders. There was no escape; she got a wet kiss on her face

"Lenny! Off! Don't worry, he is very friendly." The dog obeyed the command, waging his tail. Pleased that she was not knocked down, Sasha exhaled all the air she was holding in her lungs. "I am so sorry. Hi, I am Helena and you must be Sasha," said the young woman, who was visibly older than Sasha. Helena had on a sleeveless cotton dress with a miniskirt that revealed her slim body. "Lenny loves to greet our guests and sometimes he is faster than me."

"Is he a Great Dane?" Sasha asked, her voice shaking, unsure if it was a good idea to join these people. She was thinking there should be a sign on the fence to warn people about the dog, who, done with his greeting job, was already casually stretched across the whole sidewalk.

Coming from the sunny street, the hallway seemed very dark. It was also very narrow, perhaps to save more space for rooms but it gave Sasha an impression of imprisonment. Sasha silently followed chatty Helena. "Everybody is already here, except my parents. They are traveling," she said. She led Sasha to the end of a narrow hallway, to her room. Through the partly open door Sasha heard the voices of both genders and the song "The House of the Rising Sun" wafting through. Sasha's stomach was clutched tight when Helena opened the door and Sasha was able to see everybody sitting in a room lit by the late afternoon sun. They were all smiling at her and a woman who looked to be in her early thirties stood up and put her hand out to greet Sasha. She introduced herself as Martina. Sasha intuitively covered Martina's cold hand with both of her fiery palms and looked into her dark brown eyes. Three other people who were sitting on the small brown sofa or on the floor, papers in front of them, introduced themselves. A young man, Jan, was a university student, a hippy with untrimmed beard and shoulder-length hair. Sasha was intimidated by his tight pants but he put her at ease with a serious look and a sparkle of enthusiasm. The two other girls, also university students, offered Sasha a cigarette. She felt misplaced, not sure if she really belonged there.

They asked her not to reveal to anybody what she heard during the meeting, not even to her parents. "Is this a religious group?"

she asked. Just last week they had talked about the growing number of religious cults on the radio.

She gazed at Helena for an answer, which came promptly and clearly: "No. This is a Literary Club." Helena explained that the group had to remain underground until the communist government passed a bill allowing freedom of the speech. Sasha had heard about underground movements on Radio Free Europe, and a gamut of emotions swirled in her brain. This might be part of something much larger than she had expected. She listened carefully.

"Why did you invite me to join your group?" asked Sasha peering at Martina.

"That was my idea," she admitted. Your friend Sylvia brought some of your poetry published in the school magazine and we found it charming."

"Is Sylvia part of this group as well?" asked Sasha after a little hesitation

"Yes, but she comes rarely." Helena said, noticing Sasha's tension. She hurried on to explain that they were reading the poetry and prose of authors who were still officially banned in Czechoslovakia, and for that reason they asked her to keep it secret, that this was why they were still underground.

"Besides, you have the right to refuse our invitation," Jan pointed out. "Please have a seat," he offered Sasha his chair and found a comfortable place on the floor. Then he took out a small, well-worn book. The title was Ferlinghetti Lawrence, Poetry. The book was translated by somebody from the underground opposition movement. It had been published in West Germany and smuggled to groups of opposition in Czechoslovakia, Jan explained. On the coffee table there were some other books of American Beat poetry and forbidden domestic writers.

"You might take a look at these two books and pick one." Jan offered Sasha Allen Ginsberg's Poetry book or The Joke of Milan

Kundera. Sasha preferred poetry. In her school they read the love poetry of French poet Jacque Prevert – everybody from her class fell instantly for those verses, and also for the poetry of Guillaume Apollinaire, but she had never heard about Ginsberg. So Sasha took the Ginsberg and was ready to rush home to read it. From the large window on the west side of the room she noticed the sky was darkening with clouds. Two of the people at the meeting read poems they had been inspired to write during the meeting. Jan was smoking and all of them looked relaxed. Every single detail left an imprint in Sasha's inexperienced mind.

It was starting to drizzle so Sasha had to race the storm home. Once there, she made sure nobody would find her treasured book. Both parents were busy so, unnoticed, she sneaked into her room to climb to her asylum place. Hanna was reading a book but dropped it when Sasha entered.

"Will you play a card game with me?" Her large blue eyes were begging for attention.

"Sure, just a minute I have to read something." Sasha tossed her bag up first, and climbed on top of the armoire to sit in her favorite reading spot. Her parents respected her privacy when she was up there without questions. Sasha settled on the small pillow and took out the precious book. The poetry was interesting, but it didn't make sense to her why it was forbidden by the government. Absorbed in reading, she didn't detect her sister climbing up until it was almost too late.

"Hanna, you can't climb here! There is not enough room for two people," she said as she hastily closed the book and waved her back down.

"Promises," said Hanna, "That's all I hear."

"We are going to play cards now but we need to sit at the table." Sasha was proud of herself for finding a quick solution.

This was the time when reality knocked at Sasha's door and she began to pay more attention to the news. She learned that

Czechoslovakia was part of the Warsaw Pact[12] and that the Soviets controlled the military; she learned that the Soviet model for industrialization of the Eastern Bloc wasn't working for an already-industrialized Czechoslovakia. The politicians of her country were talking about a 'New Model of Economy' requiring political reform. Young writers like Milan Kundera were urging freedom of speech and she was reading the forbidden poetry of Allen Ginsberg.

---

[12]There was not a presence of the Soviet military in Czechoslovakia after President H.S.Truman and J.V Stalin reached an agreement to that effect after WW II, until the invasion in 1968. The Warsaw Pact was established in 1955

The Detective

Dave Becker

My name is Detective Sam Saturday, Dalkon Shield Badge number 4321.1, which equals 11, which is my favorite number. I've been with the LAPD, BFF, EMT, PTSD, STD, LOL, VFD, Mountain/Beach Division for 14 years. My partner, Detective Tuesday, has been with me off and on, mostly on, for about three years.

We've been temporarily assigned to the Robbery/Theft Division to monitor a local "Wally World," correction: Walmart, complaint about a series of shopping cart thefts. These shopping cart thefts have taken place in broad daylight, and they usually are full of merchandise from the store.

We got a report Monday that a theft occurred last Sunday, but I went out of town Friday, hoping to return Tuesday, but my car didn't start Tuesday, so I couldn't make it back to work until Wednesday. Payday wasn't until Thursday, so I took the bus to work Wednesday, and met up with Tuesday Wednesday. Thursday, we got our first briefing. I got paid, and got my car back Thursday. We started our first stakeout at Walmart Friday. Nothing happened all day Saturday. Then we got our first hit on Sunday.

After a lunch consisting of three Chicago dogs, fries, large soda, an apple and a nap, we got our first hit. I was awakened by a short homeless person with a full shopping cart surrounded by a group of Walmart associates. We approached the group of Walmart employees, identified ourselves, and said that we would take over the investigation.

The perp was a local well known jaywalker, horse thief, rapist, burglar, drunk, drug dealer, scam artist, runaway child molester, bad check passer, little person named, I.M.SAM. That's Ichabod Michael Sam (short and mischievous). We cuffed him, read him his rights, and seized the shopping cart full of merchandise from Walmart.

In the shopping cart were a 12 pack of beer, Ding Dongs, Skittles, Milk Duds, a fifth of vodka, M&Ms, Hershey bars, Twizzlers, Bon Bons, the latest copy of True Detective, and an ice cream sandwich. So the ice cream sandwich wouldn't melt, I ate it.

After booking the suspect and questioning him, it was time to log the shopping cart and its contents into evidence.

To my surprise the evidence had disappeared during the questioning of the suspect. The only items left were the shopping cart and the Milk Duds.

Of course it was still lunch time in the squad room, and everyone was eating my evidence. The beer went to the men in the drunk tank to keep them quiet. The Ding Dongs went to the court-appointed attorneys. The Skittles went to drug enforcement. The Hershey bars and the Twizzlers went to vice. The M&Ms went to the front desk. The True Detective magazine went to the Chief of Detectives. The girls in the typing pool got the Bon Bons. And my Russian captain got the bottle of vodka.

All I had left was the shopping cart and the Milk Duds. Walmart offered to drop the charges if they got the shopping cart back, then they would charge the whole thing off to "associate training."

My little friend said that he would keep off police radar for three hours if I let him go and give him the Milk Duds.

The Key to Fear

Laurie Wilson Fatland

She caught his eye long before it happened. A tall, slim girl, whose shoulder length dark hair swayed with the rhythm of her walk. She moved like a cat, with long, liquid strides; determined and predatory. He followed, his own hunting instinct honed in on his prey.

Every victim of the hunter makes its fatal mistake, and she made hers. She stepped aside suddenly to avoid a homeless man, his shopping cart piled with the smelly remains of a miserable life. Her quick move tilted her shoulder bag at just the right angle and a set of keys fell to the sidewalk.

His lips turned up into a grin as he reached down without stopping and pocketed the keys. Following discreetly, he sifted through the possibilities of this gift, pulling his dark ball cap over his face and turning up the collar of his black jacket. Blending in was a skill he cultivated, just like any successful hunter. No one ever noticed him, no one ever remembered him except for the victims, and their memories were extremely short.

He crossed the pavement and melted into the shadows as she paused before a pretty brownstone on a narrow street overhung with trees. Its green door gleamed in the reflecting streetlight, the glow illuminating her face. He watched as she opened her bag and began searching, no doubt for the missing keys. Again he smiled to himself, fingering the keys in his pocket like a lucky talisman. Her search became more desperate as she rummaged through her bag and then her coat pockets. In frustration she turned and sat down on the step, chin in hand.

This was his first clear view of her face. She had a sculpted beauty, high cheekbones, well shaped lips and dark eyebrows that set off her light blue eyes. He imagined running his knife over those features as they froze in fear, her lips parted in agony. It made him hard and desperate.

She jumped up and began to move aside all of the potted plants that lined the small doorstep. Triumphantly she held up a key to the light and grinned. The spare key opened the door easily and she slipped inside.

He waited a long time in the shadows, watching as she moved around the downstairs, a blurred shape behind gauzy curtains. Finally, the lights downstairs went off and the upstairs lights came on. Now was his chance. He had a plan; adaptable of course, should the situation change.

This was a new sensation for him, choosing and killing so quickly. Usually he followed his victims for days, their nearness and ignorance feeding his growing need. It was a game of cat and mouse, the mouse totally unaware until the killing pounce. It made the final act so fulfilling. But the keys changed everything. The keys were a gift, a sign he should act tonight, and by now his excitement was palpable. He could imagine his body over her lean, taut one; his knife making him squirm with desire and her with fear.

He licked his lips in anticipation and moved over to the door, slowly unlocking it with her keys. Edging the heavy door open, he crept in and noiselessly closed it behind him, listening for sounds in the house. A dog would ruin his plan, or another person, but there was no one. There was no noise but the distant spraying of the shower upstairs.

Taking the stairs one at time, he carefully placed his weight to check for creaks that might alert her to his presence. He peeked into her bedroom, feminine and neat, her clothes lying across a chair. He fondled her underwear as he listened to her humming in the shower. He was throbbing with excitement. Quietly he slid under the bed.

He waited patiently, listening as she finished her shower and dried her hair. He was good at waiting. Every hunter learned this. Conceal yourself and wait for the unwary victim to come close. Footsteps, and a view of her slim feet as she came near and he heard her lie down on the bed, the springs sagging above him. He forced his breath to mimic hers as he lay beneath her, reveling in the sweet ache of eagerness and anticipation. Finally she turned off the light and allowed darkness to permeate the room. He listened, her breathing slowing into sleep.

When he was sure she was unaware, the hunter quietly pulled himself out from his hiding place. Ever so slowly he lowered himself above her, his knife hovering over her pale, slender neck. He licked his lips again as he ran the blade of the knife over her face, gently, gently, no need for pain yet. There was plenty of time to enjoy that later.

Her eyes flickered beneath their lids as she sensed his presence. He smiled. He waited for her eyes to open and the full blossom of fear to take root in them. He felt her move slightly and felt the sudden shock of cold steel on his temple. Fear surged through him, an electrical current of terror as he heard the click of the gun. She smiled, and pulled the trigger.

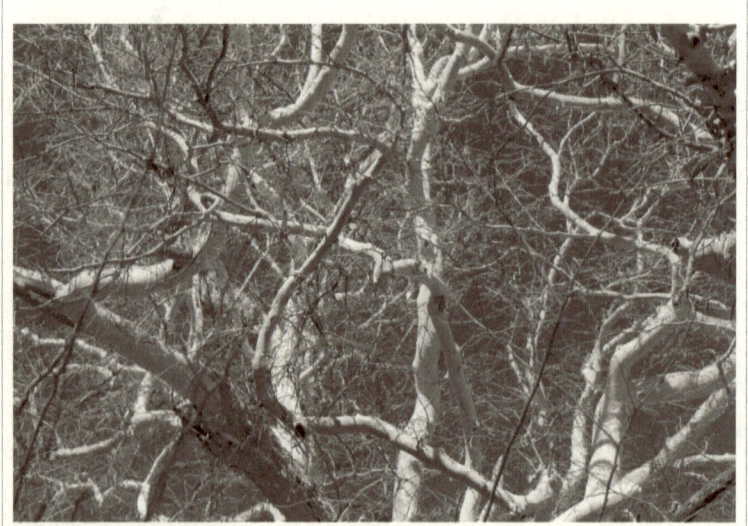
Photo Credit: John Fatland

FIRST WORDS

What We're Working On

The Miracle *du jour*

The frenetic modern world tries to make us to think that the miraculous is not to be found in our harried work-a-day lives; that the sacred resides at some distant remove, in some other-worldly place. This whimsical collection of tales, fables, parables, confessions, and essays begs to differ. *The Miracle du jour* notices that joy, redemption, and absolution surround us every day in a million small ways from acts of kindness, to taking responsibility for ourselves, to the myriad ways Mother Nature can bring peace and the manifest presence of the miraculous into our lives.

Enchantment isn't gone from the world; we've just forgotten how to find it.

This excerpt is from the Spiral of the Year section of *The Miracle du jour*. It explores all those little miracles to be encountered early in August, when we first sense the turning of the season. *The Miracle du jour* will be published early in May, 2015

'Tis the Season – Lughnasadh

Terryl Warnock

Lughnasadh (loo-na-sa) is an understated change, more a sweet little tug on the heartstrings than a fully-formed thought. It doesn't so much spur us to actually put another blanket on the bed as it imparts nostalgic fondness for the cedar chest safeguarding those extra blankets we were so glad to be rid of last spring; a tiny recollection of the warm, welcome weight of that wintertime nest. This first vague awareness surprises a bit because it's not chilly, not yet, it's only a mild, nearly subconscious impression early in August. This trifling surprise triggers the sudden recognition that the vibrant yellow of the clover has faded a bit gray now and the bee people are no longer very much interested in it; recognition accompanied by a prayer that the season has been kind to them and that they have enough put up and put by for winter. The spider people start their insistent efforts to move into the house. The season hasn't turned, not yet, but we can see it from here for the first time. We realize it's time to start thinking of putting up and putting by for winter for ourselves. Apples litter the sidewalk and it's time to make cider. Lughnasadh is the subtlest touch, presaging fall's more adamant caress.

As summer gives forth these first delicate hints of farewell, the air in quiet rural neighborhoods comes alive early of a weekend morning. It starts early because it's still summer enough to make what is a pleasant job early in the morning too miserably hot to enjoy later in the day. The stillness is banished before full light by the baritone buzz of chainsaws, harmonized with by the tenor voice of the weed eaters. Few run mowers here, there are too many rocks. The cut weeds of the mountain Southwest fill the air with the tangy perfume of sage mingled with sweet, cloying clover, and the harmony of these two voices make each breath taste like the purification ritual it is—we're just more aware of it than usual this particular early morning because we can taste it and smell it. Scent and taste invoke powerfully.

Like all of us, plants have magical, spiritual and physical presences and power. Plants and trees create aromas by means of the essential oils they generate. These oils are the plant's immune system, the perfumes attract or repel in the plant's best interest. The bright colors and aromas of flowers attract pollinators, while resins are anti-microbial and anti-fungal to keep plants and trees safe from predation. In a spiritual sense, these powerful aromas and bright colors are what make the plant people engaging and welcome neighbors. Sage is a balancing aroma used in purification rituals since ancient times, and it's the terpene alcohols in the cedar wood we line our linen chests with that smell so good to us and so bad to the moth people. Sweet flower smells like the clover act as gentle nervines, they make us breathe deeply, relax, and smile a little.

The chainsaws may add the vocal bass note to the sounds of this early August morning, but their work adds the aromatic treble of heady cedar to the attar in the air. It's a species of juniper, actually, but people around here call the fragrant shaggy-barked trees just off the rim cedars. We can't help ourselves, they smell like cedars and scent invokes powerfully. Just a short drop in elevation from here lives a vast, diverse Pinon/Juniper forest and beloved aromatic cedar is so plentiful there we burn it in our stoves and fireplaces in winter. We only take the ones that have already died a natural death, of course. No hard work ever smelled so good as going out to get a load of cedar to warm your bones through the dark of the year. Oak here is rare—solid gold—and we'll take it if we can find it of course, but the majority of the woodpile is fragrant, beautiful cedar. The deep red body of the perfumed wood is shot through with brilliant yellow streaks. It looks like it's on fire already and smells more fragrant than any burning incense ever could. Although it makes a lot of ash, it burns hot and long. We burn it preferentially to the closer and more plentiful pine because pine has more resin and doesn't burn as hot, so it makes more creosote to gum up the stovepipe. You want to have a little pitchy pine on hand, though, (fatwood) to splinter down for kindling. One match, no paper is a worthy goal for the family fire starter and if you have some nice fatwood under some small-ish pieces of cedar, it is an eminently attainable and satisfying goal—lighting the fire in this way becomes a ritual of thanks to the tree people who capture the light and warmth of the sun and bring it in to warm our homes in the dark, cold of the year.

The subtlety of the season is most eloquently spoken by a minuscule shift in light, and the first taste of it each summer at Lughnasadh is a Miracle *du jour* that makes hearts sing with anticipation of the coming turn. The light somehow tastes slightly different. We know on a rational level the arc of the sun has slipped a fraction lower toward the horizon with the noticeable shortening of the days, but oh, the magic in that fraction! The microcoating of resiny sap on the pine needles makes the trees shimmer in a way they didn't just a few days ago. The blue of the sky is somehow more deeply blue, anticipating the black, black nights to come that will ultimately embrace longest night at winter solstice. Gossamer spider webs, invisible only yesterday, float lazily in the breeze animating and illuminating what was darkly inanimate. The spider people spin two sorts of webs. One is fixed, a home to live and work and make babies in. The other is a means of transportation; they anchor one end and jump off. Kowabunga. Arachnoid repelling. They spin their way to their destination, tie off, and continue on their merry way. The tethers they leave behind are as beautiful in the Lughnasadh light as tinsel hanging from a Christmas tree. From close up they float and wave in the breeze and tiny rainbows play up and down along their ethereal lengths. From afar, the entire forest glitters and dances each tree meticulously and individually decorated by uncounted industrious tiny elves.

Ancient pagan folk celebrated Lughnasadh (after the god Lugh, The Shining One, skilled in the arts) at the beginning of August as the first of three harvest festivals. It marked the time to start putting up and putting by for winter. This holiday was also called Lammas, the Feast of the Bread.

If you should happen to see a beautiful, garnet-colored, sun-kissed raspberry as you walk past the bush you've been carefully tending all spring and summer, you are well-advised to grab it and revel in its sweet magic right then and there. This isn't the Pacific Northwest, where people have to hack and hew to defend their personal space from the encroachment of the wild berry people. Nor is it the Midwest with the agricultural abundance of its deep black soil. This is the desert Southwest, and aside from the odd Mesquite pod or Prickly Pear fruit we are not accustomed to chancing across fresh fruit here. The Stellar's jays have a sharp eye and a bold manner. They are no respecters of other people's berries and lurk in the adjacent pine tree waiting for those raspberries to achieve the perfect color that proclaims ripeness. The berry will not be there later if you pass it up now.

The family of Cassin's Kingbirds, of the Flycatcher clan, who have miraculously survived the cat to raise their family in the eaves of the house all summer, have fledged their young and are starting their long journey to winter in warmer climes. Their cheerful *chee-wheet!* calls are missed, as are the complicated and spectacular aerial acrobatics required of them in front of the dining room window to gain entrance to their sequestered nest.

The great, pulsing artery of life in the desert Southwest is the Rio Grande. Its magical presence touches vast stretches of Southwestern barrenness with Element of Water; the life-giving miracle here in the drylands. This is the time of year our mouths start watering in anticipation of the Hatch chili harvest. Mother Earth has blessed the Rio Grande valley in the vicinity of the village of Hatch, New Mexico, with a symphony of miracles that include the Water of the Rio, the Earth of the Hatch Valley, and generations of the expertise and passions of People who are connected to both. In concert they grow the best chili peppers known to human kind.

Communities throughout the Southwest begin to buzz about this miracle *du jour* when the roasters are set up. We know the harvest will not be far behind and we couldn't be more excited if

Santa Claus had parked his sled in front of the Farmer's Market. The day the trucks rumble in with their brightly colored boxes the assessment begins. The bravest among us taste first. "How hot are they this year?" Us wimps get them early, at Lughnasadh. Those with stronger constitutions wait till later, nearer the equinox. They get hotter and redder as the harvest goes.

Darn right we tip the young farm hands who come to work the roasters, and we tip them well. We get to enjoy the delicious fruits of their labor all year long. Theirs is heavy work next to a large fire in the August heat. You can buy the chilies raw, but that means you get to spend time in the company of your oven or BBQ for long periods of time during the hottest part of the year, too, getting chili juice in the myriad little cuts, cracks and hangnails you didn't even know you had on your hands till you got chili juice in them. Do NOT rub your eyes for any reason. Try as you might though you'll never get them roasted as perfectly as the big rotating drum with its propane burners. When the pros do it every surface is done to a turn so the blackened skin slips off easily leaving only the fragrant, delicious chili underneath.

These are the miracles *du jour* my plant, animal, and human neighbors share with me at Lughnasadh. You have neighbors who will do the same, wherever you are. If we look to find the small miracles in our lives, the local folk, both human and nonhuman, will share them willingly.

Fall is in the air, you can taste it.

Migration

Migration is a tale of promise, kinship, and discovery at the Fall of Western Civilization. Global climate change has brought about the Armageddon people always feared: the end of the world they knew would be painful, but trusted and hoped would be quick. The end of the world is proving a long, drawn out, dismal affair. The American Southwest is becoming uninhabitable. Partners Lee and Willa, Fire and Air, set out for the North and a new life. They decide to go the old-fashioned, low-tech way; on foot. Not because they are fearful or Luddite, but because they want to experience Mother Earth and those who inhabit Her; both as they were and as they are becoming. Willa and Lee set out hoping to find or found genuine, supportive, diverse community. All are welcome to join them provided they agree to only one limitation; that they harm none.

The first to join Lee and Willa's family of choice is a strange, fierce, nameless child. This excerpt is from early in the pilgrimage. Lee and Willa teach the child about the gift of Mercy.

Watch for Migration in 2017

Mercy

Terryl Warnock

We been walking across the desert northeast from Tuba City most of the summer. We ain't smelled or tasted nothing but crunchy sandy desert dust for so long we can't remember what nothing else tastes or smells like.

It was blistering hot every day when we first started out and we weren't never so happy as when the sun went down at night. You could tell summer was almost over now though because the sun wasn't so high in the sky in the daytime no more and it was cold at night. That big black sparkling sky we were so happy to see when it was so hot sucked the heat right off of that desert now and left us shivering under the wagon. We were stopping earlier, way before dark, so Lee could take the sides of the wagon down. They folded down like windows once you took them poles out of the brackets on top that were holding them up. They made a cool fort underneath, like me and my little brother used to make with a blanket over the coffee table. Them side boards on that wagon, they had windows and everything so we had us a nice little house underneath that wagon when the sides were down. We put the pads from on top of the storage boxes down on the ground in our little fort so we had a nice soft bed under there and now it was cold we would get all them blankets out and Lee and Willa would stack up like they did in the evening time. They stacked up like that even when it was hot; Lee would sit with his back against a wheel and Willa with her back against his chest and if that silly old hen was broody, Willa would even let her stack up with them too. Dottie would drop her wings and spread 'em out as far over Willa's lap as she could and just sit there and look around like she was sitting on them eggs, like she was trying to hatch Willa or something. Silly old bird.

I never cuddled like that before in my life. It wasn't just me, and it wasn't just my Dad and my Uncles being so mean like they were.

My people keep their respectful distance from one another. I remember my mother picking up my little brother and carrying him around bouncing him till he'd quit crying, but this was different. It was like Lee and Willa (and Dottie if she was broody) needed to touch each other, like they felt better doing it somehow. At first I'd just sit across from Lee and Willa and Dottie and watch them be sweet and all stacked up with each other at night before we went to sleep. Me and my puppy would sit across from them after we first started walking across the rez with them. My puppy would just sit beside me, hardly never taking his eyes off from me except to look over at Lee and Willa and that chicken sometimes. He would just lay there with his head down between his front feet watching me and thumping his tail on the ground like he did whenever I would look down at him, but then he would look over at Willa and Lee and Dottie sometimes, too, and it was like he got the idea. One night he curled up on my lap and pushed his nose under my hand. Every night after that while we were sitting around he'd get up in my lap and watch Lee and Willa, thumping his tail and I couldn't help it, it made me smile on the inside.

Then it got cold though and one night I was so cold I was shivering. I still didn't have nothing to wear but my mom's old blue t-shirt and her fancy shawl. Willa didn't say nothing, she just pulled the blanket aside they was curled up under and got up and put Dottie back in her cage and came back and settled up against Lee's chest. She opened her arms so I knew I could come and sit with my back against her if I wanted to, if I was cold. I got up and walked over and settled in with my back against her and she pulled the blanket back over us all and my puppy bounced over and curled up on my lap smiling with his whole self the way those dog people do. We were warm and cozy as we could be. From then on we'd stack up every night and eat our handful of sand-crunchy, dust-flavored pemmican and stare at our one candle. Willa said we had to have one candle at least for a little while every night, and we would stare at it and she would tell us a story.

At first I just stacked up with them to stay warm, but later on it started to feel different, stacked up with them people who took us in and shared their food with us and let us walk away from that awful smoldering stinky trailer outside of Tuba City with them. The stack became a safe place. I couldn't never remember feeling safe before, not really. I started to feel like no one would hurt me there, sitting on Willa's lap with my puppy sitting on top of me. I was a sandwich. I wasn't scared there. Willa would pet my head sometimes, or braid my long, thick black hair. She'd scratch the puppy's ears while she told her stories and my gut wouldn't feel so clenched up for a little while and I'd take these deep happy breaths and sigh 'em out and feel happy, really happy, like I never did at home in the trailer with my dad and uncles.

We'd been watching a way off bluff for days and days that had a fuzzy top on it. Lee couldn't see it very good through his binoculars it was so far away at first, but as we got closer to it he started to say how he thought that fuzz might be trees up on that bluff. None of us could remember how long ago since we saw a real, living tree and Willa got more and more excited about maybe seeing one as we got closer to the bluff. We scrabbled our way up the side of it at last one day, them poor burros pulling for all they were worth and all of us pushing the back of the wagon. All them trees up there were crunchy dead or almost dead. But Lee said he was tired of crawling under the wagon every night anyway and going to bed with the sun just because there wasn't nothing else to do and because we were cold and scared someone would see us. He wanted a fire. He wanted to stay up and sit around a fire and talk, he said, like civilized folk do. He wanted to be brave and warm.

I don't know nothing about civilized folk, everybody always told us we were ignorant savages. Even other Indian people told us that. Who knows, maybe they were right. I don't know nothing about that kind of stuff. I don't care.

Willa didn't say nothing about being civilized folk but her eyes said she was tired too and she thought it would be nice to stop early and rest a little and make a nice camp and have a fire, so we did. Willa could say a lot with her eyes like that.

We found a little bowl-like place up on top of that bluff. Lee said we could camp there and have our fire without people down below being able to see us, maybe, if there were any people down below. It was nice to set up in a different kind of place for once. The desert went on forever. All our camping spots looked the same. There wasn't usually no shade or nothing for the animals, and we hadn't found no streams or nothing for at least a week now. We were down to our last five gallon can of water and we had to be stingy with it. Everybody got some to drink, but nobody got enough and we didn't even wash our faces, much less our clothes or anything else. I figure we all probably smelled pretty bad but we couldn't smell each other so we didn't mind too much.

So we got in our nice little bowl-like place and Lee and Willa made up the bed under the wagon and I made up some shelter for the burros like I did every night by tying the big tarp off from front of the wagon for them. It was so heavy I couldn't hardly unroll it by myself, but that big waxy canvas would stretch out long enough that if I could find big enough rocks to hold the edge of it down all the way out at its end and brace it up halfway in the middle with the poles that came off the brackets on our fort, it made a nice place both burros could get in under and get some cover.

Well, my burro shelter would only stand up if the wind wasn't blowing too hard. If the wind was blowing that heavy old dang tarp flapped and knocked my poles over and pulled the edge out from under my rocks and then them burros would just be under there getting flapped and not being too happy about it neither. Lee would help me tie the tarp and hold it down if it was windy though. His big strong hands could pull that rope tight and he could pick up rocks that were big enough to really hold it down.

There wasn't no wind tonight though and my burro shelter was good and it was good for all of us to have some shade from them trees, pinons probably, even if they were dead. Them chickens always had a good spot between the burros and the wagon, so they were happy. Them burros and their tarp broke the wind from bothering them chickens and gave them shade, too, when there wasn't no dead trees.

Willa had been showing me how to notice all kinds of things about these animal people we were traveling with. They were our family too, she said, and they spoke to us just as plain as day if only we would listen to them. She was right, too, them animal people would tell you if they were happy or not. Them chickens made a nice soft cooing sound when they were happy. It was like "put, put, put," not like "GACK! GACK! GACK!" when they were scared or unhappy. That's how I knew my job was done right, when them chickens started their "put, put, putting," and after I had been traveling with these people for awhile, when them chickens and burros were happy then I was happy too.

Lee was getting the fire started and Willa was out getting some more wood. I gave the animals their small portions of water and got them some grass out of my basket. They were hungry and happy to see it. That bluff still had some grass growing on the top of it, so I had got two punched-down baskets full that day so them chickens were happy pecking away at it and them burros were happy crunching away at it. We were so happy up under them dead trees. Lee was saying maybe we could stay a day or two and rest up, enjoy ourselves and Willa had said we were going to celebrate our freedom with a nice, big bowl of pemmican that night. She had four bowls out like she always did and it wasn't the first time I thought how nice it was that my puppy counted for one of the family with her, even when it came to food and water. Me and my puppy, we were looking forward to our fire and our story and our nice, big bowl of sandy dust-flavored pemmican. I had got a couple of lizards for him that day, so my puppy wasn't starving or nothing, but it was like he knew it was a celebration and we were getting extra that night. He was excited. He kept bouncing around me and walking figure eights around my legs while I was putting them burro and chicken people to bed. I tripped over him twice, and had to pick up my grass again, but I didn't get mad. It made me laugh and he licked my face and said "buh, buh, buhbuhbuh" and wagged his tail till I thought his butt was going to fall off.

The little fire was going and me and my puppy were pulled to it like it was a magnet or something. You just can't hardly help yourself but look in a fire, same as you can't hardly help but look at a candle in the dark. Lee had got up and walked away from the fire to go get some more wood when we both looked up and saw Willa was walking back towards us real slow. She didn't have no wood in her arms neither. She was holding her hands open and up and close to her chest like she did when she was praying. When she got closer I could see there were tears streaming down her face. Lee musta seen them tears too because he walked back over to the fire quick so he got there the same time as her.

"Willa?" he said, "What's wrong, love?

"Oh, Lee," she said. Her voice was so sad it was like a fist clenching around your heart. "We must have disturbed the nest when we took wood for the fire from that brush pile over there."

She opened up her hands and leaned down so I could see too. There was a little bitty baby squirrel lying along her finger like a person would lie down longways on a big log. His little legs were hanging down around the side of her finger and he was panting. "eep, eep, eep, eep," he would say with every breath. His whole self wasn't as long as Willa's finger and half of him was tail. He was so tiny. He had a silky gray back, I touched him, and his eyes were closed and he had a little pink square nose. We all stared. "eep, eep, eep, eep." In between each "eep" there was a tiny tiny little sucking sound, like "thk." He might have thought Willa was his mom or something and was trying to suck off her. She turned him over, gently and held him on his back in her palm and petted him with her finger. His little white belly was all shriveled up, like my puppy's was that first night out at the moenkopi, and something closed up, like, in the back of my throat. I had to clear my throat. He had little bitty miniature boy parts. "eep, thk, eep, thk, eep,thk, eep, thk,." he panted. He kept saying the same thing over and over, whether he was on his back or on his belly, making those sucking sounds with his mouth. He was so little. So weak. Willa turned him back over so he could lie on his belly on her finger again.

"eep, thk, eep, thk, eep,thk, eep, thk,," He was calling for his mama. It was getting dark. It was getting cold.

"Should I go get some grass, Willa, and make him a bed?" I said, "He can have some of my pemmican, I don't mind. I'll make sure puppy leaves him alone too."

She looked at me with sad, sad, wet eyes, and the big guy waved his hand for me to come aside and talk with him where she couldn't hear. Willa just stood by the fire staring down into her hand. Every now and then she'd lift the little squirrel up to her face and blow on him, soft, like she did when she wanted to protect someone. She blew little spells like that at me and my puppy and Lee and the burros and the chickens and all the other people we met up with all the time on our way. She said they were like bubbles, those little spells, and she blew them like kisses. Soft, warm little bubbles of protection and friendship. A small kindness. A little blessing, she said. Sometimes I thought I could even see them, too. They were kinda pink and blue and swirly, like soap bubbles and they curled and twirled themselves around you, like a little puff of breeze that just barely tickles the hairs on the back of your neck, like, and you felt a little better when she blew one around you because you knew you were a little safer. Blessed. Loved.

Lee lowered his voice so just us two could hear. "He ain't gonna make it, kid. Not without his momma to feed him and protect him and keep him warm. He's too little and weak and I don't think he can eat pemmican anyway."

"Oh." The corners of my mouth turned down all on their own and I clenched my teeth. I swallowed hard and my chin went up a little. My little brother didn't make it because his momma wasn't there to feed him and protect him and keep him warm, neither.

"Do you understand?" he asked me.

I nodded.

"All right then." He leaned his face down close to me and his ice eyes bored deep down into me and made my heart hammer. I was breathing fast and shallow. I was scared, but I wasn't scared of him no more, I was just scared. "You remember we talked about mercy, right?"

I nodded.

"How it was sometimes hard to figure out who deserves it and what to do about it? "

I nodded.

"Well, this time it's not hard to decide who deserves it or what to do about it. None of us intended any harm to that poor little baby squirrel, but we tore his house apart and scared his momma off because we didn't know he was there. You know Willa, she would rather freeze to death out here than hurt that poor little guy. He didn't do anything wrong except get born in the wrong time and at the wrong place where we happened to stumble through and tear his whole world apart."

I nodded.

"He's the one who's going to pay for it, even if we didn't intend him harm. His momma's gone and she won't be coming back to get him because we're here. He's going to die. Tonight. The only question is whether it's going to be quick and merciful or slow and painful, from cold and hunger. You know the right thing to do?"

I nodded.

"Can you do it?"

I nodded.

"You sure?" He looked deep into my eyes again.

I nodded.

"All right then. I'm going to take Willa for a walk, and you take care of it. You know Willa would want you to send him on his way with a prayer."

I swallowed and nodded and we both walked back over to the fire. Lee put his arm around her shoulders and said "Come, love."

"eep, thk, eep, thk . .. eep, thk,"

I reached up and carefully took the tiny squirrel from her hand as he gently led her away.

It was like the poor little thing was getting a little weaker with every 'eep.' Lee and Willa walked out of the firelight, slowly. Lee looked back over his shoulder and lifted his chin, once, ever so slightly in my direction. My heart was pounding and there was a quivery feeling down in my gut. My puppy was standing next to me ears up and all at attention, smiling with his tongue hanging out and wagging his tail thinking this was just another lizard and he was about to get a treat. "No," I told him, "he isn't for you. This is different. He's family and we got to do right by him." My voice cracked a little when I was telling him that. I got out my knife first, but then I put it away. I don't know why. I put the sweet little eeping squirrel on a warm rock by the fire for a second or two and watched the flickering light play over his tight shut eyes. They were like teeny tiny little gray marbles.

"eep,... eep,... eep ... eep,"

Now that Willa was gone he didn't make that little sucking noise no more. He kept calling for his momma that couldn't possibly get here in time. I petted his silky heaving little gray back one more time and whispered to him "Goodbye little guy, I hope you get a better life next time. If you see my little brother over there on the Other side, tell him I said I love him and I miss him." And I picked up a rock and smashed it down on him, hard. My eyes were hot and wet, too, but I sucked it up. Willa had been telling me she figured I was Element of Fire, and that meant I would probably be a warrior and a judge someday and that wasn't no job for no coward like her. She was Element of Air, she said, and although she sure didn't seem like no coward to me, her feelings did get hurt real easy. Her heart was real soft. I had to be brave for her and for the little squirrel.

I took the rock away and picked up the small, limp body in my hands for a few seconds. It was still warm but the pathetic 'eeping' had stopped with the heaving of his little sides. Somehow it was like a great big sad silence settled down around the whole world without that 'eeping' even with the crackling of the fire and the 'put, put, putting' of them chickens and the panting of my puppy and the crunching and shuffling of them burros and all the other noises around.

I held him in my hand and blew on him. Not soft, like Willa when she's blowing them spell bubble kisses, but harder, like when you blow on a spark to try and get it to catch fire. I blew on him a few times till I thought I saw a little bit of red light blowing toward the fire, like an ember trying to light, and then I put his little bitty squashed body in the fire and prayed for the fire to make him into something new and wonderful right away. I put a piece of wood over him because I didn't want to watch him burn. Somehow I had come to love him in just the few minutes I knew him. He was my friend. He was my Teacher. He changed me. He taught me it didn't always have to be hateful and awful and scary like it was with my dad, but that death could be a gift to someone so they didn't have to suffer, so they didn't have to die alone and cold and hungry, eeping for a momma that wasn't never going to come. It was a hard gift to give, though. I felt happy for the little squirrel, but sad for me. I swallowed hard.

I was proud I had the guts to do it.

Me and my puppy were sitting by the fire, staring into it when Lee and Willa got back. We were all missing the magic of the tiny squirrel that had passed through our lives so powerfully but for such a short time. He made me know a lot of things I didn't know before. When I looked up into Willa's eyes she saw it. She knelt down and took my cheek in her hand and looked deep into my eyes and leaned forward and kissed my forehead and said "Thank you,

Beloved, I'm not strong enough to give kindnesses like that. I'm very grateful you are brave enough, and I'm more happy than I can tell you that the Great Goddess brought you . . . you and your puppy, of course . . . " she smiled and scratched the puppy's ears, "into our family and into our hearts."

A tear ran down my cheek. I scrubbed it away. Maybe she is a witch, I told myself, but she's my witch. She's my family now and she ain't no coward, and I love her, and in some ways she's just as weak and vulnerable as that poor little bitty squirrel and if anyone ever tries to hurt her, I swear I'll kill 'em. I'll give 'em justice, like Lee was saying.

Willa turned away to put some pemmican in the bowls and we were quiet as we ate our dinner sitting around our fire. I wondered if the big guy felt civilized. I felt sad for Willa. Her eyes were far, far away as she stared into the flames. It was like she was looking into the Other World, hoping to see her tiny little squirrel friend again. "It was quick, Willa," I finally said, "and merciful. I asked forgiveness from him and his momma and all the squirrel people. I told 'em we didn't mean 'em no harm, and I put him in the fire, after, and prayed he didn't suffer none and that he gets a better lifetime next time."

She got up and came and put her arms around me and laid her cheek on top of my head for a little bit and said, "Then so he surely shall," and as she turned away I heard her whisper "as above, so below." She went to the shoulder bag she carried all the time and pulled out a sage wand. She put the end of it in the fire for a minute and then held it up to my face. I blew on it to get it going good, hard, like I did on the body of the little squirrel, and when it was glowing brightly and smoking good, Willa waved it all around me and I washed off in the smoke.

She stubbed the sage out on the very same rock I had used for mercy for the little squirrel, and turned to start putting stuff away. Lee squeezed my shoulder and looked me in the eye and nodded and said, "Good job, kid."

My heart swelled up so big I thought it might spill out my eyes.

After the bowls and spoons were cleaned, first by the puppy's tongue and then by a good scrubbing with some crunchy desert sand, Lee went back over to the fire but instead of sitting down on top of his box like I figured he would, he sat down on the ground with his back propped up against it. We stacked up against him like we did and as our fire died down Willa told us stories about how the squirrel people used to jump off of this big pine tree that was right next to her house in the woods and run back and forth across her roof and make her smile all the time with their little feet going skitter skitter skitter over her head and making her cat stare at the ceiling.

The Little Tomato

A story for younger children, The Little Tomato, by Katarina Karjala, describes the world of a pear tree and a tomato plant.

Carly, a shy and polite tomato plant, hopes to forge a friendship with a grumpy pear tree. The pear tree, frustrated with its inability to produce fruit, is plagued by character flaws. Ralf, a rat, searches for fruit to eat and becomes friends with the diplomatic Carly.

Through this story children will learn about plant pollination, and fruit-bearing differences between pear trees and tomato plants. *The Little Tomato* also teaches those who are "different" to overcome hostility and utilize forgiveness to build true friendships. Watch for *The Little Tomato* in 2016.

Carly and the Grumpy Pear Tree

Katarina Karjala

A pear tree was stretching her branches on the narrow, sunny side of the big house. Her dark brown trunk was short. Light green leaves just began to bud from her thin branches. There was not another tree to accompany her. In the early spring, the mother of the house brought a tiny plant in a bulky pot and placed it in an empty spot. The plant was very small, so she was pleased to see a tree not too far from her.

"Who are you?" the tree asked the plant with a harsh voice. Not waiting for an answer, she continued, "I need another pear tree here, not a seedling growing in a funny pot!"

"My name is Carly, I am a tomato plant." She moved her dark green leaves growing from a weak stem to greet the pear tree. "What is your name?" asked Carly.

"My family name is Anjou and I am a pear tree. I don't have a first name because I don't want one," the pear tree announced.

"My family name is Champion. I am Carly Champion." Carly said proudly. "Pleased to meet you. I hope we can be friends," said Carly.

"Not really," the rude answer came.

Carly was well-mannered. She just looked at the pear tree with respect, but also with disappointment. She didn't understand why the pear tree wanted to have another pear tree there but she was still very young and had to learn a lot. Carly wished they would be friends.

The next day, Carly held her branches up, hoping to make her companion smile.

"What are you doing? Exercising?" the pear tree asked.

"I am just pretending to be a pear tree." Carly said.

"Pretending doesn't count."

Carly decided to work hard to make the pear tree feel happy.

"Pear tree, maybe you should pull your roots out of the soil and walk to find another pear tree."

"Hmm, I have never tried that," said the pear tree. So the pear tree tightened her roots and attempted to pull them out of the dirt. The dirt moved little bit. Some hair-like roots came to the surface but that was all.

"It doesn't work. Trees can't walk," said the pear tree.

Then Carly thought she should try some magic

> "Abracadabra,
> Candelabra,
> Cobra and zebra,
> The pear tree will walk now!"

The pear tree examined her roots. Nothing had changed, so she was not happy.

The Voice on the Ground

The following night, the moon was sending thin light to the garden. Carly heard a squeaky voice coming from the dark ground.

"What is this? Who put this big pot in here?"

Something jumped into Carly's pot.

"Who are you?" asked Carly. "Oh, you scared me!"

"You must be new here. Let me introduce myself. My name is Ralf the Rat," the rat said bowing politely. "Who are you?"

"I am Carly, the tomato plant."

"I love to eat tomatoes!" exclaimed Ralf with excitement. Then he did a little dance, stamping his feet. After that the rat stood on his hind legs, stretched tall, and sniffed the plant.

Carly sensed his skinny body and smelled his breath. Ralf's whiskers scratched her leaves as he sniffed around. She almost felt his sharp teeth. "Go away Ralf!" she hollered with her strongest voice.

Carly was very scared, so she looked up at the pear tree hoping for help. The pear tree pretended she didn't hear anything because she wanted to have another pear tree next to her, not a tomato plant.

"I will go for now, but I will be back, to check if you have red and nicely ripened tomatoes," Ralf said, and he disappeared.

Soon the days and nights were warmer. Carly looked up and saw the pear tree was covered in something white. She was puzzled, so she asked: "Are you making snow?"

"I didn't hear. What did you say? Is that whispering the best you can do?" the pear tree grumbled. Carly shouted her question one more time.

"I am a tree, I can't make any snow. These are my flower petals," the pear tree said.

"Does it hurt to have flowers? Is that why you are so grumpy?" asked Carly. She didn't have any flowers yet so she couldn't know if growing flowers would hurt her.

"No, it doesn't hurt but I want to bear pears. In order to do it, I need to have another pear tree here, not you! Look at the stump over there! They cut the old pear tree down." Then pear tree explained that when the other old pear tree was there, bees flew from her flowers to the other tree's flowers and pollinated them both. Later, they both could produce pears.

"OK, I got it." Carly said. "Pear trees need to grow in pairs, two of them, to have fruit. I can pretend that I am a pear tree but it wouldn't help with the po, pol. What was that big word starting with the P?" Carly asked.

"That word is pollination! Stop talking nonsense, Shorty," said the pear tree.

The small Carly thought, 'My name is Carly, not Shorty. Just wait, one day I will be tall as well.' As much as she would like to have another tomato close by instead of the nasty pear tree, she was glad that tomatoes don't need to have another tomato plant close by to be pollinated to have tomatoes.

Sins of the Fathers

Leaving behind a cheating husband and a high-paying career in Los Angeles, Allison Masters trades it all in for an historic farmhouse on the coast of Maine. Her longing to become a professional artist drives her drastic change in life. Settling in to her new world, she begins seeing a ghostly figure beckoning her to the nearby woods.

Allie and her newly-adopted dog follow the mysterious figure and discover a body uncovered by recent rains. The body is found to be a murder victim from the Civil War era and the discovery attracts the attention of the State Anthropologist. Together, Allie and the Anthropologist find more bodies, evidence of a serial killer from the past.

As she researches victim and murderer, Allie is drawn into relationships with the State anthropologist, a local fisherman whose sister has been missing for over twenty years, and the son of a wealthy politician. The past begins to unravel and when more modern murder victims are found. The present begins to unravel when Allie finds herself being hunted by a living serial killer with ties to the past.

The sins of the fathers have been carried on by the sons and Allie has uncovered them. Allie races to tie the past and present together before she becomes the next victim in a long history of horror.

Chapter 1

Laurie Wilson Fatland

Allie was walking by the kitchen window when it stopped her in her tracks. It had to be a trick of the eye, or perhaps her fanciful imagination. A heavy mist, thick as cream, was swirling through the bare knuckled trees on the hillside. Suddenly it coalesced into the shape of woman; a woman in a long, flowing dress. As she turned to look, it faded back into the darkness of the woods.

"What did they call that in art school? Oh yes, *trompe l'oeil.* Fool the eye. When something looks real, but isn't. Well, I'm certainly the fool today." Allie muttered to herself. "This weather must be getting to me." It was true; the dreary weather of coastal Maine was an immense change from the sunny climate of Los Angeles she had left only a month ago.

Allison shook her head and smiled. The major upheavals in her life over the last six months were sure to cause her some issues; she could forgive herself for an overly sensitive imagining.

The divorce was the beginning of it all. No, really it all began when she decided to leave her high paying job as an advertising executive and pursue her dream of being a professional artist. Mark had not been able to handle it.

It would have meant lowering their standard of living, giving up the house in the Hollywood Hills and moving to something less opulent. Mark's salary would have to cover everything until her art began to pay for itself. Allison had talent, she knew that, and she had a solid marketing plan. She expected her paintings to be earning her a living in just a few years. But it would never be at the same level they were used to. I was a fool, thought Allison, I thought Mark loved me enough to help me fulfill my dreams.

Mark had used all his lawyerly skills to talk her out of it, but Allie felt the pull of art so strongly she began hating her job. Creating silly ad campaigns to sell over-priced merchandise to gullible consumers was the absolute opposite of everything she had gone to school for. It had nothing to do with what she believed herself capable of accomplishing. It was a waste of time and skill.

The landscapes she had been able to produce on weekends or vacation sold quickly. She found a small gallery in Santa Monica that took them whenever she had a new one. But the paintings were rare and becoming rarer. She had no time and no energy left after a full week of work. Allie knew she needed to improve, but that would only come with time and practice. She was 38, she had no children, now was the time.

Mark had fought her every step of the way. Finally he had given the ultimatum. "You choose", he demanded, staring into her eyes. "It's either me or the art." She chose art.

The divorce was surprisingly painless. Which, I suppose, says a lot about our 12 year relationship, Allie thought wryly. She took some satisfaction in knowing Mark lost the house in the hills anyway, and it was the sale of the house that gave her the money to buy this pretty little farmhouse in Maine.

She also discovered during the divorce proceedings that Mark had been having an affair with a colleague at his office during the last year or so. That made it even easier to push for a quick, uncontested divorce. No looking back. Allie was focused on her drastic lifestyle change and her art.

When she started searching for a place to start her life over, she knew it had to be near the ocean. It had to be picturesque, a place that stirred her soul and inspired her to paint. It had to be far away from Los Angeles and cheap enough that she could buy a little place to call her own. After months of searching she found White Acre Farm on the coast of Maine. It was as far as you could get from L.A., both physically and culturally, and it was surrounded by endless coves and villages that made her eager to pull out a canvas and paint.

The farmhouse had a history. It was built in the 1830s and had been home to some of the famous Whittaker family until the early 1900s when it was sold to a series of farmers. Eventually the land and the orchards that surrounded it were sold off and now it stood on one acre of old apple orchard, a weathered barn standing solidly behind the house. A pretty meadow opened up before it giving a view of the hillside that bordered a state park. When she first looked at the property it was late winter. She walked among the bare apple trees, their twisted limbs reaching accusingly to the pale sky as if pleading for a break in the cold, and she felt a sense of the past that called to her. She wanted to a part of that continuity.

The state park was land donated by the Whittaker family that stretched along the coast, preserving some of the most beautiful coves and forest. That was the real appeal of this house; she could smell the ocean and on stormy days hear the waves crashing onshore. The mile and half walk to the sea was a joy, winding through thick woods and coming out on a cliff overlooking a rock strewn cove below. She walked it almost every day, sometimes armed with a camera and sometimes with her easel and paints.

The closest town was Harborview, well-known because of the Whittaker family mansion that stood on the coast. The Whittakers had produced a long line of Senators and amassed a fortune. They were one of America's wealthiest families, well-known for their good looks, power and the jet-setting antics of the younger members. It was the little town's claim to fame. Allie loved Harborview; it had a collection of small restaurants and pretty shops that made her trips there interesting. The clapboard and stone buildings built around the harbor were so different from anything she had ever known. Windswept gardens and sturdy houses were reflections of the hardy people who built them. Every building carried its own history, a collection of individuals with their own story to tell. Allie wished she could get to know them all.

Today, Allie had decided to forego her usual walk to the cove. There were some repairs she needed to do to the house; a board on the wraparound porch was loose and she wanted to get the flowers planted she had bought in town a few days ago.

The weather wasn't great for doing anything, overcast skies and fog that swirled and thickened around the house. Still, she grabbed her hammer and a box of nails and went out to take care of the loose board. She pounded in a few of the nails until the board felt secure, but realized now she would have to touch up the paint. Maintenance was going to be a big part of her future with this old house. "They're going to get to know me pretty well at the hardware store," she sighed.

"Now for the flowers, at least they like this weather." She looked over her collection of hollyhocks, anemones and impatiens, all in pinks and purples and decided the layout she wanted in the flowerbed by the porch. "This is going to be lovely next to the white house with its dark green trim," she said to herself. Allie began to dig up the weeds and work the soil, getting it ready to plant. When she had set the hollyhocks, she began to get a little chilled from the fog and decided to go in for a cup of tea to warm up.

The house had been remodeled not long ago. Large windows in the living room looked out over the hill that marked the state park boundary and made the house bright and cheery on sunny days. The original small-paned windows in the kitchen and the French doors that led to the porch gave it character and charm. There were two small bedrooms on either side of the bathroom at the back of the house and stairs to a large loft she had turned into her studio. The honey-colored wooden floors were worn, but smooth, she loved walking barefoot on them and imagining all the others who walked on them before her in the long history of the house.

She came out onto the porch, steaming cup of tea in hand and sat down on the steps. Looking around, she imagined the porch when she finished her decorating. Adirondack chairs painted to match the green trim, a small dining table for al fresco meals and lots of potted flowers. She planned on putting a bird bath out front and feeders to attract the wildlife. She was eager to see what might be living in the woods around her.

As she sipped her tea, the fog lifted or started to lift . Tendrils of it clung to the apple trees near the house, Allie looked up to the hill again, thinking about the strange shape she saw. There! It happened again! This time, though, she was staring right at it. The fog drew together into the outline of a woman; it grew thicker until it was a definite figure, looking directly at her. It paused and then floated toward a thicket of trees and disappeared.

Allie sat shaking her head, and the hairs on the back of her neck stood up, sending chills down her back. What is wrong with me? Allie had never believed in ghosts, but this was strange, very strange. OK, there has to be some explanation, she thought. Maybe I have a neighbor who hikes around in a long white dress. Well, that's not very plausible, is it? It has to be this weather; it's just getting to me. Allie got up and went back in the house to build a fire and read for the rest of the afternoon. She was determined not to look at the hill again today.

Runners

What would you do if you knew you would be terminated when you reached the age of 50? Would you lie down and take it or would you run? Here is a tale of one man brave enough to run and the consequences of his actions.

Chapter 1

Dave Becker

It was my 50th birthday and I knew three things were going to happen.

I noticed a very large chocolate cake in the fridge in the garage.

I was having some good friends over for a BBQ.

And I had to say goodbye to my wife who I'd been married to for 12 years, and my two kids ages 7 and 9.

You see, when you turn 50 you are slated for termination. It was an ongoing understanding that after 50 years old, you'd lived your life, you had worked for 35 years, plus or minus, and health issues were starting to creep up on you. You voluntarily terminated your life which kept society young and healthy.

You had a yearly mandatory check-up. Those who were terminally ill, used crutches, walkers, and wheelchairs were automatically terminated regardless of age. They understood they weren't useful to society anymore.

I would be a fugitive from termination and be called a "runner."

My best friend, and a runner, Zeb, was coming. He'd been a runner for about 15 years. Runners were hard to catch and always carried weapons. Police wouldn't usually approach them because runners would just as soon shoot you than be caught and terminated.

But Zeb had been doing this for a long time. He was smart, could live off the land, and had a mechanics degree in engineering. I trusted him. But then, I had to.

I thought I had everything I needed packed in a duffel bag. I went over my choices again with Zeb.

It was getting dark, the guests had left. Zeb was anxious to get going. I said good bye to my wife and kids and reassured my wife I would be alright, and I'd get word to her, about when we could get together in the near future.

Tears were running down all of our faces as we pulled away from the house. I asked Zeb where we were going. He said, "Sedona." I thought that would be great: no snow, not too far from my wife, and vortexes to play with my mind.

The ride down the hill from Flagstaff to Sedona was interesting. I hadn't been down Hwy. 17 for quite some time, but you couldn't speed (40 miles per hour is the max) because the state has abandoned vehicles straddling the lanes randomly on all major highways to prevent speeding and it made chasing suspicious vehicles easy.

Our vehicle was state of the art. Zeb's father left him a Nissan Z and when the drivetrain got tired, he swapped it out for a Tesla drivetrain. It was fast, quiet, used no fuel, had about a 300 mile range, used no lights because the windshield was infrared and you could see about a quarter mile in the dark. It could go about 160 mph flat out. Our motto was, 'Run silent, run deep.' No one could catch us, no one could see us, and no one could hear us. It was a brilliant piece of engineering.

We did see a couple of cops, but they had no idea we are in the area.

So 17 South was a breeze. I79 North had less traffic than that, and 89-A through Sedona was uneventful. The ride through the canyon was dark, lonely, and very bumpy, but the four mile trip went by like a flash.

We came up to a gate that ran from Campus Way to Canyon Wall and was chained shut and had a truck blocking the road. Zeb gave me the combination to the gate and showed me where the keys to the truck were hidden.

We made our way in, locked the gate, and put the truck back across the road.

It was a pleasant drive in; well landscaped, but overgrown. I looked at Zeb with a surprised look on my face realizing where we were. On an abandoned golf course...and no country club! I could make out homes, casitas, a club house, private range, ponds and high cliffs on both sides of the canyon.

We drove, climbing gradually up the canyon until we stopped at a rather large house at the end of the road overlooking the whole canyon.

I got out of the car, amazed at the silhouettes of the mountains against the partially moonlit sky, and the number of stars in the sky, staring down at us.

Chapter 2

Dave Becker

I woke up to the sound of dishes rattling and the smell of coffee. I looked around my room and noticed 10' ceilings, 8' doors, heavy drapes covering the windows, travertine floors, heavy marble topped furniture, wrought iron accents, and my four poster bed.

I made my way down the hall and was pleasantly surprised that the rest of the house was decorated the same way. It opened up to a large family room, dining room, and kitchen.

I saw Zeb take pancakes from the grill and put them on a large platter in the oven to keep them warm. We exchanged morning greetings and sat down to pancakes and coffee.

I asked him, "Why so many pancakes?" He said that the brains and the brawn of the community were coming over to meet me, discuss my future here, and explain the everyday lifestyle. It sounded perfect because I had questions and concerns, too.

I met with security who explained the security was tight there and that people were well armed and always on duty, monitoring the whole property.

There was a building and maintenance department who made repairs of houses and grounds and did maintenance on the property and golf course.

There was a medical team (who, I found out, I was to be a part of) who needed a surgical technician to assist our doctor and nurses who weren't as familiar with new techniques as I was.

There were work groups that did whatever came up with no qualms about the work, and always showed up. You were on for five days and off for 20.

I met with some more departments and came away with the feeling that this was a well-equipped, well organized, tightly-knit group who had a large sense of pride and a deeper sense of survival and community. Heaven forbid someone try to take us down.

Zeb cut in, figured I'd heard enough and gave me a binder with all of the rules and regulations. He also handed me a watch which was unique to the community. It glowed green when everything was all right. It glowed red when we had to head to the hills and mesas above the property to escape an eminent threat for an extended amount of time. It could also transmit and show a surveillance video onto a flat surface which monitored any current situation in real time.

Zeb nodded his approval, and made a small cutting motion across his throat, to wrap it up. I thanked everyone and assured them that I would become a valuable citizen of the country club, and that the pancakes were plentiful and the coffee was hot.

Forever Love Rescue

A young woman finds she has the gift of healing to offer animals and establishes an animal rescue she calls Forever Love Rescue. Abused as a child, she is wary of people but through working with abandoned and injured animals, finds unexpected healing and love for herself.

Chapter 5

Keli Becker

The drive to the restaurant was uneventful. Char was a careful driver and gave other drivers a wide berth. She talked to Rolo to pass the time.

They arrived safely, and even though she was prompt and it was early in the evening, parking was hard to find. The parking lot was situated on a steep incline and standard shift transmissions were a disadvantage. Char was good at shifting, though, and was able to situate the Bug with little difficulty.

She found a space about 50 feet away from the door to the restaurant. She had driven barefoot as she was not used to driving in 2 inch heels, and the sandals made the walk downhill from the car to the entrance tricky. Char was a little out of breath when she got to the hostess podium.

"I'm meeting someone here at seven. He probably isn't here yet so can I reserve a table for two?"

The hostess, a cute young thing, glanced at her seating chart. "Might you be meeting Gavin?"

"Yes." Char was surprised. "Is he here?"

"Yes, he is. He told us to expect you. I'll take you to his table."

There goes my battle plan. A cup of tea had factored heavily in that plan. Char's nerves, which had begun to settle, started their dance again.

As she and the hostess drew close to Gavin's table, a sinuous full-figured redhead sitting at Gavin's table noted their approach. She wore a sprayed on full length red dress that accentuated her amazing body. She stood, bent over and gave Gavin a full-lipped kiss that went on much too long. When she straightened up, the redhead looked at Char with a mean, self-satisfied smile. "A little crowded in here tonight, isn't it?" she smirked.

Char stared at her. What had she interrupted? Who was she? Char almost turned to leave. She felt like a fool. "Don't let me drive you away." Char threw Gavin a stricken look. "You were here first. I'll go," she said to the redhead.

Char turned and started to walk away. Her cheeks burned. The hell with Gavin! It seemed she would be hurt again.

Gavin caught up with her and gently took her arm. "Please don't go. That is my ex-wife, Liz. She can make trouble anywhere she goes. She especially likes to make trouble for me."

Char was confused about her feelings. She still wanted to get to know Gavin better. She wanted to have a first date, if that was what this was although it looked pretty shaky right now. She had felt so good at the park when she first met him.

And she was hungry! She hadn't had anything since the donuts Gretta had brought that morning.

"Will she be joining us?" Char shot Liz a scathing look.

"No, she's leaving right now." Gavin turned his back on the woman and escorted Char to the table. The redhead watched them with a nasty gleam in her eyes. She turned and sashayed toward the restaurant's front door.

Gavin held the chair out next to him for Char. She pulled the chair across from him for herself.

"I took the liberty of ordering a bottle of wine. I hope you like it, or we can get something you would enjoy more." Gavin now seemed more nervous than Char.

"I just want a cup of tea. I don't drink alcohol." Her upbringing made her avoid the stuff. She remembered all too clearly the drunken rages her parents got into. The rages usually ended in either her mother or herself getting beaten.

This sure wasn't going the way she had imagined. No one had ever mentioned that he was married before. She felt like crying. It's silly, she thought. I hardly even know him. Why should I feel hurt? What did I expect? Instant love and undying devotion? Well, yes, especially the way she felt at the park when they met. I could have sworn he felt something too. Maybe I read too much into the whole thing.

Char took a deep breath and looked at Gavin. "Maybe I should go. I didn't know it was going to be a double date." She shook her head angrily to get rid of the tears that threatened. "Then you can work out your issues with Liz."

Gavin reached for Char's hand. She jerked it back.

"Let me explain, please. I'm so very sorry about this. I had no idea she would come here. My soon-to-be-unemployed assistant told her where I was going to be tonight. Liz thought she would 'surprise' me. She had to pick now as the perfect time to tell me she's taking me to court to sue me for a larger portion of my ranch's profits." He took a gulp of wine. He motioned toward the bottle. "Sure you wouldn't like some?"

"No, thank you." Char didn't know Gavin well enough yet to share her background with him. Maybe she never would.

"Look, I'm truly sorry. Can we please start over?" He seemed sincere, and really hopeful. "I want to get to know you. We keep seeing each other at the feed store and around town, but never say more to each other than 'Good morning' or 'Good afternoon' or whatever, but today was different."

Char considered this. She tentatively held her right hand out. "Hello, I'm Charlotte Moore. I'm owner and manager of Forever Love Rescue. Marshal is a wonderful dog. You two should get along really well together." She knew she sounded rather prim and proper but it was a start. "Are you expecting anyone else, maybe Wife #2 to show up?" Gavin laughed. He has a really nice laugh, Char thought against her will. He took her hand.

The sparks were still there!

Char gasped. A small smile started on her face. She hadn't expected any kind of feeling to be left after Liz's attack.

"I've ordered an appetizer, antipasto. I hope you like it." The server, a clean cut young man brought three different kinds of bruschetta, a roasted eggplant and focaccia dish, and marinated vegetables.

"It looks wonderful. If I eat too much of that I won't be able to eat dinner," observed Char.

"We can make a meal out of antipasto and a bowl of minestrone soup. If you want an Italian dinner, you can have that, too. Whatever you don't eat you can take home in a doggie bag. Enjoy yourself. I know we got off to a rough start tonight but can we leave that incident behind us where it belongs?"

"Ok." Char's small smile grew to light up her face. Maybe everything would turn out alright after all. She felt herself relaxing. She reached for a marinated carrot. It was delicious. And that was just the start. She tried little of everything and was not disappointed. "The bruschetta is absolutely fabulous." Char's appetite took over. "Maybe a cup of minestrone would top this off perfectly. That's all I would need."

She and Gavin shared a little bit of themselves with each other. Gavin's passion for his quarter horses was obvious. "I ride them myself. I don't just breed them to sell although I could with the bloodlines I've combined. I have a professional trainer working with the young ones, to get them started. I don't have the time to do it with all the colts and fillies I've got. But I know enough to take them through show-ready training. They're in high demand for show and pleasure riding."

"They sound fabulous. Are they in any publications I could get my hands on?"

"I'd love to show them to you some time. We can go riding. Do you ride? When's the next time you have free?"

Oh yikes! What do I do now? Do not panic! Too late. "I...I...I'm not sure. I have to check my schedule. And I've never ridden a horse." Great, let's stammer a little. No nerves here.

"That's ok. I can show you enough to go for a short trail ride if you like. I know you must have a lot to do around the Rescue since you're owner and manager. That must take up most of your days."

Safer ground. "Yes and it's how I met Rolo, my three legged Heeler. But don't tell him he only has three legs. He doesn't know it and doesn't act like it."

"How did you two get together?" Gavin asked. He really sounded interested.

"He was beaten and abandoned. A good-hearted restaurant owner heard cries coming from one of his dumpsters and checked it out. He called us. We were able to save him."

"Is that where your passion for saving abused animals comes from?"

"I felt that way before Rolo came to us. I have been on a campaign since I was a kid."

"How were you able to start the Rescue?"

Oh boy, too close right now! "Through a lucky accident, you could say." That her parents had actually left her an insurance policy was miraculous in itself. She could always tell him the whole story at a later time if things worked out. She just wouldn't let herself go so far as to tell him that out of something as toxic as her relationship with her parents, something good like the Rescue had come about. The accident that had taken her mother and father resulted in her own freedom from abuse.

"I've got to stop eating. This soup has topped it off for me right now."

"Whatever you say. Maybe save a spot to share a dessert with me? They're just as good as everything else. The next time we come here, we'll have one of their main courses."

The next time? Is he already planning for the next time? Wow! Is this too fast? Maybe too fast for her. Char's emotions were in turmoil. Sonya would know how to handle this kind of thing, but Char couldn't call Sonya right now. Not in the middle of this soup. Char would wait, bide her time. Tomorrow is another day.

"If I finish this soup, I won't have room to breathe." Char was pleasantly full. Time to visit the ladies' room. "Please excuse me, I'll be right back."

Gavin jumped up to pull out her chair, startling her. She wasn't used to this. She patted his hand. "I'll be right back. I'll even leave my purse here to prove it."

He laughed. "My gentlemanly skills are just a little rusty, sorry."

"No problem. I'm just not used to anyone pulling my chair out for me, and I work with a bunch of men."

She walked off in the direction of the hostess podium. The hostess pointed her in the direction of the restroom. It led past the bar area.

Char thanked her and turned to go. And stopped dead.

Liz was sitting at the bar. She didn't lack for company. Four men surrounded her. She leaned back slightly on the bar, thrusting her admirably shapely bosom out. She had a drink in her hand and one waiting for her on the bar. Char noticed that Liz also had a pretty good view of the table where Char and Gavin sat.

Suddenly, Liz reminded Char of Jessica Rabbit. That thought made Char giggle. Liz frowned. That wasn't the effect she was aiming for. Char gazed at Liz a moment. She felt sorry for the woman who seemed to be trying so hard to rattle her.

Then Char, with a small smile on her face, continued on to the ladies' room.

In the restroom mirror, Char noticed that her cheeks were becomingly pink and her eyes sparkled. The clothes that Sonya had picked out for her showed her figure off to good advantage. Bring it on, Liz.

She laughed at herself. She looked good. And that was good enough.

Chapter 6

Keli Becker

As Charlotte walked back to the table, she exchanged dirty looks with Liz, who was still leaning against the bar with her posse. The thought of a once popular cartoon character with a voluptuous figure, red hair, and painted-on scarlet dress threatened uninhibited laughter from Char. It was only the strictest of control that kept her from giggling out loud. It kind of ruined the disdainful look she aimed at Liz. The man with Liz leered at Char, who suddenly felt like she needed a good hot shower.

Tall and slender, the man had long, dark slicked-back hair that just touched the bottom of his shirt collar in back. He was good looking in a sleazy kind of way. Not my type thought Char. Mr. Sleaze had three big muscular men surrounding him and Liz. They each looked like they could each bench-press an elephant.

Char wondered if Gavin was aware that Liz was here with 'friends,' that she hadn't left at all. Char had felt she was being watched while sitting at the table with Gavin. Maybe it had been Liz, who had a front row seat at the big ornate bar.

Char picked up her pace. Should she mention the little congregation at the bar to Gavin? She decided not to. This was none of her business. Why get involved with Liz's vendetta? Besides, Char had no relationship other than business with Gavin. Yet.

Char arrived at the table. Gavin stood up and moved to pull out the chair across from him, the chair Char had been sitting on. Char smiled at him and went to the chair next to him. He hurriedly pulled that chair out for her. She sat and settled herself. Gavin seated himself, looking pleased. They gazed at each other. Char's core was getting warm, parts of her quivering. She sensed her feelings from the park that afternoon returning.

"So, how did you get started rescuing abused animals?" Gavin asked.

"I'd been hearing about dog fighting in the area since I moved here. My staff goes out to pick up the victims, like my Rolo. The poor animals are more than half dead when they are discarded after the fights, like so much garbage, but in some of them the spark of life is so strong that, with the care they get from us, they can survive and become the most loving of rescued companions. We do all we can to get all of our critters good homes. We have a pretty good turn-over."

Gavin was captivated. Char's passion clearly showed on her face. She glowed.

"When they come in, we try to save the dogs that are used to fight and have been cast-off for whatever reasons the dogfight people have. It may be that the animals don't fight the way they are supposed to; or they're too old to fight or breed. Or they've been used as bait for the fighters and are at the end of their lives. Usually they fight Pit Bulls but other breeds are used too. Those people will fight just about any species that will fight."

"Can the Pit Bulls be turned into pets?" Gavin was interested.

"Most can be, they're really good dogs. They were originally bred for bull-baiting in Britain. That so-called 'sport' was banned in 1836. Then attention was turned to the show ring. One breed was standardized into several. Pit Bulls were developed in Staffordshire, England. As the breed was introduced to America, it became known as the American Staffordshire Terrier. It's a larger heavier dog, and a different breed than the Staffordshire Bull Terrier in England.

"They are athletic, intelligent, versatile dogs. They were used in World War II for a variety of jobs. As family pets, they are affectionate, social and protective of their people. They can be fantastic in a family that will take the time to get to know them. They do need serious training and socialization to start at an early stage in their lives. Whew!" Char stopped to breathe and take a drink of water.

"Wow, you are really up on these dogs." Gavin was impressed. "Would you ever consider one of them as an addition to your life?"

Char considered. "Yes, I probably would. I think they are great dogs and have been misused for sport and money by unscrupulous and cruel humans. Plain old greed. THEY should be treated the same way they treat their dogs!" Char realized that her voice had increased in volume. She blushed and looked down.

Gavin reached for her hand and this time she didn't pull away.

"Don't be embarrassed by your passionate beliefs. They are what makes you, you." And totally fascinating, he thought. "It's very admirable that someone is standing up for those dogs."

Char felt the warmth of his hand holding hers. The tingling in her stomach and adrenalin-like feeling were giving her a rush. She felt a little bit dizzy.

"Sorry, I didn't mean to get so worked up but I'll fight against animal abuse any way I can. The Rescue is trying to help the other shelters become 'no-kill facilities.' We've helped change two shelters already."

She reached for her water glass and raised it to her mouth. She looked at Gavin and saw his attentive face looking at her change to one of alarm as he looked past her.

Char turned to see what was going on and wasn't really surprised to see Liz gazing at them with haughty distain. Her entourage surrounded her. Mr. Sleaze stood closest to her, protectively. Char giggled.

Gavin glanced at Char in surprise. Char shared her observation that they looked like a boy band with a guest female singer with him in a whisper that must have carried to Liz.

Liz frowned at Gavin's hearty laugh. She whirled to make a dramatic exit, long red hair flying, and ran smack into a wall of elephant-bench pressing boy band thugs. Sort of ruined the effect she was going for.

Liz threw a furious look at Char and Gavin, then at Mr. Sleaze and pushed her way between the bodyguards who made up the wall.

Mr. Sleaze glared at Char, then Gavin, turned, gathered his minions and followed Liz out the door.

"I don't think we've made any friends tonight, do you?" said Char, still grinning.

"I thought Liz left," remarked Gavin. The humor had departed his face. He withdrew his hand from Char's.

"Is anything wrong?" Char felt the change in Gavin as well as saw it. It was like a splash of cold water in the face. "I saw them at the bar when I went to the ladies' room, but didn't think anything about it. Should I have told you? I didn't say anything because it's really none of my business." Char felt herself withdrawing. Was the evening, which had been so special, now a mistake?

"No, no, don't worry about it," reassured Gavin. "Liz is hanging around with some unsavory characters and it worries me. It's nothing you should be concerned with."

I guess this date is a go nowhere affair. If he was interested in taking this any further, it would concern me. Char's eyes stung and the restaurant appeared in teary prisms. I will not cry dammit! She used the cloth napkin to carefully dab her eyes. She would not ruin the makeup Sonya had so painstakingly applied. Char determined to walk out with her dignity and eyeliner intact.

"I think it's time for me to go home. Rolo is waiting for me in the Bug and I'm tired. It's been a very long day." Char realized, with those words that she was exhausted. Enough was enough.

"Would you like dessert?" Gavin didn't sound very enthused.

If only he sounded like he really wanted to spend just a little more time with me, rescue what was left of our evening.

But no, Liz had won. Liz was a force; one Char didn't feel like butting heads with. Gavin was obviously still involved with her. Char did not want to intrude.

"No, thanks. Here's money for half the bill." She got up from the table and turned to go.

"Hey, wait, please." Gavin stood up. "Can we get together again? I'd love to see you as soon as you can make time. This was not how I imagined the evening would go. We won't be interrupted next time, I promise." He genuinely looked sorry.

"Maybe, we'll see." Probably not. Char didn't plan on getting burned a second time. I guess my 'glimmer' doesn't work for me. Tears threatened again. Oh, no, he is so not worth it. But I thought he might be.

Char strode to the door of the restaurant without a backward glance. Gavin hurried after her.

"Wait Char. Please give me a second chance."

Char stopped. Her thoughts were going in circles.

"I don't want to go on another 'double date'. We were supposed to get to know each other tonight, not introduce me to your ex-wife and her boy band. They look like Mafia rejects."

"I'll explain everything to you, just not tonight. I have to find out about some things and I'll fill you in next time. If you'll give me a next time." Gavin looked desperate. His denim-blue eyes pleaded with her. She gazed coolly back at him. "We'll see. I'll let you know when you pick Marshal up. He should be ready to go home Wednesday."

"Okay." Gavin was still anxious. He leaned in to hug her (he better not expect a kiss!) and she backed up. She held her hand out for a formal shake.

"Good night, Gavin." With that, she headed uphill to her car and the only male in her life she trusted.

Rolo was ecstatic to see her. She felt the same way about him. It was nice to have somebody who loved her completely.

GRATITUDE LIST

It Takes A Village

And finally, we've saved the best for last. The writing and production of this anthology has been like dropping a stone in the middle of a still pool. The *From Spark To Fire* project has rippled outward from the Sacred Circle Writers to involve and encompass the lives and creative work of many people. This is but a partial list of them.

First, this book would never have seen the light of day without Moonlit Press's computer guru, Al Brown. His tireless coaching, unfailing support, and kind-spirited willingness to correct the digital errors of writer, editor, artist, photographer, and publisher alike cannot be overemphasized in the successful culmination of this project. The quality of this volume is due entirely to his diligence and expertise, and any mistakes remaining in it belong entirely to the writer, editor, artist, photographer or publisher, as the case may be.

Al is a hacker in the truest and best sense of the word. He is a person who is willing to bring his prodigious computer skills and expertise to bear to better his community whether that community is a small one like the Sacred Circle Writers, or the larger community of computer users. 'Hacker' is a much perjured term in contemporary parlance, but hackers like Al in fact work to free their communities, large and small, from corporate tyranny.

The Sacred Circle Writers as a whole wishes to express their gratitude to Dave Becker, Keli's husband, for his kind and fearless guidance, for his indefatigable sense of humor, and for all his great ideas. He left us, unexpectedly, in the middle of this project, and we miss him dearly.

The Sacred Circle Writers as a whole would also like to offer heartfelt gratitude to John, Laurie and Bernie Fatland. The book you hold in your hands is as beautiful as it is because of this extraordinarily gifted and generous family: John's incredible photography graces this volume throughout, Laurie's painting lends *From Spark To Fire* its arresting and vivid cover, and we only look as good as we do in our portraits because Bernie made us beautiful on picture day.

As individuals, the Sacred Circle Writers would like to thank the following:

Katarina Karjala would like to thank Linda Radosevich, Barbara Wineka and Brenda Hershey for their help in writing *The Little Tomato,* and to Jane Johnson for her invaluable insight and feedback on the text from her perspective as an elementary school teacher. She would like to thank Keli and Marilyn for welcoming her into the Sacred Circle Writers and encouraging her to continue writing. She thanks Laurie Wilson Fatland for her valuable comments and corrections, and Terryl Warnock, Editor at Moonlit Press, for her endless help and guidance.

Katarina offers many thanks to her dear friend and supporter Judy Leary, who has been helping her from her first writing steps, her daughter-in-law Helena Marinovic, her daughters Sylvia and Barbora, and friends Christine Orr and Stephany Smith for their excellent advices.

Laurie Wilson Fatland would like to thank Claudia Barlow, Jaime Lopez, Jennifer Wilson, Niki Stepanian, Jo Bakes and Judi Fatland for being our beta readers. We will be looking forward to wonderful reviews posted all over the internet from them.

Keli Becker would like to thank Dave for his love and unwavering support through all the years; Tami, her daughter, for being her cheering section, Joel, her brother, for being there for her, and all her dear friends for their support and gentle criticisms.

Terryl Warnock would like to thank the Sacred Circle Writers for their warm welcome and unflagging enthusiasm and positive feedback.

Moonlit Press would like to thank the Sacred Circle Writers for the opportunity to introduce the world to their work. We expect great things in the future from each and every writer in the Circle.

Earthshine Writer's Guild

It is a daunting experience to empty your soul into words. It is even more terrifying to hold those words out, with shaking hands, exposed, for all the world to see. Moonlit Press was founded in part to support writers, particularly writers who are just starting out. Moonlit Press is proud to be the first to publish these important new voices. They are all worthy writers with something important to say.

Future themed anthologies to showcase the work of experienced and inexperienced writers alike will be developed by the *Earthshine Writer's Guild*. Each submission will receive professional developmental editing and will be taken into consideration for publication. Watch for further details and calls for submissions as this exciting new opportunity to publish develops at http://moonlitpress.com/

Colophon - Hacker Attribution

Moonlit Press advocates free speech and, importantly in this digital age, the freedom to **express** that speech. As such, Moonlit Press supports hackers who are working to free the digital community from the despotism of large corporations who would control or withhold information and the means of its expression. *From Spark To Fire* has been created exclusively and entirely with open source computer software, which is offered free to users with only the request for attribution in return. Moonlit Press offers that attribution, and our gratitude, willingly and proudly.

We live in a culture corrupted by large avaricious institutions from the political to the corporate. To counteract and subvert this culture of fundamental dishonesty requires public organizations dedicated to protecting the rights of the individual and the ability to exercise those rights freely. FLOSS, Free/Libre Open Source Software is such an organization. It is a concept, a movement, and a business structure at once. FLOSS is the Internet equivalent of free speech, it is synonymous with individual rights and freedom of expression because to exercise freedom in any meaningful way requires both the legal right and the tools to do so. Hackers demand open access to information and the tools to disseminate it. They trust that wide collaboration ensures both integrity and accuracy of information and its wide dissemination. They labor under a moral responsibility to the human race at large, and because it's fun.

The ability to have and use Free Software is supported and defended by the Free Software Foundation; [http://fsf.org/] among others.

The text of this book was prepared using LibreOfficeWriter; [https://www.libreoffice.org/].

The graphics were prepared using Gimp;

[http://www.gimp.org/], and Inkscape; [http://inkscape.org/]. Gimp is a high quality continuous tone image editing package, and Inkscape is a sophisticated scalable vector graphics editing package.

All of the standard fonts used in the creation of this book are licensed under the Open Font License (OFL). [http://www.sil.org/about].

The main body of this book was typeset using Gentium Book Basic typeface. The name Gentium is Latin for "of the nations," and is a typeface family designed by Victor Gaultney to enable diverse ethnic groups around the world who use the Latin, Cyrillic and Greek alphabets to produce readable, high-quality publications. Gentium Book Basic was released under the SIL Open Font License which permits modification and redistribution.

The back matter of the book is composed using the Quivira typeface. Quivira is a labor of love by Alexander Lange [http://www.quivira-font.com] in Germany. He has created a large set of characters, over 11,000 and counting, and made it freely available to the world.

The poetry and titles in this book have been typeset using the versatile Kaushan Script, which was designed by Pablo Impallari and offered as open source software. He wanted it to feel like writing with an inked brush and can be utilized in 93 languages.

The back cover image is an example of the FLOSS ecosystem at work: the background image was created and integrated with the 3D modeling and animation system Blender [http://www.blender.org/], using a 3d model of a stone henge created by Mark, screen name *hypnagogia* at [http://sharecg.com/]. The image utilizes textures licensed from [http://cgtextures.com/]; has been manipulated with Gimp;

integrated with Inkscape; exported in the PNG format (a FLOSS graphic image standard); and converted to a printer ready file format using Convert [http://www.imagemagick.org/].

Supporting all of the powerful open source tools used to create this book has been the FLOSS operating system Linux/GNU.

We offer our humble and sincere thanks to all the hard working and under-appreciated people around the world who build the tools we need to keep freedom and integrity alive in the high-tech world. Moonlit Press supports these dedicated champions of social and technological justice who are working to ensure that technological advances do not erode our rights.

Community Hacker Series

Moonlit Press is a job shop. Authors employ us to help them *self publish* their work. We are frequently contacted by authors who wish us to work on a project for a share of the royalties only, as would a traditional publisher. That is not our business model so we generally turn them down.

We are, however, initiating a standing exception to this rule. Moonlit Press supports the FLOSS movement and the hackers who fuel it because hackers work in community and Moonlit Press is absolutely convinced it will only be through genuine community—the synergetic and just interconnectedness of people, resources and the nonhuman world—that human beings and planet earth can learn to thrive in one another's company.

Moonlit Press is currently seeking proposals for the inaugural volume of our Community Hacker series. Your research proposal may be of a scientific or social nature. You must have a committed source of funding for your project and demonstrate its benefit to community. That community may be human and/or nonhuman.

Moonlit Press will publish the winning project at no initial cost to the authors. We will assist with the writing process, donating developmental editing, ghostwriting and proofreading services. We will publish your results, and bring the publication to market. Watch for further details about opportunities to participate in this program of community service as it develops at http://moonlitpress.com/, and if you have an idea you'd like us to consider now, please write to the editor, Terryl, at terryl@moonlitpress.com with "Community Hacker" in the subject line.

www.ingramcontent.com/pod-product-compliance
Lightning Source LLC
Chambersburg PA
CBHW050544260626
47157CB00002B/430